MW01601358

CHRISTMAS HOME

A SWEET CONTEMPORARY GAY ROMANCE

BLAKE ALLWOOD

BLAKE ALLWOOD PUBLISHING

Cover designed by Samrat Acharjee

Blake Allwood
Visit my website at BlakeAllwood.com

Printed in the United States of America
Box Elder, SD

First Printing: Dec 2024

Blake Allwood Publishing

Ebook ISBN: 978-1-956727-67-8
Paperback ISBN: 978-1-956727-68-5
Library of Congress Control Number: pending

CONTENT WARNINGS

Abandonment
Past abusive relationships
Burning/burns and scars
Past domestic abuse
Recovery from abuse
Family conflict
Fear
Violence
Harassment
Panic attacks
Physical attacks
Weapons

Join Blake's email list to get advance notice of new books and receive his occasional newsletter:

www.blakeallwood.com

MM Romance
By Blake Allwood

Transitions Series
Aiden Inspired
Suzie Empowered (MF Romance)
Bobby Transformed

Chance Series
Love By Chance
Another Chance With Love
Taking A Chance For Love

Romantic Series
Romantic Renovations (1)
Romantic Rescue (2)
Romantic Recon (3)

Melody Series
Melody of the Heart
Melody of the Snow

Hearts of Rock and Roll
Changing His Tune (1)
More Than October (2)

Coming Home Series
A Long Way Home
Family Home
Discovering Home
Finding Home
Bound For Home

Fallen Fairytales
After Midnight

Novellas
Tenacious
Moon's Place

Romantic Fantasy
By Adam J. Ridley

Big Bend Series
Love's Legacy (1)
Love's Heirloom (2)
Love's Bequest (3)

The Witch Brothers Series
Emerald Earth (1)
Diamond Air (2)
Ruby Fire (3)
Sapphire Water (4)

Tales from the Tarot Series
Twisted Fates

Haunted Hearts Series
Cordelia Manor

Science Fiction
By Adam J. Ridley

Superhero Series
Emergence

ACKNOWLEDGMENTS

Special thanks to the following amazing people who helped me get this book finished and into your hands.

Jo Bird: Editor
Barb Toth : Editor
Renee Mizar: Editor

And of course, a big thank you to my husband who puts up with my endless stories and handles the formatting and final publishing of all my books.

ONE

PROLOGUE – RUTHERFORD CRAWFORD

T HE BIG OLD HOUSE was creepy when I was home alone. Mom and Dad had put a TV in my bedroom—the big kind with all the "gadgets," as my dad called them.

Mostly, it was to entertain me since I had no friends and didn't know a soul my age in the area. We lived in New York but spent holidays and summers here at the family estate in Tennessee. Usually, Dad's sister and her husband joined us, bringing my older cousin Farlow with them. But they weren't here this year and I didn't know why.

"As Quakers," my dad loved to say, "getting away from the city and all that Christmas nonsense is what we should be doing."

I was only ten years old and despite not having my cousin to keep me company, my parents left me home alone. They'd gone to Nashville and I knew it was to celebrate the holiday in their own way—their breath would be smelling of alcohol and they'd be laughing hysterically over nothing when they returned.

I turned off Cartoon Network. It got weird this late anyway. I stayed in my bedroom and hadn't gone back down after Mom sent me upstairs with cookies and milk before they left. The house was too spooky to wander around at night by myself.

I fell asleep with my clothes on. Mom always kept the house so hot that I preferred my shorts over pajamas anyway. This side of the house was newer and had central heating, which meant it got superhot upstairs. Then it got cold when the Tennessee winds blew through the windows.

I never heard the fire. I woke up to the sound of sirens and saw flames clinging to my bedroom ceiling. Then, I didn't know what to do. I hoped the sirens meant firefighters were coming. I hoped they'd come and get me.

I drew the covers over my head and cried out for Mom just as I felt blinding pain hit my stomach. Moments later, something else fell on my legs. I couldn't see what it was. "Help me!" I screamed, unable to move.

Then I felt the fire burning through the blankets, scorching my skin. "Help!" I screamed again but no one answered.

2

The flames were eating me alive, blazing a path from my stomach to my chest and making their way up toward my face. "Help. Please." I knew my cries were growing quieter. I was dying. I was going to die in this old house, alone and in unbearable pain.

I squeezed my eyes shut but couldn't escape seeing the glow of the fire. Then the pressure on my body lifted and the burning covers were pulled back.

As I was picked up, I blacked out. I didn't remember anything else until I woke up in a New York hospital room. I never learned who my rescuer was.

As horrific as the burning had been, my nightmare had only just begun.

Two

Clyde Griffin

"Lewellen, you get yer trashy white ass back here!" I yelled as the seventy-six Boss Hog Cadillac convertible sped off, spewing mud and gravel back toward me. "Lewellen, yer such a bitch!!!" I screamed, but it was no use. It's not like I should be surprised. My underhanded cousin was hightailing it and there was nothing I could do to stop her.

"What a shocker," I could imagine my sister saying. "Lewellen betrayed you again, stole yer money, and left you high and dry."

"Well, I ain't a calling you for help, Emmylou. How about that?" I said to myself, and imagined sticking my tongue out at my ass of a sister.

I turned back toward the old, run-down motel and walked to my room.

4

"Crawford City looks nice," Lewellen had told me when I needed to get away from the latest jackass I'd met. The man had a lot of fun using my face as a punching bag and almost put me in the hospital. So that night, after he'd gone to sleep, I'd taken his wad of cash and foolishly called my cousin.

Lewellen was my mama's first cousin's daughter, which made us second cousins...or maybe third? Hell, I don't know. All I know for sure is she loved doing this shit to me. Thought it was funny that I kept falling for it. I felt a whole lot like Charlie Brown on them cartoons when Lucy pulled the football away every time Charlie Brown got close to kicking it.

I looked around the dingy little motel room. Lewellen had agreed to stay here with me for a month. We'd used my jackass ex's money to buy enough groceries to last until then. The idea being that until he or the authorities caught up to us, we would have food and shelter, at least.

That'd been one week ago. Now, the ol' hag had run off with the groceries that were still in the car and what money I had left. Oh well, at least the motel room didn't have bed bugs, and I had a safe place to lay low from my ex.

God, I hoped he hadn't gotten the law involved. This wasn't the first time a man had taken to hitting me, and it wasn't the first time I decided not to be a punching bag. My old man used to hit me enough. I didn't need a boyfriend doing the same damned thing.

Still, last time I'd had to sit in jail for just under a month while a judge decided my part in the fight had been self-defense. Not sure I'd be looked upon as kindly this time, considering I'd taken his money. That was a first for me.

If I was lucky, which I never am, I could avoid Georgia for now. Even if my ex did call the law on me, maybe Tennessee wouldn't send me back down there for a legal whupping.

Why hadn't I just left the man the first time he raised his fist to me? Isn't that the million-dollar question? Why don't people just leave? I mean, first it's, "Oh, I was drunk. I didn't mean it." Then it's, "Oh, you deserved it." Then it goes on and on. Well, after this last time, I didn't wait around to hear more excuses. I knew how it'd turn out. And I knew if he found me now, he'd whup me good. Kill me if he could.

I flopped on the old, musty bed. God, I hated sleeping in motel rooms. Even though I'd done it plenty growing up.

My stomach grumbled but I ignored it. There'd be no food if I couldn't find a job or some church willing to let me eat while they prayed over me. I'd go searching for both tomorrow. Besides, if I liked it here, I might stick around.

The town looked quaint. Like in them Hallmark movies. I was ready for quaint...well, ready for something, at least. Something besides the same shitty life I'd lived for the past thirty-four years.

THREE

RUTHER

"SIR," MY ASSISTANT SAID sarcastically, "are you sure this is a good idea?"

"If you ask me again, Corey, I will be forced to fire you."

He looked at me skeptically, like he always did when I threatened to fire him, and shook his head. "You've already sold the Crawford City estate, and you know what happens when you start thinking about—"

I put my hand up. "I'm forty years old, and I'm tired of facing that demon over and over. Indulge me. Keep the therapists you insist I see on speed dial, but I know deep down if I don't face this once and for all, I'll never have peace."

Corey shrugged in his dismissive way. The guy was a decade younger than me—tall, regal, and one hundred percent New York elite, although I knew he hadn't come from that. But, when I'd taken him on as my personal assistant, he'd undertaken the job with relish, and to my dismay, he was now extremely involved in planning my life.

Regardless, between running a multimillion-dollar company and managing my PTSD nightmares, it helped to have someone who could hold things together.

"So, this is happening then?"

"I'm afraid so. Sorry, Corey, but you don't have to come. I can handle it myself."

"Pfft," he interjected. "You'd fall apart in less than a day without me. I've already begun to make arrangements. Jake Hudson, the man who helped me process the sale of the estate, owns a nice hotel downtown. However, because I'm the best assistant known to man, I've secured you a condo adjoining the hotel. Mr. Hudson assures me it's up to par with your accustomed lifestyle."

I laughed. "You mean the lifestyle *you* are accustomed to."

"Don't put words in my mouth, sir. I'm fully capable of talking for myself. So, when do you want to begin this terror quest?" he asked, stopping me in my tracks.

It was becoming real, and dammit, if that wasn't probably the very thing Corey wanted me to feel. "Let's go next week," I said. Corey sighed and shook his head.

"As you wish, sir."

When he was gone, I stared down at Central Park below me. I'd liquidated the family business and our real estate holdings in Pennsylvania and Tennessee after my father passed away. That'd been over two years ago, and I'd be damned if the nightmares hadn't increased.

The therapy didn't work, and neither did the medication. I had hoped selling all the stuff connected to my family, the old Crawford City place being at the top of that list, would end it, but no. I'd close my eyes and be back in my childhood bedroom alight by fire. Surrounding me. Burning me. Killing me all over again.

Since I'd read a self-help book my therapist recommended that said facing your fears was the best way to overcome them, I'd decided, why not? I'd go back to where the incident happened. I'd return to the scene of the crime, so to speak—my ground zero.

I'd storm the gates of hell and face the devil himself if it meant I could have a full night's sleep again. That's what Crawford City represented for me, my own personal hell. The devil, though? I needn't worry about him. My dad was already dead.

Four

Clyde

"WHATCHA NEED DOIN'?" I asked the lady currently looking me up and down.

"Well, I need a short-order cook, but that's only from four in the morning until Lydia comes in by six. After that, I need someone to bus tables, clean bathrooms, mop floors, and keep the trash cleared. You think you can do all that?"

"Seems like that's what I's made for, ma'am," I said, and she smiled.

"Well, it's not a glamorous life, running a restaurant, but it is a living," she said.

"So, I'm hired?" I asked.

"As long as you've got your social security card and ID. I'll sign you up right now."

I'd never been so relieved to have a job in all my life, even if it was back to the same shit I'd done since I was

10

sixteen. I knew how to clean a toilet and how to keep the back end of a restaurant running. I also knew how to keep my damned mouth shut and avoid the drama that got other folks fired.

As long as I was in Crawford City, I was sure I'd have a job. Well, until the cops found me and dragged my ass back to Georgia, that is.

Just as Mrs. Cole brought me the paperwork, my stomach let out the loudest hunger roll imaginable. She just laughed. "Son, you fill that application out while you fill your belly. Go on and get you a plate."

I looked at the older woman with my mouth agape. "Um, I don't got no money for breakfast," I said, embarrassed.

"I didn't figure you'd be giving me money, son. Since I'm now your employer, the money will be comin' from over here, don't you 'spect?"

I smiled but blushed from embarrassment. "Maybe you can put it on my tab."

"More like she's gonna take it outta your ass when she gets you up and working," a smart-looking young woman said as she dashed out the back and past our table.

"Oh, she's right," Mrs. Cole said. "I don't have time to be messing with lazy people, and since I 'spect you to work hard while you're here, I need you to be in tip-top shape. Someone who ain't been eatin' proper can't work proper. So, like I said, go get your plate filled up, *then* finish that application. When you're done," she said as she stood to go, "I've got some chores need doing, and I can use you right away."

It was still early. I'd made a point to get here at six in the morning, and boy, I could use a bite to eat. I looked at the steaming buffet full of real eggs, bacon, sausage, and biscuits and gravy. Not to mention hash browns, cheesy potatoes, and grits, which I normally hated—

Now's not the time to be choosy. If these people are willing to feed you, don't be an idiot. Pocket your pride, eat, and be thankful.

I tried gulping down the food so I could get started, but damn, I savored every mouthful. Oh, my soul, it was delicious food. Obviously made from scratch and nothing like the rubbery eggs, hockey puck-like biscuits, and pasty gravy typical of buffet breakfasts. I practically licked my plate clean, then hurriedly completed my application, and didn't protest when Mrs. Cole encouraged me to get a second helping before she disappeared into the back.

I'd just popped the last bite of biscuits and gravy into my mouth and moaned for what had to be the hundredth time when Mrs. Cole refilled my coffee cup, then sat down across from me.

"So, I checked your references while you, well, while you devoured that," she said, her eyes twinkling before becoming serious again. "Your last place of business said you lit out of there like your hind end was on fire. Wanna share anything about that?"

I thought about all the reasons I could give her. I was an expert at lying about being hit and hiding my bruises. But I liked this woman and decided I'd had enough lies to last a lifetime, so I pulled my turtleneck down and showed her the evidence of where the SOB had tried to strangle me.

"It was run or die," I said as I let the turtleneck slip back into place.

"Good heavens, that does explain it. You worried about him coming for you?" she asked.

I shrugged. "Only my cousin knows I'm here. Hey, how did you know it wasn't a she?"

She just smiled. "Could've been, but I get a strong vibe you aren't the kind to have a *she* on your arm."

"Is that a problem?" I asked.

Mrs. Cole leaned back and laughed out loud. "Oh, son, if it was, half the town would boycott me. No, you're welcome here, and if that one," she said, pointing at my neck, "comes here looking for trouble, you let me know. We don't have much stomach for that sorta thing around these parts."

I breathed out a sigh of relief. I'd already started looking forward to working at the café and not just for the free food that hopefully came with the job.

She gave me a knowing look, then said, "I told your previous employer they could mail your last paycheck here. I didn't know why you hadn't told them where you were going, but I know to respect someone's privacy, Mr. Griffin. As long as that privacy don't bring trouble to me and my establishment, you've got nothing but respect here." She stared at me until I nodded in understanding. "Now, you finish that coffee, then I'm going to show you the back. I need my freezer cleaned up and reorganized. I figure after that big breakfast, you can handle the cold, and I'm expecting another shipment this afternoon, so I need that shelf space cleaned off."

I nodded, took another swig of my coffee, and followed Mrs. Cole to the back. She appeared pleased that I'd picked up my plates, silverware, and cup and placed them in the sink without being asked.

As I stood in the freezer, rearranging and discarding the old boxes, I couldn't help but feel I'd landed in a different kind of place. A special place. I reached up and gently rubbed along the tender bruises beneath my turtleneck. I really hoped I was right about Crawford City because I was due for some good fortune.

FIVE

RUTHER

I STOOD ALONG THE main street. Very little had changed since I'd seen it last, though the trees lining the street were fuller. At one time, I could see my old home on the hill from this vantage. Now, I couldn't even tell the house or the Queen Anne near it were up there.

A shiver went through me as I thought of the house and, inevitably, the fire. For a split second, I could feel the flames lapping at my skin and smell my burnt flesh before Corey put his hand on my arm.

"You okay?" he asked.

I shook off the terror. "Yeah, I'm fine. Let's go face the demons."

Corey followed my gaze toward the old house and shook his head, clearly understanding. "No need to face that one quite yet. Why don't we go to the café for

15

breakfast first? You can get your bearings and decide where to go from there."

Corey had begun preparing the moment we boarded my private jet to fly from New York to Nashville. He'd told me at least half a dozen times that he'd arranged a hotel in Nashville, just in case Crawford City was too much for me to handle.

The man was a menace most of the time, but as the years progressed, he'd also proven to care about me. I'd often wondered if there was any hope that we could be more than employer and employee, but I always reached the same conclusion.

The idea was preposterous. Corey wasn't my type and although I loved him, he was like my family. Not a lover in any way.

I snickered as I thought about it while we walked toward the café. I was never going to be his type either, as evidenced by the string of models he'd dated and dumped over the years. I wasn't anywhere near perfect enough. The smile slipped from my face as I thought of my scars.

I kept my burned body hidden from everyone, Corey included. Even the few men I'd dated over the past twenty years had only caught glimpses. The surgeries had helped, but the scars would never be gone, at least not entirely. They spanned across my torso, so keeping my shirt on usually hid the worst of them.

We walked into the Crawford City Café and were immediately confronted by a smiling woman. "Welcome, gentlemen," she said before waving her hand around the cute little place. "Sit anywhere you like. We've got the buffet, or you can order. There's a menu on every table."

I followed Corey to a booth and slid in as I watched him check the seat for crumbs, then wipe his pretentious finger across the top of the table. When it appeared clean enough, he sat down.

"My God, are you always like this?" I asked.

He stopped unfolding a paper napkin to use as a placemat and looked at me. "Like what?"

"A pretentious snob?" I asked.

He promptly ignored me, picked up the menu, and began to peruse it.

When the same woman who'd greeted us approached with coffee, I gladly allowed her to pour me a cup. We'd left New York in the wee hours of the morning to avoid a storm that was building over West Virginia, so I needed a caffeine boost.

"So, what'll you have?" she asked.

"I'll have the buffet," I announced, and Corey cringed across from me. Hoping the woman wouldn't pay him any mind, I asked her about the town.

She smiled and answered my questions while Corey continued to peruse the menu. When the woman finished giving me her elevator pitch for the town, Corey said, "I'll have the eggs Benedict."

The woman frowned. "I'll warn you, I just hired a new short-order cook, and this will be the first breakfast he's fixed, so you're gonna hafta be a guinea pig. Is that okay?"

Corey sighed and shrugged. "If it sucks, I'll let you know."

I shook my head as the woman nodded and disappeared through the back.

"How about we try not offending the locals. This isn't New York, and since our dining options here in town are extremely limited, we may be eating here a lot."

Corey laughed. "Hardly. I'll cook until I can hire someone to do it for us. But I'll try not to be so...myself," he said dryly.

"Thank you," I replied and took a swig of my surprisingly decent coffee.

Corey flipped through his phone as I looked around the café. It was dated, almost like it hadn't been updated since I left thirty years ago. But, for the life of me, I couldn't remember eating here.

Like Corey, I searched for signs of the café being dirty, but everything seemed clean. It appeared as if someone had scrubbed the floors on their hands and knees. That spoke volumes about the place, and I just hoped the food was good.

The woman returned with a plate for the buffet, told me I could go help myself, and that Corey's food would be ready soon. Then she promptly disappeared again.

My grandmother had grown up in the house on the hill. She always considered herself a Southern woman instead of a New Englander like the rest of us. As I surveyed the buffet, I smiled when I saw the same types of food she'd cooked when I was young.

As our server had predicted, Corey's food arrived just as I returned to the table. She placed the steaming food in front of him as I sat down. For a moment, before he could contain it, I saw pleasure in Corey's expression.

"You boys let me know if you need anything else," the woman said.

I dug into my food, ignoring the fact she had called me a boy, while Corey looked at me in disgust. "You know there are probably more germs on that buffet than on the floor."

"It's possible," I conceded, "but I've literally watched someone wipe down those serving utensils three times since we arrived, and even you can't say the place isn't spick-and-span. So, if you don't mind, I'll take my chances."

"Well, it's your funeral," he said and, using his knife, cut through the eggs Benedict. I'm not a foodie. Most of the time, I eat what's put in front of me and don't worry so much about what I'm eating, but even I could see Corey's meal was cooked perfectly.

The poached eggs poured over the rest of the meal as he cut through them, and the creamy sauce mixed beautifully with the eggs.

Corey cut a small piece and placed it in his mouth, and I watched as my pompous assistant lost control just long enough for pleasure to wash over him at the taste.

"That good, huh?" I asked, and Corey's eyes popped open.

He finished chewing and nodded. In a conspiratory voice, he said, "This is five-star quality. What's it doing being cooked in a two-bit country café in the middle of nowhere?"

I couldn't help but laugh out loud. "Corey, you are just wrong."

I dug into my own meal then, and as the rich flavors swarmed in my mouth, the same pleasures swept through me that I'd seen on Corey's face a moment before.

"The food here is excellent," I said as our server passed our table.

"Best for miles around, so I'm told," she replied with a proud smile.

"This really is excellent," Corey told her. "I can't remember when I've had eggs Benedict as good as this."

She eyed him for a moment, clearly looking to see if he was being honest, and when she accepted the fact that Corey wasn't someone to give idle compliments, she nodded. "That's good news. I haven't had time to test my new cook's skills. I'll let him know you approved."

Just as she said that, a young woman rushed into the café and straight back to the kitchen. A flash of annoyance crossed our server's face before she masked it and refilled my coffee cup.

I watched as she followed the woman, then I glanced at my watch. Considering it was a quarter past the hour, she was probably late for work. From the look on our server's face, I guessed there was a serious talk going on in the kitchen.

I finished my food and contemplated going back for seconds, then remembered I couldn't work out at my home gym or see my personal trainer in Crawford City and decided to pass. Southern food was designed to keep hardworking people fueled to work, and it'd be all I could do to somehow work off what I'd already eaten.

I leaned back in my seat as Corey finished eating and returned his attention to his phone. "Crap, really?" he said, then swiped the phone and made a call. "Denise, it's Corey. No, you are supposed to go to the house today and begin the repairs. I have no idea how long we'll be here. That's why I asked you to—"

I stopped listening. Since I'd sold the business and was spending more time at home, I'd learned that several things in my apartment weren't conducive to being there so much. The toilet downstairs was fashion with no form. The kitchen wasn't much better. So, I'd asked Corey to arrange to have some work done on the place while I was away. Clearly, he was now dealing with the predictable issues that come with overseeing a remodel.

Once again, I praised the universe that I had the resources to hire someone to handle this sort of thing.

I heard a commotion in the direction of the kitchen and glanced up just in time to see a man emerge from the back with a large gray tray. I watched transfixed as the extremely handsome man began bussing tables.

He wasn't what I'd consider tall, maybe five-nine, five-ten at most. A thin build but strong arms. The kind that came from working hard for a living rather than hitting the gym. I watched as he circled the restaurant, cleaning tables and wiping down booths.

My temperature rose when his lithe body leaned over a table to gather dishes. His perfectly round butt was a lovely sight.

"Like what you see?" Corey said, and my face immediately blushed bright red.

"Hush," I said and took a swig of my now cold coffee. I usually would've cringed, but I didn't want to give Corey the satisfaction.

He just chuckled, and my blush deepened as the man came to our table and asked, in a sexy Southern drawl, if he could take our plates.

"Um, yes, that'd be nice," I stammered, giving Corey the stink eye as he chuckled into his water.

The handsome man smiled at me and disappeared into the back with our plates. Unable to help myself, I watched him go.

"You should ask for his number," Corey said, and thinking he was teasing, I looked back, ready to nail him for it. His face didn't register humor, though. Instead, he looked concerned.

"I don't know if he's gay or bi."

"So ask."

"This isn't New York, Corey. You can't just go around asking strange men about their sexuality."

"I could give your number to him, if you're interested. Are you two gonna be around for a while?" a server asked. I hadn't even seen the younger woman come our way.

"No...well, yes. Or, well, maybe," I stammered. "But no to giving my number out. I'm here on personal business, not to find a date." I gave Corey a withering look, then smiled at the server. "Besides, I'm here for at least a week, so I'm sure our paths will cross again."

She returned my smile. "I'm sure," she repeated, placing our check face down on the table. "You can pay me whenever you're ready." Before she could leave, I handed her my credit card.

Once we'd paid, I looked around, hoping to see the sexy man again. Unfortunately, I had no such luck. With nothing left to distract me from my mission here in Crawford City, it was time to face the demons ingrained in my psyche.

Six

Clyde

I CRINGED AS MRS. Cole tore my coworker a new one. "I pay you to be here on time, and no, it's not okay that you show up thirty minutes late, causing everyone else here to work double time." The girl lowered her head, but I could see the smirk.

Well, that one ain't gonna last, I thought before grabbing the bussing equipment to make myself useful. Experience taught me when a restaurant owner started firing, they didn't tend to stop at one, and I needed this damn job.

I wasn't two steps out of the kitchen when I noticed the silver fox but forced myself not to make eye contact. Besides, the sharply dressed man sitting across from him was likely his lover. Again, I reminded myself to keep people happy and keep my head down to keep my job.

24

By the time I returned to the kitchen, I expected to be told to get back on the grill, but the snarky woman had somehow managed to keep her job. I carried the dishes to the dishwasher and separated the food and trash in the bins. Then I ran the dishes through the cycle.

I'd worked in a heck of a lot of restaurants, and dishes were a never-ending job. No exception here. Luckily, Mrs. Cole ran an organized place because I didn't even have to ask where anything went.

I finished with the dirty dishes and dashed out the door with a stack of clean plates and silverware to re-peat the process. There's not much glory working in a restaurant. It's hard, backbreaking work, but if someone knows their way around a kitchen, it's mindless, and they can spend time on their thoughts...when they want. I didn't want to, but that didn't mean I could escape them.

Mrs. Cole had spoken to my last employer, which meant they knew where I was working now. My ex might be an idiot, but even he would eventually figure out to ask where my last paycheck was sent. I didn't think my previous job would give a shit about confidentiality.

Most likely, the cops would be the ones to ask, which was worse. *Extradition*, that's the word. I'd heard it on *NCIS*, my favorite TV show, many times.

I'd taken just under a thousand dollars from him. It made sense he'd want it back. But I was here now, and there wasn't a dang thing I could do but work and hope.

"You about done?" Mrs. Cole asked, catching my at-tention.

"Yes, ma'am. Do you need me for somethin' else?" I asked.

She laughed. "Son, it's past your working time. You should've clocked out half an hour ago. Come on, leave that for Tommy to deal with, and have a bite before you leave."

I was shocked. How had the day gone so fast? I did as she instructed, once again feeling hungry. I hadn't eaten during my lunch break, telling her I didn't like to work on a full stomach, but now, well, I was ready for a bite or a hundred.

I grabbed a couple of pieces of fried chicken because it had enticed me all day long, and if the dirty plates that'd rolled in at lunchtime were any indication, it was as good as it smelled. Peas, potatoes, homemade rolls. It all looked so yummy.

I sat near the kitchen door, since that seemed to be where employees sat, and dug in. "Oh, Mother Mary and Baby Jesus," I whispered to myself as the juice from the chicken almost dripped down my shirt. How on earth was this so delicious?

I was well into my meal when Mrs. Cole joined me. "Son, I understand now why your other employer was upset you were gone. You are one heck of a good work-er." I blushed. Accepting compliments wasn't my strong suit, probably because they were rare. "I'm gonna have to let Lydia go. Bless her, I've given her every chance under the sun," she said and shook her head. "Don't you fret about that, but I'm gonna need a short-order cook more than I'm gonna need a busser. I'd do it myself, but

I try to spend most of my time out on the floor these days."

I nodded and swallowed the chicken I'd just bitten off. "I'm willin' to do whatever's needed, ma'am. Just point me in the direction you want me."

She chuckled. "You're a breath of fresh air, Clyde Griffin. I'll see you before the crack of dawn tomorrow. Now don't be comin' in late on me, you hear?"

I smiled. "No, ma'am. I'll be on time." In fact, I'd get here early just to show my gratitude. It's not like I hadn't pulled early mornings in the past, even though I'd never been a morning person. I preferred lounging in bed, not that I was a man of leisure. I doubted I ever would be. *Some of us are supposed to be silver foxes*. I thought of the sexy one from earlier. *And some of us are meant to be peasants.* Clearly, peasant was my destiny.

Seven

Ruther

I 'D JUST COME OUT of the café when a familiar face nearly walked past. "Amos?" I asked, and the man looked up.

"Rutherford Crawford?" Amos asked, sounding shocked. "I never thought..." His words trailed off, but I knew what he must be thinking.

Amos cleared his throat. "Did you just finish at the café?" he asked, quickly changing the subject. I nodded, pasting a polite smile on my face. "I was just going in to get something for my husband. Do you remember Emanual?"

"Vaguely," I responded, but *husband* resounded in my mind. I knew Amos and my cousin had fooled around one summer when Farlow came to visit. I was a lot younger than them, but I remembered Amos as being a handsome man. Hell, he still was.

"What're your plans this afternoon? I know Emanual would love to chat," Amos said.

I looked at Corey, who recognized my cue to respond for me. "We're meeting Jake Hudson to get the keys to the condo we're staying at. After that, we don't have plans."

I nodded. Corey was ever the efficient one. "Do you have time later today?" I asked, suddenly wanting to catch up with people I'd known years ago.

"I do. Not sure about Emanual. I could text you after I speak to him?"

I nodded just as Corey handed his business card to Amos. "Text me, and I'll let him know."

Amos smiled and looked at the card. I knew having a personal assistant must seem strange here. Hell, it was strange enough for me, and I'd had one most of my adult life.

"That's wonderful. I'm Amos," he said, reaching a hand out to Corey.

I narrowed my eyes at my assistant to make sure he knew not to snub the man, but Corey smiled and shook Amos's hand without missing a beat. "It's my pleasure. I'm Corey King."

"Nice to meet you. I'll see you both later today," Amos said. Then, after saying his goodbyes, he disappeared into the café.

"An ex?" Corey asked.

I laughed. "Um, no. He's a bit too old for me, or was, but I had a boyhood crush on him when we were younger. He did have a fling with my cousin, though."

Corey frowned. I didn't have much to do with my extended family. Farlow, my eldest cousin, had been the exception to the rule. He'd been my father's right-hand man in our company and had taken as much abuse from him as I had. As a result, Farlow and I had been close.

"That reminds me, you need to get in touch with Yamato," I said. "I forgot his birthday is coming up."

"I remembered for you," Corey said. "I've already purchased his gift—tickets to see *A Beautiful Noise*." I nodded, thankful for my assistant's efficiency. Ever since Farlow had died, I'd been trying to stay close to his widower. Most of Yamato's family still lived in Japan, and he was the only family I had left. Or the only family I had contact with.

We walked along the street to where a large brick building stood. I had noticed the new construction project when we first got into town. It definitely hadn't been there when I was growing up. I couldn't quite remember what had been, but it was nowhere near as nice.

A smartly dressed woman met us as we entered the hotel, and I was shocked when I recognized her Manhattan accent. "You're from New York?" I asked, getting a cocked eyebrow from her.

"Yes, you?"

"Off West Fifty-Seventh," I said, not mentioning that it was Central Park South.

She regarded me momentarily, then looked at Corey, and I knew she must've picked up on the fact that I'd come from money. Oh well, I *had* come from money. There was no use hiding it.

"We were supposed to meet Jake Hudson here," Corey said.

"Oh, yes. Sorry, Jake got pulled away. Come with me, and I'll show you to the condo. I'm surprised Jake was able to get the owner to agree to this. Jesse is usually rather protective of who stays in his condo."

Neither Corey nor I responded since we didn't know the circumstances. Whoever this owner, Jesse, was would be well compensated for leasing us the unit, I'm sure.

The woman, Catherine, wore a name tag but hadn't formally introduced herself. We followed her up a short flight of stairs, she pointed toward a door. "You're welcome to use the elevator or the stairs. Enjoy your stay."

She handed us the key and left.

I honestly didn't expect much. A simple room with maybe a modern kitchen. But the high-end, stylish furniture and tasteful décor were pleasant surprises. The appliances were as nice, if not nicer, than my own, and the bedrooms and en suite were equally impressive.

A small balcony led off the side of the building and faced an old railroad track. I stepped out for the full view and could see that across the track was a little park with a gazebo. I remembered sitting in that gazebo as a boy. My gaze strayed from there to the hill, and I caught sight of my old home.

Cold sweat immediately broke out across my forehead, and I quickly slipped back through the door and pulled the blinds shut. *Guess I won't be using the balcony.*

Forcing myself to calm down, I walked back into the living area, where Corey was speaking on the phone.

"Yes, you can have the luggage delivered here. I'll be waiting, yes."

I knew he'd made arrangements with the limo service to bring our luggage from the airport. It was still early, and the limo driver hadn't arrived when our plane landed. I also didn't want to show up in Crawford City in a limousine. So, despite his disappointed stare, Corey had arranged for them to deliver the luggage once we were settled.

"If you're going to wait here, then why don't you let Amos know I'm going to walk back into town."

I should've gotten Amos's number myself, but if I asked now, Corey would pout. He was already upset enough about the circumstances that I didn't want to upset the applecart more than I already had.

I went to the kitchen, pulled a sparkling water out of the refrigerator, and sat at the counter to drink it. I was about to consider returning to the bedroom for a nap when Corey said Amos and his husband were available to meet.

"Where?" I asked.

"Town hall," Corey said.

I nodded and left him to do his million phone calls and whatever else he did when I was occupied.

I remembered the old town hall, which, to be honest, looked about as ragged as it had in my childhood.

The old school next to it had been refurbished and was now a public library. The café sat just across the street. I could see the improvements now I didn't have Corey clouding my vision. Most of the buildings were occupied. There was even construction going on across from where the hotel and condos stood.

Most small towns this size were dead or dying. Crawford City, however, seemed to be moving in the other direction. I had to wonder what was behind that.

I climbed the old stairs to the second floor, where I found Amos sitting across from another man in an office. Amos smiled when he saw me, then stood and opened the door.

"Hi, Rutherford. I'm glad you had time to visit. This is my husband, Emanual. You weren't sure if you remembered him or not."

I noticed the frown on his husband's face and for a brief moment, I wondered if maybe my family or I had said something that offended the man back then. Maybe it was just my imagination because he quickly smiled and shook my hand.

"It's been a long time since you've come to these parts. How does it feel being back?" he asked.

I nodded. "It's...well, it's time, I guess."

I looked up and saw the same man in a painting behind his wide oak desk. It was titled, *Mayor of Crawford City*.

"You're the mayor?" I asked. "That's unexpected, assuming you and Amos are out."

The mayor smiled. "Crawford City is special, and compared to the rest of the state, it's rather progressive."

We spent the next hour catching up. I learned Emanual had been the town doctor until his son took over the practice, then he decided to run for mayor. Amos also had a son, apparently a construction manager here in town, and they were in business together.

It felt like we were long-lost friends, but nothing could be further from the truth. Our lives hadn't been remotely similar, and had barely even intersected in our youth, but I enjoyed hearing about their lives. Given their prominence in town, maybe I wouldn't have to deal with bigots while here. That was something, at least.

EIGHT

CLYDE

B LAST THAT STUPID WOMAN. The same one that showed up late yesterday didn't show up at all today. Mrs. Cole was hot enough that we could fry eggs on her forehead. I'm guessing my new boss was trying to give the poor soul one last chance but she was, for sure, getting fired after this.

I put my head down and worked at whatever needed doing. By the time the noon hour hit, the kitchen was in full meltdown. Knowing what was needed, I simply handed the bussing equipment to the kid who'd just come in, slipped into the back, washed up, and joined the line cook.

At first, the guy looked at me funny, then nodded. "You do the chicken. Crawford City can put away a lot of fried chicken, and it never does well for us to run out."

I nodded as I reached for the flouring tub. Mrs. Cole walked in and spotted me tossing battered chicken in the fryer. I almost expected her to complain about me taking the initiative, but a smile crossed her face instead.

Okay, well, I'd done right.

We rushed through lunch, then I joined the kid bussing tables to help clean up the dining room before the dinner crowd hit. Once again, as the crowds increased, I slipped back to the line and helped keep the food coming.

I worked an extra couple of hours before Mrs. Cole sent me packing again. "I don't have the money to be paying overtime, so you get on back home," she chastised, but then patted me on the back, letting me know she appreciated my efforts today.

I ate quickly, knowing from experience I was so tired that I'd probably fall asleep standing up, and I hadn't been wrong. Even though the sun still shone, I knew I had just enough energy to walk back to my motel room and take a shower. Then I'd crash like a lead balloon.

The old motel sat across from a beer joint. I knew to stay away from there. It seemed every man I'd ever dated came out of a place like that, and every man I'd ever dated was about as worthless as a cracked tooth and just as painful.

As I rounded the corner, I ran headlong into someone walking in the opposite direction. "Ouch," I said, grabbing my head where I'd bumped it after ricocheting off the man's hard frame.

"Oh, sorry, are you okay?" he asked, and I felt a couple of large hands reach over to steady me.

"I think so," I said before the words died in my mouth. The silver fox from the day before stood in front of me. Damn, why do attractive men have such a visceral impact on me?

I felt my face flush before all the blood rushed from my head down to my lower regions. I immediately shook it off, or tried to. *No more men!* I chastised myself.

"I-I've got to go," I said, slipping out of the man's grasp.

"Wait, what's your name?"

I almost didn't answer, determined not to get involved. I knew no one put their hands on someone like he had if they weren't interested in exploring more. His touch had lingered a little too long, and damned if I didn't like the feel of it.

"Clyde," is all I said as I darted past him, forcing myself not to look back.

I could almost feel the silver fox's eyes on my back. If I were lucky, he'd only be a town visitor. He certainly didn't seem to fit in this part of the world with his fancy haircut, perfectly trimmed beard, and designer clothes. No, he was a tourist, and damn, it'd be better for me when he moved on from Crawford City.

I knew I was being silly, thinking Crawford City would be anything but a stopover for me as well. Nothing lasted long when it came to me and small towns—cities, too, for that matter. I always made some bad decision, almost always regarding some loser, and then I'd be off without any foundation to keep me stable.

I sighed as I closed the door of my motel room and began stripping out of my clothes. I needed a shower after working all day in the hot, sweaty kitchen. I'd let myself indulge in thoughts of being able to stay put for a change. Crawford City seemed nice. If Mrs. Cole was correct, it was even nice to people like me. That still seemed off to me. I couldn't imagine any small Tennessee town tolerant of gay people.

The world was changing, though. Maybe I was wrong. Anyway, indulgences were for quick showers, then it was time to get your head back on straight. Although anything straight for me was impossible, I'd try in this case.

Images of the man I'd run into forced themselves into my head as I scrubbed off the day. I'd always dreamed of having a loving husband who cuddled me after a long day of work. Those dreams had been behind all my troubles, though. Sorry, sexy silver fox. Starting now, there will be no more men to keep me from finding peace.

I dried off, hung my towel over the shower rod, and climbed into bed. I thought about watching some TV, but I needed rest more than anything. Unfortunately, my stubborn brain thrust images of the man front and center, and no matter what I did, I couldn't stop thinking about him.

Who was he? Where was he from? So many questions. All stupid shit that would sink me again. I banged my hands against the mattress and sighed. You'd think someone who still had the bruises from his last mistake would know better than to obsess over the next bad choice.

I guess that's just what I am, a loser who couldn't learn from his past mistakes. "Well, screw that!" I yelled into the room.

Banging on the wall shocked me enough to calm my inner thoughts. I closed my eyes and, this time, fell into a fitful sleep. Fitful was better than none, though.

NINE

RUTHER

REAL ESTATE WAS IN my blood. I knew it was fool-hardy. I wouldn't be in Crawford City long enough to start or manage a new project, but I couldn't help myself from looking. The little motel facing the local bar at the edge of town was for sale, and it'd caught my attention.

Well, not so much the motel as the fifty acres that came with it. I could tell the property wasn't attractive to most investors because, behind the motel, the land dropped down into a ravine. There was also an old railroad track that separated the land from downtown.

A quick search online told me it was unlikely the rail line, which came out of Nashville, would ever be restored. More likely, it would go the way of so many other abandoned railways across the country in becoming a running and biking trail.

Of course, that just made it that much more appealing to me.

When Corey looked over my shoulder to see what I was looking at, I quickly closed my laptop, but not before he caught sight of the search.

He squinted but didn't say anything. I did a lot of research when it came to property. Corey knew it was just how my mind worked. Being stuck here in the little town where so much had happened to me, things I'd far from overcome, it helped to keep my brain busy.

Corey got up to take a phone call, and since I was just across the road from the property, I decided to look for myself.

There was a trail around the motel into the woods—too many years in New York told me not to enter the woods alone. Crawford City didn't strike me as a place where a lot of dangerous street people posed a threat, but one could never be sure.

Not only that, but lessons from my childhood told me there were snakes. No, I'd just explore from the street.

The ravine wasn't as bad as I'd thought. It descended quickly, but because of it, there was a natural separation between the land and the commercial development of the motel property. That made a potential residential development possible. I'd have to ask Emanual and Amos what the town needed.

I also remembered that Amos said his son was in construction. Maybe this was something I should consider. I was just about to walk back to the condo to ask Corey to get in touch with Jake about renting the condo long-term when I collided with the handsome guy from the restaurant.

When he bounced off me and hit his head against the building behind him, I immediately reached out to steady him. I can't say I got romance novel electric shocks as I touched him, but my body certainly took notice.

I took the opportunity to study him close-up. Cropped chestnut brown hair curled stubbornly against his head, making me wonder what it would be like to see those locks grown out. That made me think about running my fingers through them, and just as the heat of the day got significantly hotter, he pulled away and all but ran toward the motel.

"Crap," I said to myself—way to be a creep. I didn't really have control over my attraction to him. He was handsome and in every way my type, but he was certainly not looking to get involved. Based on his reaction to me, though, I was almost sure the server had been correct in that he played for my team.

I watched him rush away, then realizing I was still being creepy, I forced myself to move on. The man had not left my thoughts as I entered the condo to see Corey working on his laptop. "Hey, I've got a question."

Corey looked up, and his eyes narrowed again. "You've got that look," he said. I laughed. There was no use denying it. Corey had worked with me long enough to know when I'd found an interesting project.

"Just ask Jake if we can keep the condo longer, and before you get upset, you don't have to stay. Corey, I need to make peace with this place, and a project will help me do that. Crawford City holds absolute horrors for me. I need to replace that with something else, something good."

Corey nodded. "I'll make inquiries, but, boss, if you're staying, I'll be here for you."

My assistant seldom showed anything but professionalism in his demeanor, but for a brief second, I could see his concern. Corey had become so much more to me than an assistant over the years. He'd dealt with my father's narcissism while he was still alive, helped me through the loss of my cousin, and now, well, Corey was family.

Yes, that was sad because I paid the only person I considered family besides Yamato, who was actually a cousin-in-law, but I knew that relationship would change now too. Yamato was still a young man. He'd been significantly younger than my cousin, and I knew he'd eventually remarry.

Maybe knowing how little family I had left—well, family I associated with—was another reason I needed to come to terms with my childhood. I needed to fill in the gaps in my past so I could move toward my future. Whatever that might look like.

Ten

Clyde

THE WEEK WENT BY fast, faster than I'd anticipated. I got my former employer's final paycheck in the mail and only had a brief pang of worry that my ex might find me and haul my ass back to Georgia. Then I got too busy to even think about it.

I honestly don't know what got into me. I never put down roots in a new town. I usually don't stay in one place long enough. But, in a moment of weakness, I set up a checking account.

Banking, really? Me? I chalked it up to my brain not being quite right. Besides, if my money wasn't sitting around, Lewellen, who still had a key to the room, couldn't steal it when I was at work. And the heifer would. She *totally* would.

The silver fox slipped up on me almost daily, and, each time, my heart began beating a mile a minute before I

44

could remind the treacherous thing that men and I didn't mix. Luckily, he'd stopped looking my way, and even the few times he showed up when I was bussing tables, he didn't ask questions or leer at me.

Although, I'll admit I liked the idea of him leering. Well, no, that'd be too much. Looking my way, though. Dang it, there I went again. I was a weak man. For the hundredth time this week alone, I asked myself why I was so bad at ignoring handsome men.

I finally shrugged it off as an internal flaw or something. I had Monday and Tuesday off and had no idea what I would do with myself. Honestly, I could use a day outdoors getting some fresh air. I didn't mind hanging around the motel, so long as I kept to my room. Too many unsavory folks lurked around the place, especially in the evenings. More than once, the sheriff had shown up and hauled someone off. I needed to stay off her radar if at all possible.

I laughed at that. Staying off anyone's radar in this tiny town was impossible. Already, I'd met the sheriff and her deputies, and truth be known, I liked them. They were funny and got along with everyone. Still, I had impending legal troubles south of here, so it'd be best if she only saw me as the guy that worked at the Crawford City Café and not the guy living among what I assumed were meth heads at the Daylight Motel.

I slept in on Monday and ignored the jibes from my coworkers when I came into the café on my day off to eat. The food was too good to pass up, and I was getting used to a big breakfast early in the mornings.

Trails wound into the woods from the motel, and I hadn't been hiking in years. I always did like exploring, though, and having been at the motel for over a week, I knew none of the regulars ever went back there. The only reason the trails were there was because a family of deer showed up in the evenings around dusk.

So, after breakfast, I dashed over to the drugstore where Mrs. Cole's husband worked, found some bug spray that hopefully might keep the ticks at bay, and then went for a walk.

The smell and quiet of the woods hit me the moment I slipped through the undergrowth. Damn, I had forgotten how healing this kind of place was for me. The trails were open and clear, which I was thankful for.

I was reticent to walk in heavy underbrush, though, knowing copperheads liked this terrain, especially with all the mice the downtown buildings must attract.

I'd only gone a short distance when I heard someone shout, "Shit!" and then yelled, "Ouch!"

He said a lot more, but even I didn't want to acknowledge when someone used the Lord's name in vain. I could do without any bad luck brought my way.

"You okay?" I asked, then immediately regretted saying it, thinking I might've accidentally run up on one of the meth heads doing a backwoods deal.

"Hey, over here!" I heard, and the educated accent eased my concerns about running into a thug.

I pushed my way down the path that wound along the side of a gully and into the ravine. I'd only gone a few feet when I spotted my silver fox—yeah, like he was mine—sitting on the ground.

"Hey, you okay?" I asked when I saw him holding his ankle.

He shook his head. "No, I tripped trying to step over that fallen log. I think I sprained my ankle."

"Here, let me help you up. See if you can put weight on it."

Too many years caring for my big-ass family caused me to lean toward nurturing rather than concern for myself, so I didn't hesitate to kneel next to the man and help him up.

When he put weight on the ankle, he sucked in air. "It hurts, but I don't think it's broken."

"How can you tell?" I asked.

He chuckled. "Let's just call it hopeful thinking."

I smiled. "Well, best we get you to the doctor. Can you lean on me while I lead you out?" I asked.

He nodded, and we slowly made our way out of the woods and into the light of day.

Fortunately, we emerged on the backside of the town, where two of the café's regulars, Dr. Gib and Dr. Ash, ran a medical clinic. We weren't more than a block from there.

My injured silver fox didn't complain when he saw where I was taking him, thank goodness, because I didn't have any more minutes left on my phone to call anyone, and he hadn't pulled his out. That was a bit weird since I'd have thought he'd call someone right away.

Before I could think about that, I had him sitting in the waiting room, filled to the brim with crazy kids running around and a couple of old folks coughing up a lung.

I grabbed one of the face masks they had set out for patients, determined not to get sick when I'd just started working, then explained to the lady behind the desk that I'd found the guy, who was currently bent over in pain, after he fell in the woods.

"Dr. Ash," the woman hollered toward the back, "we've got an emergency."

I'd seen Dr. Ash quite a few times while working at the café, and he'd introduced himself once when he and Dr. Gib had come for lunch. So, I felt comfortable enough to explain what'd happened.

I looked around self-consciously as the folks in the lobby fell silent when I relayed everything to the doctor. I hated that I'd shared the man's private business in public, but hell, with the pain he was clearly in, he needed medical attention.

"Okay, thank you," Dr. Ash said, and with my help, we took the man to an exam room.

"I don't got no more minutes on my phone," I said as I was leaving, "but if anyone needs me, I'm over at the Daylight Motel."

"No, wait, you're leaving?" the man asked.

I stood in the doorway, not sure what to say. "Um, yeah, do you need me to stay?"

He nodded and then sucked in a breath as Dr. Ash lifted his foot onto the exam table.

"Oh, okay," I said and went to his side. "Don't you have someone you can call? That man—"

I stopped. Maybe he was up to something in the woods that he didn't want his man to know about. It was none of my business anyway. He looked like he was about to respond when Dr. Ash pulled off the guy's shoe, and I saw his face contort with pain.

"Easy does it," I said and reached over to pat the guy's shoulder.

When the sock came off, I noticed scars and wondered what had caused them, but quickly pushed that out of my head, knowing that was none of my business either. I stood next to him as the doctor examined his foot and said he needed X-rays, which was no surprise. I'd broken a lot of bones growing up, playing hard and running wild across the fields behind my granny's place.

I still doubted such a short fall would break his ankle. Hell, I'd had worse falls at work this week and had a couple of bruises to show for it. But I figured he might've managed to twist the ankle.

Once the doctor left to get someone to take the X-rays, I took that as my cue to leave. "I-I'll leave my number at the desk, but I should probably go."

The man didn't try to stop me this time. "Thank you for your assistance today," he said. "I'm Ruther. You're Clyde, right?"

I smiled and nodded. I didn't like giving my name to strangers. I'd spent enough years on the road to know how easy it was to be vulnerable. It was too late, though.

I'd already told him when I'd run into him the day before. At least now I could put a name to his face as well.

I hesitated and almost went back to shake his hand or something, and felt a magnetic pull toward him when the look of longing swept through his handsome features again. I knew if I let myself, I'd buckle under my own attraction. "If the doctor needs me for anything," I said, intentionally making sure I didn't say if *he* needed me, "he can find me at the motel."

I left without looking back. I couldn't get caught up with this guy. I just couldn't. No matter how much I wanted to ignore the warning bells in my head.

ELEVEN

RUTHER

---

*D*AMN, WAY TO MAKE *a fucking impression*, I thought, as the guy I couldn't stop thinking about all but ran out of the exam room. I really was losing my cool.

Of course, as I looked down at the burn scars on my swollen ankle, I doubted a man as handsome as Clyde would look my way again. Damn good thing he was there when I needed him, and damn lousy timing for my...well, shit, I was a freak show. Who was I kidding?

The only men interested in me were just after my family's wealth. In my miserable life, you'd think I'd have figured that out by now.

I sighed heavily as the tech showed up to take me to get an X-ray. While they worked, I laid back and thought about everything. When I'd spoken to Emanual, he'd said there was a significant need for development, but so far, the small town just wasn't enough to attract a reliable developer for the job.

Of course, I'd let the cat out of the bag, just asking the question. Emanual and Amos both knew of my family's business dealings. It wasn't a secret we'd been in real estate for the past century. If I did dig into a project here in Crawford City, there probably wasn't much money in it, but that didn't matter. I'd be doing it more to keep myself occupied while my mind healed than for any profits I might make.

If the project fell flat on its face before I could get started, so be it. I thought of Clyde again. He was handsome, yes, and he talked like he'd just walked out of a Del Shore movie, which was part of what made me go weak-kneed around him.

Had it not been for the fire...shit, no, don't go down that road. I all but screamed at myself and almost screwed up my X-ray by letting the trauma freak me out again. I rarely had flashbacks like I used to, but—

I closed my eyes and concentrated on the image of a beach with the waves slowly rolling onto the shore. Imagery sometimes helped calm me, stopping the thoughts that sent me into a panic attack.

Thankfully, it worked this time, and the tech finished the X-rays and took me back to the exam room. *Shit, I have to call Corey.*

He'd know my interest in the project had gone from curiosity to action when he found out I'd been snooping around the property. Oh well, it's not like I'd be doing the project without him. Before we'd liquidated the business holdings and my father's estate, Corey had handled a majority of the details. Over the years, he'd become as integral to helping manage my business dealings as my personal life.

I doubted I'd do a very good job managing a new project, even a small one, without Corey's assistance. I didn't know if this would make him happy or angry. Angry, I guessed, since Corey belonged in the hustle and bustle of New York City, not a gossipy small town like Crawford City.

I know he said he would stay, but I didn't expect him to. Before he left, though, I did need him to help me set up the process so I could manage the project on my own. If, that is, I decided to go ahead with it.

I chuckled at myself acting like I hadn't already decided. Yes, I needed a feasibility study to ensure I didn't lose my pants on a development deal. The liquidation of the business and my father's assets had given me more money than I'd ever be able to spend, but that didn't mean I should throw money away.

Years spent watching my father hoard money like a dragon hoarded its treasure was too ingrained in me to throw caution to the wind. However, the more I thought of it, the more I was convinced a project was just the thing I needed to keep my mind on task long enough to face my Crawford City demons.

Demons that were somehow tamed at the moment, though I'd actively avoided visiting the old homestead. Sweat popped out on my forehead at the thought, but Dr. Ash walked in just in time to distract me.

"Well, the good news is it's not broken. You've got yourself a mild sprain."

"And the bad news?" I asked.

He sat down across from me. "The bad news is Jake has heard rumors that you were snooping around the property behind the motel. He's going to hound you like crazy if he catches the scent of you wanting to make some improvements to our town. He's even worse than my father in that regard, like a dog with a bone."

I shook my head. "Jake Hudson? How would Jake know where I was?"

Dr. Ash just laughed. "Welcome to Crawford City, Mr. *Crawford*," he said, emphasizing my last name. "The gossip flows faster here than high-speed internet ever could."

I chuckled. "I seem to remember that from my earlier days."

"And I assure you, it hasn't changed. The good news is, if you are seriously looking at the motel property, Jake is the one you want to talk to. He has his finger on the pulse of Crawford City more than anyone else, except maybe my dad."

I smiled, thinking of Emanual and Amos. "Okay, so what about all this?" I asked, pointing to my ankle. "Just keep it elevated?"

"Yep and soaking it in Epsom salts will help too. I'll get you a wrap to help with the swelling, but keep your weight off it for now, and I'd avoid trampling through the woods until it's healed."

I nodded. "Oh, the man who brought me in said his name is Clyde. I don't know his last name, but he works at the café. What can you tell me about him?" I asked. I knew I was overstepping and that this would probably help fuel the flames of gossip, but didn't care that much. I'd been the subject of gossip and speculation most of my life anyway.

Dr. Ash shrugged. "I don't know much. He's as new as you are, newer considering I don't think he has much of a past here, but if you want the scoop, you've only to ask Mrs. Cole. She owns the café and if she's hired him, you can bet your entire bank account she's researched him. Mrs. Cole is a kind, welcoming person, but she doesn't suffer fools."

I chuckled at the old saying. "I'm sure you're right. No matter, though. He rescued me, and I thought it'd be nice to thank him."

Dr. Ash studied me a moment, clearly seeing where my interest lay. "Well, the man could probably use an ally. As far as I know, he's not got anyone here, and we can all use a friend. Wouldn't you agree?"

I smiled. "Yes, I do."

I heard Corey asking about me through the thin walls of the clinic, and I smiled at the doctor. "Speaking of friends, I think my ride just arrived. Is there anything else I need to know?" I asked, and he looked at me funny.

"About the foot," I quickly added.

Dr. Ash laughed. "No, just what I've already told you. Clara Sue will check you out, and you can take regular acetaminophen or ibuprofen for the pain. As long as you don't put weight on it, it shouldn't hurt you much."

I nodded and stood to follow him out. He helped me hobble into the waiting room, where Corey had clearly already given my insurance information to the receptionist. By the time I reached them, the woman smiled and said we were all set.

Corey didn't say anything. He just slipped his arm around me and let me lean on him as we walked outside to our rental car.

"Don't start," I said when he climbed into the driver's seat.

He pursed his lips and started the engine. "You get one day's pass. Then you're going to tell me what's going on in that scheming mind of yours."

"Might I remind you that you work for me?" I said, teasing him like I always did.

"You might provide the paychecks, but I do the work, and you had no excuse crawling around the woods of this backwater town without someone knowing where you'd gone. You didn't even take your phone!" He shook his head. "Now, see, you've got me arguing with you, and I promised myself I would give you time to heal before I did."

I chuckled and put my hand on his shoulder. "Thanks, Corey. I've got some ideas, but I wanted to see if it was worth the effort before I got you involved."

"More like you wanted to scheme behind my back," he said, sounding annoyed, "but your business is your own.

I will remind you, though, that *my* business is to keep an eye on yours."

I smiled but didn't respond. I'd been thoroughly chastised, and, honestly, Corey had let me off the hook easily. Had I not been injured, he would've come down on me like the overprotective diva he was. Not that he still wouldn't, but ultimately, I'd dodged a bullet this time.

On the short drive to the condo, we stopped at the drugstore and Corey ran in to buy me crutches and over-the-counter pain medicine. Given stairs were no longer an option, we rode the elevator to our second-story accommodations. Corey helped get me situated in bed, checked the bandaging, and gave me the pain meds before retiring to his own room.

The last image that came to my mind before I fell asleep was that of my very handsome rescuer. *Clyde*. What an old-fashioned name for such a young man. It didn't match his persona. He looked more like a Kyle or Drew to me.

A smile curled my lips as sleep began to take me. Leave it to me to feel entitled enough to change someone's name. Must be the Crawford blood running through my veins.

Twelve

Clyde

By THE TIME I left the clinic, it was after lunchtime. I wondered if it'd be too much for me to go to the café for my lunch after having already visited that morning. I thought it probably would be, at least for eating in, so I decided to get takeout.

I didn't mind takeout, really. Fried chicken, for example, was just as good to me cold as it was hot. Today, though, I had a hankering for a hamburger. Mrs. Cole saw me come in and immediately asked about Ruther.

"You found him in the woods?" she asked, and I noticed all the interested faces around me.

"Yes, I think he was out for a walk. It's easy to trip over things while exploring. I think he's going to be okay."

"Well, you did good. I'm glad you found him before he had to linger out there. So, what can I get for you?" she asked.

I forced myself not to look around at the eavesdroppers. "I think I'd like a burger to go, and I'm gonna grab some sides too. I'm up for a night at home watchin' TV," I announced, knowing the gossip would have me and Ruther in the throes of some torrid love affair if I didn't put them off the subject now while I could.

"Well, nothing like a night *alone*," Mrs. Cole emphasized before winking at me, "to put the body right. Especially after the week of work you put in."

I smiled and nodded. She left to get my burger started while I filled one of the to-go containers with goodies for tonight's supper. I loved fried chicken, and Lord knows I'd worked hard enough and got enough steps in this week that I could eat it without guilt, not that I gained much weight anyway. No, I was born skinny, and unless my very obvious genetics wore off, I'd die that way.

Despite that, I knew I needed more nutrition than greasy chicken provided, so I dished up some turnip greens, green beans, and sweet potatoes to go with it.

I looked at the desserts and moaned happily as I saw the homemade chocolate meringue. I hadn't had that yet, but Mrs. Cole made all the desserts herself, and I'd yet to eat anything she made that didn't make me want to cry with joy. Nutritional value be damned.

I grabbed another to-go container and dished a big slice of pie into it. By the time I got to the checkout counter, Mrs. Cole came up with my burger, also packed to go. She'd also included some plastic cutlery and heaps of napkins, which was kind of her.

I walked from the café, happy until I got to the motel and surveyed the unsavory crowd that'd already begun to gather in the parking lot. It's unlikely they were from Crawford City. Of course, I didn't know for sure, but I did know that it didn't matter where you were, whether in a big city or a small town, these old motels seemed to attract the same type of people.

I mean, I had to stay in them too, but the addicts seemed to flow from one seedy motel to the next, always leaving havoc in their wake. Staying off their radar, if at all possible, was how to survive.

I usually did. I was short and quiet and not very memorable. I mean, I could stick out when I wanted to, but sticking out always attracted the wrong crowd. Images of my ex as he knocked me around came to mind.

Ducking my head, I slipped by them unnoticed and sighed with relief as the door shut behind me. I flipped on the TV and pulled out my burger, pleased Mrs. Cole had doctored it up like I liked with all the fixings except lettuce. I'd never understand why people wanted it on a burger.

I contemplated Ruther as I devoured the feast. He'd been in pain but had managed it better than I thought a fancy man of privilege would. Men in his situation either gushed over me, wanting to get me in the sack for a quick fuck, or they stuck their noses up the moment I walked within sight. Ruther hadn't done either, although he was clearly interested in me. Sexually, that is.

I didn't expect there to be more encounters between us other than perhaps crossing paths again at the café.

Still, after finishing my lunch and disposing of the waste, I laid down and pondered what it would be like to have a man of status like Ruther consider me as something more than a plaything.

I ended up laughing at myself. I was as plain and country as they came. Ruther was like a shiny Lexus, whereas I was a beat-up Cadillac. Sure, fancy men like him might take me for a spin, but I wasn't worth showing off. Soon enough, they'd trade me in for a better ride. I shook my head then. When had I begun to compare myself to cars?

Thirteen

Ruther

Aﾠfter tossing and turning all night, and pain hitting me every time I moved, I somehow woke the next morning surprisingly rested. I hobbled into the living room on my crutches, and Corey greeted me with a smile.

As always, he went to the coffee pot, poured and fixed my coffee as I liked, and placed it in front of me. "I spoke with Jake Hudson about the condo, and he assured me a long-term stay works just fine. Apparently, the owner got married recently and is extending the honeymoon."

I grinned at our lucky timing. "Thanks, that's great news."

"Oh, and another thing," Corey said and peered at me over his glasses, a sure sign I wouldn't like what he was going to say next. "Word's clearly gotten out about why you were lurking in the woods. Mr. Hudson would like to meet with you about your 'development plans.'"

I chuckled despite Corey's accusatory look. "Yes, Dr. Ash warned me that Jake was on the trail. I guess he's the town busybody."

"Well, you don't need me to tell you it's never good for a development project's potential to leak before it's settled. You'll have all sorts of trouble when the locals come at you with pitchforks."

I shrugged. "There's no project, Corey. I'm simply curious."

"So, I should decline Mr. Hudson's meeting invitation on your behalf?" Corey asked.

"No, let's hear what he has to say."

Corey humphed and looked back down at his laptop. I sipped my coffee and stood to go to the kitchen for something to eat.

"Don't eat much. The meeting is this morning for breakfast. In fact, you've just got enough time to get a shower."

"Okay, help me unwrap this ankle. The tightness hurts," I said, and Corey nodded.

I washed down more pain meds with the last of my coffee, then basically crawled into the shower. I was happy to talk to Jake and anyone else about a potential project, but honestly, I was more excited to see Clyde now that I'd officially met him. Maybe if I played my cards right, he'd let me get to know him better.

I was disappointed when we walked into the café and Clyde was nowhere to be seen. When Mrs. Cole, who I now knew was his boss, caught me looking, she smiled and whispered, "Today's his day off."

I grinned sheepishly. "Am I that obvious?" I whispered back.

"You'll find this town is full of interested parties, but I think I'm the only one who noticed. You'll be looking for Jake and his posse, too, I'm guessing?"

I laughed. "You don't miss much, do you?"

Her eyes twinkled as she smiled at me. "Over in the far corner. That's where Jake likes to hold court."

I nodded and headed over. Corey had helped me into the café, but to avoid making me look weak in the face of potential partners, he let me hobble to the table aided only by my crutches.

"Good morning," Jake said upon seeing us. "Come have a seat."

Two chairs sat side by side, clearly pulled over in anticipation of our arrival. After we shook hands and sat down, Jake made the introductions. "This is Lance, my husband, and I think you've already met Amos and his husband Doc, our mayor. But I don't believe you've met Todd, Amos's son, and Linc, his right-hand man."

I smiled and greeted each of them. It probably should've been disconcerting, but it amused me how everyone in town seemed to know our names regardless of if we'd been formally introduced.

"So, I hear you paid my better half a visit yesterday," Todd said and nodded toward my crutches. When he saw my look of confusion, he added, "My husband runs the medical clinic in town."

"You're married to Dr. Ash?" I asked. Todd smiled and nodded, and the way his eyes sparkled at the mention of his husband's name, I figured there was a good story there. I also wondered how I'd missed the fact that Amos's son and Emanual's son were married, given the ever-present grapevine that ran through Crawford City.

"Before you boys get started with all your important business," Mrs. Cole said behind us, "go get something to eat. Mr. Corey, shall I get you your regular?"

Corey smiled up at her, a genuine smile, unlike what he usually gave servers in restaurants. "No, ma'am, I think I'd like to try your buffet today."

I'm not sure who was more surprised, me or Mrs. Cole, but when I glanced at her, she seemed to have recognized the honor it was for Corey even to consider eating at a buffet. His willingness to try it was testament to Mrs. Cole's cleanliness.

Corey stood and immediately solved my twisted ankle issue by saying, "Why don't you and Mr. Hudson discuss the particulars of the condo while I get us both something to eat?"

Jake clearly understood what was happening and smiled up at Corey before nodding.

"So," I began as soon as the rest of the party were at the buffet, "how did you figure out I was interested in the motel property?" I ignored Corey's suggestion we talk about the condo. I knew for a fact my assistant had all those details ironed out and they'd be contractually solid.

Jake seemed amused by my directness. "Crawford City's a small town, and not much happens here that I don't hear about. As it happens, though, I was coming back from a trip to Nashville and caught sight of you hobbling out of the woods with that good-looking fella Mrs. Cole just hired."

"And you figured we'd only be in the woods together because I want to purchase the property?"

Jake stared at me for a beat, then burst out laughing. "Mr. Crawford, you don't strike me as a man who goes for a roll in the woods with handsome strangers, so unless my instincts were off, you were there for some other reason."

I nodded, unable to hide my smile. "Between you and me, I wouldn't mind a roll in the woods with that particular man, but no, you're correct. I went there because I'm curious about a potential development opportunity so close to downtown."

Jake nodded. "Things in these parts have changed a lot over the years, I'd like to think mostly for the better." The rest of the crew returned to our table as he spoke. "However, that area has been considered blighted since the railroad split it from the rest of town."

I looked around the group as they all nodded in agreement. "So, if development is done in an area the town considers blighted, will they consider it ever being anything but?"

"Oh, that's all in the PR," Jake said. "Which, lucky for you, I'm an expert in."

I chuckled. Jake was a character and one I enjoyed getting to know. A lot more had to be figured out, though, because had I not been hesitant before, I most certainly would be now. Knowing how the rest of the town viewed that swathe of land was cause for caution moving forward.

I listened as each man talked about the need for more residential housing. Corey knew enough to question them without my involvement, shaking out more detailed information and jotting notes on his phone to review later.

Ultimately, before we all disbanded, I'd learned that the men agreed small, middle-income housing was the type most needed. Apartments were unlikely to be a good solution, at least not yet. They also didn't hold back in saying more than a few townsfolk would be happy to see the old motel leveled.

I wondered where that would leave someone like Clyde. He was staying in that motel, and to be honest, besides it being a little run-down, it didn't seem as seedy as these guys were making it out to be. I'd certainly seen worse.

Later, once Corey and I were back in the solitude of the condo, he began peppering me with questions. "What's on your mind? Do you think apartments? Will the local economy continue to grow, or will it stagnate? Or maybe it's already in decline?"

I didn't answer, instead letting my assistant's very sharp mind ferret out all the necessary questions to create a reliable feasibility assessment.

We worked the day away, both of us on our laptops, and when my body complained about sitting for too long, I told Corey I was going to the hotel gym.

"Stay off that foot, or you'll have major issues," he warned.

"Yes, *Mother*," I said as I slipped into my room to change. I could lift weights, at least, even though my body was craving cardio. Perhaps this was punishment for traipsing through the wilderness without proper footwear. Corey had yet to confront me about my poor choices, and I wasn't fool enough to think I wouldn't have to face it eventually, but for now, he was intrigued with the project enough to give me some breathing room.

That shocked me, to be honest. Corey loved a project, but always in New York or another large city. He was not a small-town guy, and as smart as he was, I knew he understood this project couldn't bring in the same revenues as our urban builds. How could it?

Regardless, I was happy for the reprieve.

FOURTEEN

CLYDE

"HEY, YOU," A MAN yelled at me as I returned to the motel after a quick run to the store.

"Shit," I muttered to myself, pretending I didn't hear him.

"No, you don't. You come here. Don't I know you?"

I looked over, knowing if I ignored him now, the consequences would be worse. "Me?" I asked.

"Yeah, you. You look like... Oh, I *do* know you. You and that faggot Jimmy were a thing."

I cringed. Less because he'd called my ex-boyfriend Jimmy a derogatory term than because he'd recognized me. "No, I'm Alan Swift, but folks tell me I favor other people all the time."

I turned to go into my room, which, luckily, was close. "No, you look too much like him, unless you got a twin."

69

I waved behind me as I slipped inside. "Shit," I said as the door swung shut and I threw the deadbolt. "This isn't good."

I set the groceries on top of the dresser and paced the room, trying to figure out what I should do. Leave. That's the solution I usually went with, and it made the most sense. The problem was I didn't want to leave.

Also, as long as I was staying in no-tell motels, someone who knew me, knew my family, or, in this case, knew an ex, would keep showing up. Small towns were notorious for everyone being in everyone else's business. The community that man belonged to, the one I accidentally fell into because I'd gone out with someone like Jimmy, well, it was small too.

I heard the motorcycles and knew the guy and others were leaving. They'd been here a few nights, and I'd avoided them until tonight—stupid, careless me. I got back here later than intended. I'd stopped by the café on the way to the store, and Mrs. Cole had said "my admirer," as she put it, had come looking for me.

Of course, I knew instantly who she meant. I was thinking about Ruther instead of keeping my head down when the jackass had spotted me. Would he tell Jimmy? The fact he'd referred to my ex as a faggot told me he didn't have good feelings for the man.

That didn't mean he wouldn't sell me out if Jimmy was still looking though. Considering the amount of money I had taken from him, he very likely still was. I forced all that out of my mind as I put my groceries away.

I flipped the TV on, hoping it would calm me, and smiled as I recognized the old movie with Bette Midler called *Beaches*. This was the part where Bette's character and her best friend had moved in together and she's banging on the pipes with a frying pan to get heat to their apartment. That scene always made me laugh.

I let the sad but awesome movie distract me until I was ready for bed. Tomorrow would be an early morning since I'd once again agreed to be at the café at four. We were all-hands-on-deck until Mrs. Cole found someone to replace the woman she'd fired. Luckily, though, thoughts of work were swept aside for more desirable ones of Ruther. With him in mind, I fell asleep with a smile on my face.

Fifteen

Ruther

I SAT ACROSS FROM Corey, who'd returned to ordering his poached eggs and hollandaise sauce, and watched for any sign of Clyde. Mrs. Cole had winked at me when I came in, so I knew somewhere back in the kitchen was the man I longed to see.

I ignored Corey, who gave me a knowing look that made me want to yell at him, but I was rewarded with a perplexed-looking Clyde a few moments later. He came out of the kitchen with the bussing tray and looked over the restaurant until his gaze fell upon mine.

He smirked as he turned back toward the kitchen's closed door, and I realized Mrs. Cole must've kicked him out of the kitchen so he could show up while I was out here.

He didn't immediately come over but bussed a few tables on the other side of the restaurant. Not that many needed it.

When Clyde came to our side of the restaurant, he smiled at me. "Hi, Ruther. Nice to see you. Your ankle doing better?" he asked.

I nodded and felt my face heat. I liked this guy a bit too much if he made me blush.

Across from me, my assistant cleared his throat and smiled. "I'm Corey King. It's nice to meet you." Then he waited for the object of my desire to introduce himself.

"Name's Clyde Griffin. Pleasure to meet you, Corey," he said. "Can I take those plates?" He gestured to the dish I'd moved to the side after I'd devoured a cinnamon roll off it.

Once Clyde took the plate, he finished bussing tables, and before slipping through the kitchen door again, he glanced back over and smiled.

"You've got it bad," Corey said.

"Got what?"

He laughed. "Just remember, there's consequences for squeezing the Twinkies!"

"You're so crass," I said but chuckled nonetheless. Clyde did have a distinctive twink quality to him, although I could tell there was more to him than the hot young model types Corey seemed to go after.

When Jake came in and asked if he could join us, I didn't hesitate to scoot over. Had we been in the city, I'd have thought it strange and intrusive if someone asked to join Corey and me for breakfast, but I'd been here long enough to realize it was pretty much how things were done.

Jake talked a mile a minute about how his buddies, who'd opened a winery, were going to expand their store in the hotel.

"A winery in Tennessee?" I asked and barely managed to suppress a shudder at how awful the wine must taste.

Jake caught the incredulous tone in question, though, and laughed. "Trust me, it's better than you'd expect, but don't take my word for it. Why don't you two join me this afternoon? Lance and I are going to drive up to the winery and have lunch with Logan and Matt, the owners."

Corey gave me a meaningful look, telling me I needed to do this since we were considering a project that Jake could influence, like it or not.

"Sure," I said, pasting a smile on my face. I dreaded the sickly sweet wine I could all but taste now. God help me, this project better be worth it if I had to swallow swill and pretend it award-worthy.

Emanual and Amos came into the café a moment later with a sweet-faced young man I hadn't met before, and they stopped by the table before sitting down.

"This is Chris, our town librarian," Amos said.

I held out my hand for a shake. "Nice to meet you, Chris. I'm Ruther Crawford," I said, and the librarian's mouth dropped open.

"Wow, I-I didn't realize you were in town. My husband is Roth Gallo. We bought and renovated your home on the hill."

Just like that, the panic overtook me. I nodded, trying to ignore the cold sweat that instantly engulfed my body—the feeling of fire burning my flesh.

"Ruther, Rutherford," I heard Corey say, but I'd gone too far. I wasn't coming back from this one, at least not yet.

"I-I..." I tried to say, but the words wouldn't come.

Then I felt a strong but gentle hand on my shoulder. I didn't know who it belonged to, other than it wasn't Corey. "Ruther," the voice said, and a soothing feeling like milk on my tongue after eating a chili came over me.

"Is he okay?" the voice asked.

A very concerned-looking Clyde came into focus. "I-I'm okay. Just threw me for a moment."

I glanced around and saw a sea of concerned faces staring at me. "It's no wonder. You probably forgot your medication this morning," Corey said conversationally. "If it weren't for me, that man would forget to brush his teeth." As my assistant expertly clamored on to divert attention away from me, the panic began to recede until I could breathe normally. Thank God for Corey.

Clyde's hand never left my shoulder, a support that sent shockwaves through me. I knew it was either the weight of that hand that had helped me calm down as quickly as I did, or the fear that he'd never look at me with any respect again if I didn't calm down.

"Sorry, I need a moment," I said and stood. Corey stood with me. "No, stay here. I'm going to go take a walk. I'll meet you back at the condo." I strode toward the door as best as I could on crutches and didn't look back to see if he was following me.

I didn't get far when someone grabbed my shoulder again. "Ruther, wait a moment," Clyde said. "Your legs are longer than mine, even on crutches." He made me slow down when I'd rather have run—figuratively speaking—all the way back to the condo and then back to New York as fast as I could.

I couldn't look him in the face, not after that. I hadn't had a panic attack in public in a long time, and prior to that, my dad or one of his lackeys always stood close to whisk me away before I could embarrass them.

"I'm sorry, I-I just—"

"You had a panic attack, honey," he said. I looked up, fear of what I would see on his face causing my chest to constrict again. But I only saw understanding.

"Here, let's sit on this bench," Clyde said, leading me over to the side of the road where the library stood. Seeing it almost sent me back into another panic, thinking of the librarian who said he and his husband had redone the old house. Even now, the thoughts of fire burning me began to creep into my mind.

"Shhh, I know a panic attack when I see one. Lord knows I've had plenty myself."

He babbled on, mostly stuff I wasn't hearing, but his voice was soothing, keeping the memories of fire at bay. Finally, I took a deep breath and relaxed. A sure sign the attack was receding. "Damn, that one was...it's been a while since one that intense has hit me."

I felt Clyde's weight leaning against me. He didn't say anything, just sat there, holding my hand, leaning into my side, and looking out over the town. I expected him to ask me what happened, or at least say he had to get back to work, but instead, he just sat there until Corey finally came out of the café, looked around, and found us sitting on the bench.

"Well, I see Clyde has come to the rescue yet again. Thank you, Clyde, and you've done a good job," Corey said, smiling at me. His smile was tense, though, and I could tell he was still putting on a pretense until he could get me out of the public eye.

I turned toward Clyde and smiled before bumping up against him slightly. "Thanks, that helped...a lot," I said, and he just winked at me and stood. He was about to leave when I asked, "Clyde, do you have plans tonight?"

He stood frozen for a moment, then shook his head. "No, but I have to work early tomorrow morning. You'll be coming in for breakfast, right? If you can come around nine, I can take my break then. Will that work?"

I smiled, heat rising on my face, but still pale from the episode. "Yeah, nine works. See you tomorrow."

He left then, and Corey sat down. "I'm sorry, boss, I-I didn't realize..." He let it hang there instead of finishing what I knew he was thinking.

I turned and looked back at the library, then quickly stood before the librarian decided to return to work. "Come on. I need a shot of something strong."

"You need to lie down and rest," Corey said, but a drink might be good too. Besides, if you still feel up to it, you told Jake Hudson you're willing to go try out his friend's winery. If you want to stay on his good side—" He paused, and I knew he was thinking about my attack. "—I think you should go."

"Yeah, you're probably right. Can you arrange a time? I think I will go take that rest, although, to be honest, the shot would be better."

"Being drunk on the job wouldn't, though."

"Yeah, yeah," I said and chuckled despite the fact my nerves were still frayed. At least I wasn't still imagining all the ugly stuff I had been. Instead, I was thinking about a sweet, unassuming, handsome knight who'd come swooping in for my rescue.

Sixteen

Clyde

I DIDN'T THINK. I saw Ruther freaking out and instantly knew he was having a panic attack. I had no idea what had led up to it, but I'd had enough of them to know how to spot one.

I went over just as his partner said something about medication. Anxiety medication, maybe, but I doubted he needed meds as much as he needed an escape. He excused himself a moment later, and before I could let Mrs. Cole know I was going to check on him, he was gone.

Shit, he shouldn't be alone, I thought, and rushed headlong after him. Ruther calmed down easily enough, and despite my curiosity, I forced myself not to ask questions. I didn't want to risk sending him into another panic attack.

Personal experience told me he just needed someone to sit with him while he got himself back under control. I didn't think about Mrs. Cole or the restaurant until after I started back. *Crap, crap, crap, crap, will I lose my job?* I mean, in most places, that's all it'd take.

I slipped back in the front door, and instead of an angry boss, I saw kindness and relief. "Thank you, Clyde. You did good," she said, patting my shoulder.

I should've known someone with a kind heart like Mrs. Cole would see what I'd done as a good thing, not a lack of work ethic. I sighed with relief as I grabbed the bussing equipment and returned to work. Lunch rush was around the corner, and the dining room was a total mess.

I tried not to listen to the table of men who remained as I cleaned up, but I caught bits of their conversation. Something about a fire years ago at the Crawford family's house that the librarian now owned.

The poor guy was apologetic, and I felt sorry for him, but I felt worse for Ruther. I remembered the scars on his foot and figured they were probably from that. He was back in Crawford City, maybe to address his past somehow? I had no idea, but I hadn't had such a strong sense to protect someone since my nieces and nephew were little.

I sighed as I collected the rest of the dishes, bussed them back to the kitchen, and brought out the vacuum. No use dwelling on what I couldn't fix, and that probably included me. At least I wasn't just lusting after the poor man. I felt a kinship with him and a need to help him get through his troubles.

I mean, I still felt attraction, but nurturing always overcame other feelings inside me. As I vacuumed the crumbs of the morning rush, I couldn't help looking forward to tomorrow morning's break. Maybe I could become friends with Ruther and his...whatever Corey was to him. Husband, boyfriend, other? The way Ruther reacted to me in front of Corey suggested that whatever the relationship, it was open. I didn't intend to get in the middle of that, but I felt connected to Ruther, so whatever happened, I'd be here for him, at least in the short-term. Not that the man needed me. The need was in me, though.

Seventeen

Ruther

Despite dreading the winery, I smiled when Jake and Lance met me at the condo door. "You know, we need to invite you two up for dinner one night, especially since you're staying right below us," Jake commented.

"That'd be nice," I said and meant it. "So, elephant in the room and all that, I'm sorry—"

Jake put his hand up. "No need to mention it except to say Chris feels horrible about making you uncomfortable. He'd like to make it up to you, but let's leave that for now. Shall we go to the winery?"

Despite my resolve to behave, I cringed just enough for Jake to catch it. Fortunately, he chuckled and patted my shoulder. "You're going to be pleasantly surprised, trust me."

Corey had tried to beg off, but I squared him with a look that said if I had to endure it, he did as well. When he said he had to work, I simply reminded him his phone worked just as well in the car as in the condo. Ultimately, I didn't back down like I usually did. No, if I had to endure the Tennessee sweet wine, he would too.

The drive to the winery was breathtaking. We drove up hills that opened onto vistas through the trees. Cows grazed lazily in fields along the route. It didn't feel real as we drove—more like watching a scene from a movie. I'd completely forgotten about the beauty of the area. Not that I had spent much time out here.

I quickly forced my mind away from those thoughts, knowing that line of thinking eventually led to a panic attack. One was enough for today.

Corey and I gasped as we pulled into the winery's parking lot and saw the old mill. The water wheel was still turning in the creek that ran alongside. When we walked toward the entrance, I leaned over and whispered to Corey that the view alone made it worth the trip.

He shrugged, not convinced, even if he'd agree the picturesque setting was spectacular.

We were greeted as we walked into the mill by a young woman who appeared to be in her midtwenties. She hugged Jake and Lance, then shook Corey's hand and mine. "Welcome. My name is Lia. Jake called ahead, telling me you were coming, so I've set up a tasting for you upstairs."

At least the setting was first-rate. The problem was sweet wines, even those prized as dessert wines from Italy, did nothing for me. In fact, they made me gag.

I'd decided to forgo my crutches, since my ankle was feeling better, but climbing the stairs took more time than it normally would've. I wasn't prepared for what I saw and the moment I was in the space, my mouth fell open. The second-floor room was open just as it was below, but original hand-hewn beams decorated the ceiling. Large picture windows stretched across the entire space, letting in lots of natural light. Then I spotted the artwork.

Like the wine, I kept my expectations low and figured it would be anything from velvet paint by numbers to amateurish art, but as I wandered over to the canvases, I saw how wrong I was. I'm not an art connoisseur, but my father considered quality artwork as investments. He and his friends fretted about it enough that I eventually learned what to look for, in case a piece of art came available.

These pieces were magnificent, with confident brush strokes that adorned the canvases with color, and shadow that contrasted beautifully with the light. I was mesmerized. I turned to see Corey had the same expression on his face. "These are stunning," Corey exclaimed, and for a brief moment, I remembered my assistant had majored in art before coming to work for me.

Lance and Jake, along with the woman, Lia, were all smiling knowingly at us. "They are true works of art," Lance said.

"Who's the artist?" Corey asked, almost reverently.

"Matt Brinks. He's becoming quite well-known," Lance replied.

"I can see why," I said.

"Well, let's get to what you came for," Lia said, leading us to a beautiful table in front of a window that showed both the wheel outside and what must be remnants of the original building before it was renovated.

She placed wine glasses in front of us, along with spit buckets and water. I'd been to enough wine tastings to know they took this seriously. In fact, even if the wine tasted horrible, the setup would make any French winery proud.

"I'm going to start you with our merlot," she said, pouring each of us a glass. "You'll notice our merlot is slightly different from what you might find on the West Coast. That's the natural acidic soil." I swirled my glass and sniffed, surprised to find the acceptable scents for a table merlot.

Lia was saying something about how the soils of Tennessee had once been an ancient sea, but the flavor burst forth enough to cause me to focus less on her and more on the taste. Perfect? No. Equal to the French or the Western U.S. wines? No. But I wouldn't hesitate to put this on my table, even if I were entertaining.

Lia smiled at my surprised reaction and pulled out another bottle. "Pinot noir is the first grape we tried here at the winery," she said as we all swished and prepared for the next tasting. Jake and Lance watched closely as we tipped the wine back, and the flavor flooded my pallet.

My eyes widened as I was overwhelmed by the taste. "This is delightful. This wasn't raised in Tennessee. You're pulling my leg," I said, and Jake, Lance, and Lia all laughed.

"I grew up on Long Island. My father was a lead physician there, and he is the biggest wine snob I've ever met, yet even he can't fault the wine here," Lance said.

Both things shocked me. First, Lance was from Long Island. I hadn't detected an accent on the drive here, or the other times I'd spent with him. His accent made me think he'd probably grown up here. Second, this wine was probably one of the best pinot noirs I'd tasted, and since it's one of my favorite wines, I've tasted my fair share of them.

"It's won more than a few awards, all of which are on display downstairs behind the official tasting area. I'll let you peruse those on your own. No one likes a boastful host," Lia said, chuckling.

She hesitated momentarily, then sighed. "I wasn't going to try this one out on you. It's a bit of an acquired taste, but we've been experimenting with one of our wild grapes here. It's called muscadine, and normally it's disgustingly sweet. Great for jelly, mind you, but not good for wine."

She paused and shook her head. "I'll just hush and let you taste it. Tell me honestly what you think."

I was back to my original fear of tasting a disgustingly sweet wine when Lia poured each of us a glass. "We haven't perfected it, but the blends are nice, and—" She gestured for us to sip. "—you will catch that intense bite of muskiness. That's the muscadine. We want to capture that while avoiding the sweetness."

I could tell where she was going with it. The bite was pleasant. The blend wasn't bad either, but she was correct, it wasn't quite right, at least not yet. "If you can figure this out, it's going to become a favorite," I said and took another sip, enjoying the different flavor profiles.

She smiled. "I'm glad you think so. Logan, our vintner, is fairly certain this year's batch will yield the results we're hoping for. Lots of people have tried to tame the Tennessee muscadine, but none have accomplished it...yet."

"Invite us back!" Corey blurted, surprising me.

Lia smiled and nodded. "I'm afraid you'll have to wait at least another year, but you're welcome to come test the new samples then. In the meantime, would you two enjoy coming for the harvest? If you're here this fall, Logan and Matt host a huge harvest festival. It's become quite the event."

"Do they share their wine?" I asked, getting a chuckle from everyone except Corey, who was still looking wide-eyed at the wine we'd just tasted.

"We do, but it will cost you. If you're willing to sit through Logan's classes, you can actually help harvest the grapes."

"But he's becoming more and more of a stickler as time goes on," Jake said, triggering a snicker from Lia.

"The man is a perfectionist when it comes to his grapes, but as you can taste, he's extracting some amazing flavors out of them."

"That he is!" I admitted before Lia left all three bottles open in front of us, pulled out a cheese tray from a refrigerator behind her, and set the tray on top of the bar. "Help yourself. This is Jake's treat. Enjoy," she said and went back downstairs.

"This wine is so much better than I would've dreamed. I honestly believed it was going to make me gag."

Both Lance and Jake chuckled. "We knew exactly what you expected, but we enjoyed watching you discover it, just like we did."

I poured myself another glass of the excellent pinot, and when Corey gestured toward his glass, I also poured him some. "I'd like to buy several bottles to take back to the condo," I said, and Jake nodded.

"That's expected, too, but just so you know, they also have a nice setup in the hotel. You can walk over anytime and buy whatever you like."

"Do they just serve reds?" Corey asked.

"No, actually. I didn't ask for any of the whites since I have to drive us back to Crawford City and I'll be tempted to drink too much as it is, but their whites are nice as well. Not quite the level of perfection as the pinot, but give our Logan some more time and he'll have those perfected as well."

"I'd like to meet this Logan," I said and was interrupted by Corey.

"And Matt, I'd like to meet the artist."

Jake patted Corey's back companionably. "I'll set it up. Meanwhile, I'd like to talk to you about your development, where the ever-present gossips aren't as likely to hear."

I nodded, figuring that was the real purpose behind this winery tour.

"Crawford City is growing fast, and we're struggling to keep up with the housing demand. We all told you true, that we aren't quite ready for an apartment complex. Even as nice as the condos are, if I weren't one of the owners, and my friend Jen hadn't bought the second, the third probably would've been more difficult to sell than I'm comfortable admitting."

I nodded, anticipating as much. "Do you think single-family housing is needed then?" I asked.

"I think it's a need we can't ignore any longer despite the town's unflattering opinion of that property's *side of the tracks*," he replied, using air quotes on the last bit. "Things have changed a lot over the years. The bar and the motel blight the area, but as you know, nothing else is over there."

"So, you think if we tear down the motel and close the bar, we'd change the town's opinion, and people would readily buy in that area?"

Jake snorted. "You'll not be tearing the bar down anytime soon. That old saloon is a local landmark of sorts. In the early eighties, the ladies of the town went on a crusade to close it down once and for all. As you can see, they lost."

"But the townsfolk still think of it as blighted?"

Jake nodded. "Yes, for the time being. As the new owner of said bar, I know for a fact it's about to go through some significant changes."

"Well, that seems like half the battle's won already," I said, and I caught sight of Corey, who couldn't quite hide his pleasure at the news. Both he and I had seen projects die in the suburbs where one establishment, hated by a community, could sink an otherwise beneficial project.

"So, you'd do the renovations soon? Perhaps in tandem with a new housing development?"

Jake winked at me and then looked at his husband. "A brilliant architect I know already has a few ideas about a potential development—"

Lance elbowed Jake and then laughed. "My sweet husband tends to speak before he should," Lance said. "After hearing you were looking at the property, we did start talking about what kind of development would do best in the area and how to help you avoid some of the pitfalls of the town council."

I nodded skeptically and glanced at Corey, who was clearly as unsure as I was.

"Let's do this. Give me a few days, and I'll put together a proposal. Not that you have to use me, but I'm the only local architect left in the area now my mentor has retired," Lance said. "There are plenty of Nashville architects you could use, but if you give me a chance, I think I have some ideas to inspire you."

I couldn't help but cock my eyebrow, and Lance grinned. "I'm not pulling a fast one on you. I promise no hard feelings if you don't like what I've got to show, but please give me the chance."

I knew Lance and Jake both held a lot of sway with the community, and considering they were also our ride back to town from the winery, there really was nothing I could do but nod and smile.

"Okay, business done. If you're finished with the cheese and wine, we'd like to show you our favorite part of this property."

"I'd like to buy a few bottles before we leave," I said, and Jake nodded.

Corey and I took our time exploring the retail shop, and I selected several bottles to purchase. Although Jake said the whites weren't quite as good as the reds, I wanted to try them all. I had always loved wine, more than I should at times, and I was impressed with this little shock of a winery. At the very least, I wanted to spend some money here to encourage them to keep up the good work.

Once our boxes of wine were loaded in Jake and Lance's trunk, they led us down a path and up to one of the most beautiful little chapels I've ever seen. My family were Quakers, and the no-nonsense aspects of the meeting houses used by the Friends, as they were called, was the polar opposite of this place. It probably would've turned the more ardent Friends off, but I couldn't help but be intrigued by the beauty and spiritual elements of the space.

I was utterly smitten by this quaint little country winery. As we drove back to town, my thoughts drifted to the man who'd smitten me in a similar way. Clyde wasn't a refined man. He had a strong accent, and despite his small build, his muscles were toned by long hours of hard work. He was so unlike the few men I'd dated in the past, and I found it refreshing.

I wondered what it might be like to bring him to the winery. Share some wine and cheese with him. Wander up the path to the adorable chapel. Maybe steal a kiss or five hundred. I chuckled at the romantic scene playing out in my mind.

There was something special about Clyde, but I got the impression that he didn't think of himself that way. I wondered how I might go about convincing him otherwise.

Eighteen

Clyde

I WAS BEYOND HONORED when Mrs. Cole asked if I'd help her with the desserts. I'd been helping cook when she asked me, and both the server, a woman who'd been working here for years, and the cook froze.

I nodded and followed Mrs. Cole into the area of the kitchen where she prepared desserts. "I bring more people into my café with my baking than with my food, and I've been waiting for someone who appreciates the need to do things right. That's why you're the first person I've trained to do this since my cousin Gloria retired a few years back. Now, I need you to watch and listen. I have my little secrets I throw in to make it all taste special and last longer. Can you do that?" she asked. I immediately nodded my head. "Good, I figured I could count on you."

I gave her my full attention as she threw together dessert after dessert. I'd tried most of the ones she put out regularly and a few she kept back for "special occasions." Although most of her dessert recipes were as old as time—things like chess pie, chocolate meringue, and banana pudding—Mrs. Cole's creations were unique.

When she tossed a teaspoon of white distilled vinegar in one of the meringue pies, I gasped. "Vinegar?" I whispered, and she winked and nodded.

"Not only does it give it a little tang, but it also helps keep it fresh longer. But mind you, if you put in too much, it'll taste like vinegar. This town would not forgive you if you made their favorite desserts taste bad."

I nodded solemnly. "So, what other secrets do you hold?"

She laughed out loud, making both the server and cook look our way. "Oh, you'll learn, but not all at once. For now, we need to get these done and out onto the serving line before the dinner rush hits."

I loved learning from Mrs. Cole. I couldn't even express how much. I had never enjoyed working anywhere as much as I did working for her. In the short time I'd been here, I'd also come to love the look of the little restaurant, the repeat traffic, hearing how customers enjoyed my cooking, and the coworkers I'd gotten to know.

What I loved most, though, was that even though this café served the best food I'd ever had the luxury of serving, I was treated like my efforts mattered. Mrs. Cole recognized my commitment and as a result, trusted me with things like the desserts. I never would've asked for that, knowing how important they were to her and her business.

I was on cloud nine as the dinner rush began to wane and knew Mrs. Cole was about to kick me out just as Ruther walked in the front door. I smiled and waved at him as I wiped down the serving utensils and buffet area.

"I was hoping you were still here," he said, walking up to me. I noticed he was no longer using his crutches, which must mean his ankle was better. "When do you get off? Can you join me for dinner?"

I glanced up at the clock and couldn't help but wonder if my matchmaking boss might've been behind his perfect timing. "Sure, let me finish here and ensure Mrs. Cole don't need me to do anythin' else."

He smiled and wandered over to a corner booth. When Mrs. Cole smiled and winked, I knew she had most definitely had a hand in arranging this little meet-up. "Shall I carry out the mop water before I'm done?" I asked her. I always did it as part of the cleaning routine, but I was curious what she'd say today.

"No, son, you go on out there and talk to the handsome Mr. Ruther. I'll have Elsie do that before she closes for the night."

I grinned. Yep, a full-out setup.

I tossed my apron onto the dirty clothes pile, knowing that'd be another of Elsie's jobs before she clocked out tonight. Then I went to the restroom, used a paper towel to wipe down my sweaty, greasy face, and shrugged when I had to accept that I wouldn't be too pretty after working an eight-hour shift in a Southern food restaurant.

When I returned to the dining room, Ruther was waiting. "You could've gone ahead and gotten your plate unless you're wantin' to order somethin' off the menu."

"I wanted to wait for you," Ruther said, sounding sincere. "I'm not even all that hungry. Mostly, I wanted a chance to thank you for what you've done for me the past few days."

I smiled at the praise, even though I didn't quite know what to do with it. "Well, I'm famished. Nothin' like a long day's work to build up an appetite. Shall we fill our plates before we chat?" I asked.

I used the time at the buffet to get my mind to calm down. I hadn't planned to spend any time with the man again, fully convincing myself to leave well enough alone, but he'd been so sweet to wait for me. Regardless of what all he wanted to discuss, and even if it included a romantic proposition I'd have to decline, I could still enjoy being in the presence of such a beautiful, dignified man, right?

Ruther bumped me gently a couple of times by accident while we shuffled along the buffet line. The brief touches caused my insides to skitter, but I packed that down quick.

"So, as I was saying," he said as we returned to our booth, "I need to thank you. You not only rescued me when I injured myself out in the woods but also this morning after I had a panic attack." He paused a moment and stared down at his food. "I-I don't have them often any longer, but when I do, I just need to calm down, and that's hard to do when people are swarming me or asking a bunch of questions. Corey is great at helping me save face, but you...you just helped me get myself put back together. I can't tell you how much I appreciate that."

His face was so pinched, I let my guard down long enough to reach over and place my hand over his. "Listen, I had panic attacks bad when I was in high school. My dad, well, he was a little free with the belt, and anytime I'd mess up at school, I'd freak out thinkin' bad things would happen at home."

"Did you get away from him?" he asked, leading me away from the panic attack conversation.

"Eventually, but not until I was grown. Anyway, I recognize panic attacks and know what you meant by needin' a moment to calm down."

"Do you still have them?" he asked, and the composed demeanor he always seemed to have slipped a moment, exposing a vulnerable soul that just made him all the more appealing.

I nodded. "I do, but they're sporadic, and I can never predict them. Luckily, I've not had one since coming here. I think it's because Crawford City's the first place I've been in a long time that makes me feel safe."

Ruther's eyes grew wide before they clouded over. "Safe in Crawford City," he said, mostly to himself, then laughed dryly. "Do you like wine?"

His abrupt change of subject made my head spin for a moment. "Um, yeah, a little."

"I got you something, but I don't know if you like dry wine. Do you?" he asked, and I laughed at how concerned he looked.

"I don't drink a lot of wine 'cause most of what I can afford tastes like someone poured a gallon of sugar in it. As for the so-called dry stuff, if it's in my pay range, it makes my face blush too hard and goes right to my head."

Ruther chuckled. "The cheap stuff does that. Anyway, I visited a little winery near town that produces surprisingly good wine. I brought back a bottle of my favorite, thinking maybe you'd share it with me."

I quickly looked around, nervous that if Ruther opened wine here in the café, Mrs. Cole would take our heads off.

Ruther seemed to understand my reaction and grinned. "Not here, but now that I think about it, there's a nice little place at the hotel that serves the wines with local cheeses. I haven't gone there yet, but it'd be fun to go there with you."

I blushed and, with my hand still over his, nearly said yes. I turned my head just enough that the almost gone bruises on my neck twinged, and I remembered exactly why I had to decline his invitation.

I pulled my hand back but kept smiling. "Ruther, you're a handsome and sweet man. I would love to say yeah, but I...well, I'm not in a place to entertain male friends right now."

"Oh," Ruther said, looking stricken. "You have a boyfriend, or are you married?"

I couldn't hold back a grimace thinking about my dating history. "That would be a no. I don't have a partner, and I ain't ever been married. Honestly, that's a blessing 'cause I've only ever dated losers."

When he blanched, I sighed. "I've sworn off men, at least until the bruises from my last relationship fade."

I could tell he didn't understand I meant literally fade, and I was okay with that. No need for him to know I tended to go out with men who used me as a punching bag, not unlike my father, whom I'd somehow mentioned in a moment of weakness earlier.

"I-I don't have the best track record with dating. I only just found my way to Crawford City, and to be honest, Ruther, I like it here. More than any other place I've ever been. It's beautiful. The people are sweet and kind and don't seem to mind that I'm a flouncing fairy. That's hard to come by in these parts, so as much as I'd like to take you up on your offer, I'm afraid I'm not in the market to find someone who might make all that go away."

Ruther gave me a bewildered look, then sighed. "I was afraid you might say that. I'll be honest, I don't know how long I'll be in Crawford City, but let me make a proposal. I'm here in town to...well, I'm here to face some of my past demons. And that's hard, as you saw earlier today. I'm struggling with it. Would you consider helping me see Crawford City the way you do? I know it sounds strange, but you said you feel safe here." He paused and looked down at the food still heaped on his plate, then back at me. "I don't and haven't felt safe in a very long time. I could use some guidance, and I can promise not to make a move on you. In fact, we can keep our meetings public, and if I need, I can have my assistant join us to make sure we keep things, um, platonic."

I couldn't help but laugh. "Are you saying you'd hire a chaperone?" I asked, and he blushed and then smiled.

"That's exactly what I'm saying, a chaperone when not in public."

"And your assistant, is he also your lover?" I asked, wanting to get to the bottom of that before agreeing.

It was his turn to laugh. "That's a very hard no. I haven't had a lover in several years, and my assistant, Corey, is special, but that's because he cares about me as a friend and an employer. Corey is one of the most important people in my life, but there's nothing romantic there, and there never has been."

The man doth protest too much, I thought, then caught myself. It didn't matter if his employee was someone who did him favors or not, and it wasn't any of my business anyway. I wasn't gonna get involved with Ruther or anyone else for that matter. But I'd seen the vulnerability when he'd said he didn't feel safe in Crawford City, and I couldn't ignore that.

"Ruther, I'm open to getting to know you, your assistant, and other people in town as friends. Right now, though, I'm also wanting to get to know this fried chicken 'cause I'm about to starve to death over here."

That made him laugh, and I didn't wait any longer to bite into the deliciousness in front of me.

Our conversation was light after that, mostly Ruther telling me about his day and the winery he'd found with his new friends, Jake and Lance. In turn, I made some small talk but intentionally kept my personal life close to my chest.

I'd already told Ruther more than I usually did with people I didn't know, but his vulnerability was like kryptonite to me. Knowing I'd already overshared made me twitchy. I'd have to be careful around him because it'd be just a bit too easy to let my guard down.

I wondered for a moment if that might be his intention. Then he told me about the chapel in the woods, and his eyes gleamed, and I thought, no, I was looking at one of the only genuine men I'd ever met. No fake promises or begging me to give him something I wasn't comfortable giving.

He'd heard me and respected me, and now we were going to get to know each other in a platonic way. Of course, my inner dysfunction screamed at me to crawl over the table and into his sexy lap. But I wasn't ready to dive headlong into a new relationship, even if Ruther was more refined than all the men I'd dated. Granted, refined didn't mean he wasn't violent, but getting to know him as a person meant I'd see his true colors soon enough. I just hoped I wouldn't be disappointed. Lord knows I was full up on that, enough to last several lifetimes.

Nineteen

Ruther

D ISAPPOINTED, YES, VERY MUCH so. I guess I had visions of Clyde jumping across the table and into my arms while telling me how much he wanted me. That's not how our meal went, but I still enjoyed myself and hoped he felt the same.

It's been too long since I've tried to date, I thought, and began my nervous talking when things felt awkward. Not that he'd made me feel that way. In fact, he'd been kind about it, and I could sense some hard scrapes must be behind his caution.

Of course, I knew Clyde had seen my burn scars when my sock had come off in the exam room. Years of therapy had helped me not be quite as fearful that everyone I met would be turned off by the sight. But not even therapy had completely gotten rid of my trepidation. I wondered if maybe my scars were what drove him away from wanting to spend a quiet evening with me.

I shook the thought off. Therapy had also taught me that letting myself go down that rabbit hole meant I didn't give anyone a chance before I chased them off. My therapist had said in no uncertain terms, though not unkindly, that fear would prevent me from opening myself up to a long-term relationship, and that'd proven true so far.

If I had been in New York, I'd have scheduled a massage with my bodywork therapist. He was good at working my body and helping me feel what it was like to have someone touch me without being repulsed. But that wasn't an option, so I needed to let the work I'd done for the past three decades kick in and keep me from falling apart.

"So, about that wine and cheese, perhaps we could still do that along with Corey? He loved the local wine, and it'd be a chance for you two to get to know each other a bit more."

Clyde nodded. "That seems fair, and Corey seems nice enough. I'm off next Monday. Will that work?"

I couldn't help but smile. "Yeah, that's perfect."

We finished eating, and Clyde rushed off to take our plates back and buss the table himself before he said his goodbyes to everyone.

"Can I walk you home?" I asked without thinking.

Clyde hesitated. "You're staying at the hotel, right? The nice one on the edge of town?"

I shook my head, afraid I'd just overstepped our agreement. "Close to that. I'm actually staying in a condo that's next to the hotel."

"I've got to go by there to get to my...well, lesser motel," he said, smiling at his joke. "I'll walk you home, then make my way to mine. Deal?"

I shook his hand to solidify our deal, and we walked out of the café. The sun had begun to set, and that magical twilight time had crept in. If Clyde hadn't nixed all notions of anything happening between us, I'd have said it was an ideal time for a romantic stroll.

I loved how the little town sounded as it was closing down for the evening. Calls from folks to one another echoed as the sounds of Southern insects chirped in the background. It really was a unique place. I just wished I didn't think of it as a prelude to a horror movie.

I hadn't been lying when I told Clyde I wanted to see Crawford City through his eyes. He said he felt safer here than he had anywhere else. I had never felt as unsafe as I did here. That didn't mean I couldn't recognize the tranquility or know my reactions were misplaced. My adult brain knew my childhood traumas were just that, but looking at things logically had never factored into how I felt about this town.

If Clyde's perspective could help me settle the fears, even slightly, it was an improvement. Something years and years of therapy hadn't been able to do.

I looked over at him as we meandered toward the condo. "You're quiet."

"I'm tired," he said, laughing. "I love what I do, but it's a lot of work. At thirty-four, I shouldn't be turning in with the chickens, but damn, that's my life."

"I don't know, you do seem to run the entire time you're at the restaurant—not that I was watching or anything," I said, causing him to laugh again.

"Sure," he said and companionably elbowed me.

"Well, this is me," I said as we approached the front of the condo, a bit too soon for my liking.

"Have a good night, Ruther, and I'll see you at the café tomorrow?"

"At nine, you said."

He nodded. "Bring your chaperone," he said, teasing, and turned to disappear around the corner.

"Chaperone indeed," I said to myself and entered the building, anxious to tell Corey his new designation. On second thought, I'd probably cause myself all kinds of grief telling him that.

Twenty

Clyde

D ESPITE THE NICE WALK, I was leery when I came
around the corner. The man who'd recognized
me the day before had probably checked out, and I
hadn't seen his bike since, but I didn't want to take
any more chances. I still wasn't sure I'd gotten off the
hook, but there was no reason to tempt fate.

I didn't see anyone lurking outside the motel. In
fact, the entire place was mostly empty, but I did a
thorough check before I crossed the parking lot to
my room. I sighed with relief as I closed and locked
the door behind me.

It's like I lived in two different worlds. On the one
hand, I had a job I loved, one I enjoyed more than
any before. I took evening strolls through town, passing fancy buildings that housed an upscale hotel and

high-end condos, to escort a potential suitor home like a gentleman.

Then I'd cross the tracks and enter my reality. A place where I had to watch my back, where I was lucky not to be found and beaten within an inch of my life. *This*, I reminded myself, *was my real life.*

It didn't pay to forget that. I'd done a bad thing when I'd taken my ex's money. I'd also asked for trouble when I'd returned the bruises he'd given me. He'd have likely have let that go, because men like him understood you sometimes had to take what you gave.

The stealing, though, wasn't something Jimmy would forget or forgive. Even if he didn't send the law after me, which I couldn't rule out, he would take revenge on me if he could. Men like my ex were just as likely to kill me as not.

Of course, I didn't realize that when I'd started dating him. Not that I was paying attention. I was drunk the night we met in a bar, not unlike the one across the street from here. I'd let the girls from work talk me into going, and we drank too much, and then he'd come sniffing my way.

Jimmy wasn't that good-looking, but was tall and strong, despite having a gut. I should've kicked him out of my life the following day like any sane person who'd woken up next to a loser after a drunken night of frolicking. Instead, I let him woo me into a false sense of security.

Then, as it always did, came the hitting and the apologies. Shit, I was pathetic. I was barely attracted to Jimmy—nothing like how I felt when Ruther looked my way—and I didn't even like him as a person very much.

Idiot! I chastised myself before I finally shook my head and headed into the shower. It did no good to rehash this time and time again. It'd happened, I'd let it happen, and now all I could do was move on with my life.

I'd keep Ruther on a very long leash, though if tonight was any indication, he wasn't one to push himself or an agenda. As long as he kept to that, I'd be fine. Well, mostly fine. I still liked him more than I had any other man in...maybe ever, but that didn't mean I'd act on it.

I wouldn't. I liked where I was too much to jeopardize it. If I could save up some money and maybe find a cute little apartment somewhere downtown, I could keep ahold of a life that wasn't quite as shitty as the one I'd had before. If that meant not having a man, then so be it.

TWENTY-ONE

RUTHER

THE FOLLOWING WEEK FLEW by. I roused Corey every day to go to the café by nine in the morning to catch Clyde for his break. The two men seemed to get along fine, although Corey was often preoccupied with dealings in New York, meaning the ongoing renovations in my apartment.

"Oh, Lord, you should've seen it," Clyde said in the middle of one of his engaging stories. Sometimes, one of the townspeople would pull up a chair to join us, but most had already come and gone by the time Corey and I got to the café. I liked it that way.

Besides, Jake and Lance had begun to pull Corey and me into their lives since we'd all gone to the winery together.

Lance invited us for dinner a few days after the winery trip and showed me his concept for a housing development at the motel site. It was impressive. None of the homes were larger than fifteen hundred square feet, and all of the little bungalows had front porches big enough for a swing or rocking chair. It all looked very homey and quaint in all the best ways.

"So, you want to recreate homes from the thirties or forties?" I asked after Lance showed me all his preliminary designs.

He nodded, as did Jake behind him. "If Crawford City instead of Mayville had grown into the town it should've, with a railroad coming through it, these are the kinds of homes we could've expected to see on the outskirts of downtown. Since the railroad all but abandoned Crawford City before that could happen, we have the land you are looking at, but we can still recreate that old-fashioned feel."

I stared at the plans and could tell Corey was excited about the idea, but I wasn't entirely convinced. "So, you think this is what people want? Not more modern designs?"

Jake stepped in then. "We have a lot of modern houses being built out in rural areas. Some rather large estates for people with money to burn. But for folks wanting to live close to town and who don't have millions in the bank, yes, we both think more traditional designs would be better. Hardwood floors, wide plank woodwork, but with a modern twist. Open floor plans, for example."

I almost elbowed Corey, who, in a very out-of-character way, said, "These are perfect. Charming with a historical feel but not dated. Brilliant."

I nodded and sighed. "I agree. How many do you think we could put in that area?"

Jake and Lance glanced at one another, then Lance clicked another page on his proposal. "We think you should tear down the motel and add townhouses across the front. You could sell them, but you could also lease them out."

Jake sighed. "We hate the idea of losing tourist money, and even though the motel is run-down, it is a place to stay for people who aren't looking for what we provide here at the hotel. The finances don't support me adding the next addition unless I can charge what we do now, but if you had a few units that could be used as vacation rentals, it could provide an affordable alternative and ensure the investment is worth it."

"I have no intention of running a bed-and-breakfast. Who do you see managing this?" I asked, already assuming I knew where this was going.

"Catherine could manage them for you. She has been in the business since she was a child, and we already have cleaning staff."

When they paused, I laughed. "Okay, I'm not going to fight you on this. I just need to see the numbers. I'm not opposed to keeping an asset, although, to be honest, if we build the vacation units, you should consider purchasing it yourself, let it become part of your portfolio."

Jake and Lance looked at each other and exchanged some sort of unspoken communication. "We can talk to our partners about that," Jake said. "Now, let's discuss a possible builder."

I listened as they sang the praises of Amos's son, Todd. My father had liked Todd's grandfather and had used him on multiple occasions to work at the estate. I forced the nerves to skim past that thought.

If all the praise Jake and Lance were giving Todd was any indication, it'd be worth talking to him. Being the third generation to provide quality workmanship in the same community also bode well.

"We need to warn you though. Todd is booked out for at least a year."

"Do I have any other options locally?" I asked. "I'm guessing bringing in a builder from the outside wouldn't be the town council's preference."

"The Richards brothers have experience building new construction, and I happen to know they're about done with a joint project with Todd and Amos." Jake looked at me thoughtfully, and I saw the shrewd businessman behind his charming persona. "Would you let us take point on this? I can find and recommend an available builder, one we trust and the town council won't balk at."

"No," Corey interjected. "I'm happy to accept your recommendations, but we have a set way of doing business. However, if you'd like to help me as I set up a feasibility plan and meet with potential contractors, I'd welcome your assistance."

I stifled a grin, having known instinctively Corey was going to nix all that.

"Yes, of course," Lance said. "Let me make a couple of inquiries, and if the contractors are available, I'll set up an appointment."

"That's acceptable," Corey said, and just like that, we were off. I honestly didn't think this project would get off the ground. There were a lot of variables. Not the least of which was me not officially living here or, more to the point, dealing with the monster on the hill that still haunted me.

However, Corey now had his claws into the project, and he'd be able to ensure it was done to his satisfaction, no matter where I factored into the equation.

With my sprained ankle on the mend, I cited needing to walk more as my reason for regularly showing up at the café around the time Clyde got off work. I knew he was tired, which made escorting him across town to his motel all the more important to me.

Corey and I had agreed we'd been eating way too much fried food, so he'd started cooking or prepping salads at the condo. But I still wanted to see my new friend whenever possible. *Friend.* I was trying to force myself to think of Clyde that way.

So far, I'd only been mildly successful in that effort. More often than not, I wanted to draw him into my arms and kiss him, but small steps were necessary here, for both of us. As predicted, spending time with Clyde and focusing on the new project were making me feel less anxious about the town.

Was I even close to being able to face my childhood house of horrors? Far from it. But at least I wasn't constantly surfing a potential panic attack. I'd take any positive I could get, and that was a significant one.

TWENTY-TWO

CLYDE

I SHOULD'VE REBUFFED ALL the attention. I knew it and beat myself up a little about not doing so, but Ruther and Corey had only come to hang out with me during my breaks. The occasional strolls home alongside Ruther were so sweet, I couldn't resist. I was a major romantic, after all, and even if we were sworn only to be friends, I had to appreciate his consistent kindness.

I already knew long after these evenings were no longer part of my life, I'd think fondly of them. Was I a sucker? Yeah, but who cared? I needed these kinds of memories to counterbalance all the nasty ones.

Ruther hadn't mentioned going to have wine and cheese at the fancy hotel with me and Corey since we'd made those plans, so I wondered if maybe he'd forgotten or wanted to back out. If we were still on, he'd either have to say something on the stroll home from work tonight, or he'd have to come to the motel and get me tomorrow.

Perhaps him forgetting or canceling would be a good thing. I'd become more and more paranoid about the motel and people recognizing me there. I knew my cousin Lewellen, as hateful as she was, wouldn't tattle on me to that slob Jimmy, but I didn't know who else might.

It was best if that world didn't collide anytime soon with this one. Ruther coming to the motel was more than I could handle. I hoped he wouldn't, even if that meant no fancy wine and cheese night.

I ended up having to put in a longer day than usual since all the tourists had begun swarming town. Lately, we spent all our time fixing more food and less time cleaning. Mrs. Cole told me it was rare, but sometimes the summer months were like this.

Regardless, since working at the café, I'd begun to take some ownership, and leaving it a mess was more than I could stomach, so I was happy to give the extra time.

By the time I finished, I didn't expect to see Ruther. To my surprise, though, I came out of the back to see Mrs. Cole sitting across from him, poking him to eat one of the chocolate meringues she'd just pulled out of the oven for tomorrow.

"I see some folks are getting special treatment," I said, smiling even bigger when Mrs. Cole blushed at my accusation.

"Now, you behave. I needed to wile my ways to get Mr. Ruther here to eat something while he waited for you to finish."

"Mrs. Cole, this is divine," he said. "I can't remember ever eating anything like it."

She laughed and the blush returned. "Well, you enjoy that with your beau, and make sure you bring that cutie pie assistant of yours in tomorrow to have some."

"Yes, ma'am," Ruther said, and I swear I heard a little Southern twang mixed in with his highbrow New York accent.

The chuckle kept me from correcting her about me being Ruther's beau, and I sat across from him as he finished his pie. "You know she guards those desserts like an old mother hen watching her chicks. She never lets anyone have a bite before she puts it out on the buffet."

Ruther smiled. "I have a feeling my privileges stem from her appreciation of you. She couldn't stop telling me all your attributes."

It was my turn to blush now. "Really? She said all that?" I asked, looking back toward where my boss had just disappeared.

When I turned back toward Ruther, he was nodding. "It doesn't take a very observant person to see you're a hard worker, Clyde. You're smart and considerate, but Mrs. Cole is clever and knows how lucky she was when you showed up to work here."

I stared at him, waiting for him to laugh or point out that he was joking. People never said nice things about me without a punch line at the end.

When he just kept eating the pie, I shrugged. Yeah, I worked hard. People like me had to. It was either that or find yourself homeless and in a gutter somewhere. As I'd been told most of my life, I wasn't anything special.

"Somebody's got a sweet tooth," I said to change the subject.

"I really want another piece of this," Ruther said and sighed after swallowing the last bite.

"You'll have to come back tomorrow. Oh, just so you know, I made that one myself. First time Mrs. Cole let me do it."

"Wait, you made it? You know how to make this?" he asked, sounding almost excited. It was cute.

"Yep, I knew how to make a chocolate meringue pie before coming here, but now I know the secret to making it taste like that," I said, wagging my eyebrows suggestively.

Ruther grinned. "Okay, that's it. Who should I ask for your hand in marriage?"

"Hand in marriage? All it takes is a slice of pie to win you over?" I asked, laughing now.

"Pie for life, you mean. I've already been courting you like some Victorian gentleman, so should I ask Mrs. Cole for her blessing?"

I was still laughing at the thought when he stood up, acting like he was looking for my boss.

"Stop that. You're gonna get me in trouble or get the gossipy tongues waggin'. Come on, I'll walk you home," I said.

I knew he'd been teasing, but I liked the old-fashioned courting like we were in an old-time novel or something. I shook my head before I got any lovesick notions and led him out the door.

"So, are we still on for tomorrow?" Ruther asked as we walked more briskly than usual did toward his building. "At the hotel's wine bar, I mean."

I closed my eyes and let the happy thrill zing through me for a moment before I nodded. "Yep, if you're still willin' to waste your money on such things, I'm game."

"Then let's meet here around noon. Corey said he's got his hands full in the morning, which works fine, considering wine for breakfast might be a bad idea."

I chuckled and smiled. "If this local stuff is as good as you say, drinking wine anytime is probably a wonderful idea," I said and paused outside the door to his building. "And yes, I'll be here tomorrow at high noon."

Ruther leaned forward, and for a moment, I thought he would kiss me. Luckily, or maybe not so lucky, he stopped short and just smiled. "I'm looking forward to it." Then he turned and walked through the door.

I walked, mesmerized and distracted, all the way to the motel, not doing my usual scan of the parking lot. I'd just gotten to my door when I heard laughter and turned around to see who it was.

The guy from before who'd said he recognized me was staring at me from the parking lot. His buddies were facing him, but he was ignoring them. When I made eye contact, he winked and gave me an evil grin that, more than anything, told me my happy days here were about to come to an end.

TWENTY-THREE

RUTHER

S O, THAT ALMOST HAPPENED. I stopped myself in time, but I'd certainly wanted to kiss Clyde. The man sparked something inside me that caused me to act like a lovesick puppy.

His reaction when I mentioned I'd been courting him on our walks was priceless. His cute face blushed with pleasure and melted my insides. Yeah, I had it bad for this guy.

He seemed almost willing to let me kiss him too. Almost. I logged that in the back of my mind because now I'd seen how he reacted, I was more determined than ever to taste those pouty lips when the time was right.

I came into the condo whistling, and Corey cocked an eyebrow at me before shaking his head. "So, I have some preliminary numbers on the project. If the costs to build are similar to what we've paid in New York, which is unlikely, considering the cost of living here is significantly less, and if we price the homes based on my initial research, we stand to make this much," he said, swinging his laptop around to show me the numbers.

I laughed before turning the laptop back. "You better double-check those numbers because that's comparable, if not better than, what we make in the city."

Corey shook his head and turned the laptop back around for me to see. "The initial investment is significantly less. We'd pay at least ten times the cost for property in the city and at least five times as much if we were building in the suburbs, even if we were building in Jersey."

I snickered at the joke. Corey was a snob and wasn't above typical New Jersey jibes.

"What about the development costs?" I asked, looking at his numbers again.

He shrugged but smiled. "I have to assume they will be at least equal to or less than it would cost in New York. Construction supplies aren't going to be much cheaper here, but labor might be. Regardless, as you can see, building the proposal using our normal cost calculator should be reliable enough to show you this is more than worth the effort."

The fact he didn't call me boss went a long way to show he really had faith in the potential of this project. "Well, Corey, I like the idea. I like those numbers even better. We also don't have to get board approval any longer, not to mention I'll be footing the costs myself.

So, do it. Let's chase this down and see if, after getting realistic numbers, it could make the money indicated."

Corey nodded. "I...well, to be honest, I never thought a development project like this would be something to consider, especially with...with your history here. However, it does seem this area is prime for development. I also like Lance's modernized bungalows idea. This has a lot of promise."

I patted his back, letting the excitement from walking Clyde home and Corey's excitement over the project propel me to the bedroom.

I looked over at the curtains I'd pulled tightly shut to hide my view of where my family's former home stood. On a whim, I threw the curtains open and stepped out onto the balcony.

It was too dark to see the house, but the little bandstand in the park was lit up, making it look all the more welcoming. I glanced back up toward the darkness, where I knew the house stood behind the trees, and was pleased not to have to fight the usual panic.

Was it because it was too dark to see? Maybe, but when I'd first gotten here, just knowing the view included it was enough to send me over the edge. No, I was better, and it was all because being here wasn't the terror it had been just a few days ago.

Now Crawford City was full of hope. Hope for a project I was getting as excited about as Corey, and hope for more with Clyde. More what? I had no idea. I know he told me he wasn't interested, and I would respect that as long as he felt that way.

That didn't mean I wasn't hopeful. Those glimmers of possibility were enough to propel me into a different place around my trauma. I wonder what all the therapists I'd gone through over the years might say about that.

TWENTY-FOUR

CLYDE

I PEERED OUT MY motel room door, double-checking the creepy man wasn't watching and waiting for me. When the coast was clear, I slipped out and through the parking lot toward town.

I sighed in relief as I approached the donut shop. I hadn't been anywhere but the café and the grocery store since arriving, and I figured I needed to expand my horizons a bit. I ordered a long John and hoped it would taste as delicious as the place smelled.

A good-looking guy behind the counter took my order. I almost thought he was gay until a woman carrying a wiggling toddler and tugging a kindergarten-age child came in and kissed him. Not that I should be speculating about who was gay or not anyway. I wasn't interested, I reminded myself for the umpteenth time. The guy, even if he was bisexual and not in a relationship, wasn't my type anyway. Too skinny, too, well...not enough. I like my men bigger, meatier, like Ruther. I inwardly sighed. No, no, not like Ruther. I'm not looking—

The young couple were cute together. The woman wanted to help, but the toddler wasn't having any of it. Eventually, she kissed the man again, then pulled the kids back out of the bakery. I watched as the sweet young family headed for the swings in the park just beyond the shop.

Would that ever be my reality? I doubted it. I think I'd have loved having a family, though. Lord knows I'd helped raise my nieces and nephew. Being the youngest—significantly younger than my siblings—meant I was a built-in babysitter for their kids.

I enjoyed watching them grow up. Now they were all teenagers and hardly had time to acknowledge me when I did come home, which was seldom. Such is life, I guess. Once again, I wish I'd been closer to my family.

They weren't particularly religious or anything, but they were also not great about me being gay. My dad's abusive nature didn't lend itself to a close-knit family either. After my parents divorced, Mom married another abusive man, divorced him, and married another. I hadn't been around enough to know if the latest husband was abusive, but I didn't doubt it, if history was any indication.

My sisters had done the same, but unlike Mom, they'd at least gotten rid of theirs and kept another one from coming in. Me, well, I'd followed the same pattern as Mom, except I got rid of mine before I could tie any knots. Fortunately for me, gay men didn't procreate without planning and outside help, so children never factored into my messy relationships.

Small blessings, I guess. I sat pondering that as I finished my donut and coffee.

"Can I get you anything else?" the cute dad asked me from behind the counter.

I smiled at the thought of surprising Ruther and Corey. "Yeah," I said before thinking better of it, "can you box me up a couple of your jelly donuts to go?"

He nodded and went to do as I asked. It was still early and probably crossing some line by just stopping by, but isn't this what a friend would do? Besides, if we were going to drink wine, we needed full stomachs. That's the excuse I could use. Mostly, I just wanted to see Ruther because seeing him kept me from thinking about my own bullshit. That's probably codependency, but it sure beat being alone to dwell on things.

I rushed out of the bakery and down the road toward Ruther's place, as I now thought of it, and was just about to go inside when I glanced back toward the street. A black pickup drove by, going way too fast for this part of town. I didn't recognize the truck, but shit, shit, shit, was that—

I shook my head. No, the creepy guy from last night had just frayed my nerves. Jimmy wasn't here, and he sure as hell didn't drive a black pickup truck. He loved his crappy old Corvette, which ran horribly and smelled like exhaust inside.

Despite being sure that Jimmy driving by was just my imagination, I dashed into Ruther's building. I took a few moments to still myself inside the front door and was just about to enter the hotel side, since I didn't know where Ruther's condo was, when Corey stepped into the hallway.

"Hi," he said when he spotted me. "How are you this morning, Clyde?"

I smiled. "I decided to bring treats for you and Ruther," I said and handed him the box, feeling way too awkward all of a sudden. "I-I figured we needed a full stomach if we're going to drink this afternoon, so...anyway, I'll see you around noon." I turned to go.

"Wait, I'm sure Ruther would like to see you. We're going to Jake and Lance's soon to review some preliminary numbers for a project we're considering, and I was about to talk to the hotel manager about...anyway, Ruther would probably like to thank you."

I swallowed hard, resisting the urge to run. Instead, I nodded and followed Corey to the second floor and into the condo.

"Ruther, we've got company, and he brought...what did you bring?" Corey asked and looked into the box. "Oh, you are naughty." Humor spread across his too-handsome face. "Ruther, he brought jelly donuts!"

I blushed. "Sorry, do you not like them?"

Corey laughed. "I've gained ten pounds since I've been here. Ten, and I'm not even exaggerating. I'm going to have to run an extra five miles on the treadmill to get rid of this, but it'll be worth it."

I smiled. I didn't run on treadmills. Usually, the only running I did was away from my exes, but I knew how Southern food could put weight on. My pitiful small frame would likely always be next to nothing but skin and bones, no matter what I ate.

Before I could go through my normal self-deprecating internal speech about how unattractive I was, Ruther came out of a back bedroom. He was buttoning the top button of his shirt, and I caught a glimpse of his delightful chest hair. I swallowed hard and had to force my eyes to the floor and try to remove the vision of running my hands through that fur.

"This is a nice surprise," Ruther said, causing me to look up at his smiling face.

"I...well, I tried out the donut place this morning and thought since we're having wine for lunch, maybe you'd both like something to fill your stomachs before, you know, we go do that."

"Smart thinking, and I love jelly donuts. Someday, when you come to New York, I'll take you to my favorite bakery. It's been in the same family for generations, and the donuts are so delicious they make you want to weep."

I blushed this time because even if I were to throw caution to the wind and jump into bed with Ruther, I would likely never visit him in New York. It was a sweet comment, though.

"Well, Corey said you've got somewhere to be soon, so I won't linger, but y'all enjoy those, okay?"

"No, wait, why don't you join us? I'm sure Jake and Lance would enjoy your company as much as me, um, us," he said, looking toward a bemused Corey.

"Oh, no, I don't want to impose. Besides, I'd like to go wander around the park. I haven't been over there yet, and I should probably stretch my legs a bit since I don't do much of anything when Mrs. Cole gets her clutches into me."

Ruther laughed and nodded, but I could tell he was disappointed. I probably should've stayed, but I was too nervous about just popping by. That, and I was still hot and bothered by the too brief glimpse of his chest. That image gave me way too many feels to deal with while sitting in front of him and his assistant.

"I'll see you around noon. Enjoy the donuts," I said, then made a beeline out their front door.

I sighed heavily and left the way I'd come, thankful I didn't have to go through the hotel lobby to exit, so no one noticed me acting like a nutjob just because I'd been foolish enough to bring donuts instead of leaving well enough alone.

I checked the street, and not seeing any signs of the black pickup truck, I darted off toward the park.

It only took a few minutes to get there, and I sighed with relief as I walked under the canopy of some old trees that cast comforting shade, blocking out the already hot morning sun. It would be ridiculously hot this afternoon in these dog days of summer, as my granddaddy called the last days of the season.

Usually, I was inside running around the café, and although it got hot while I was working, I at least had some nice air-conditioning to get through the worst of it. I wandered around the park until I came to a swing set that sat mostly abandoned. It was older, and the newer set of swings across the park, closer to town, had clearly been used significantly more than this one in recent years. For me, though, it was perfect. Sorta concealed but with a view of Ruther's building across the way.

My motel lay just around the corner from there. I swung myself up and watched to see if there was any evidence of the pickup truck. Luckily, there wasn't, just the regular folks I'd met while working at the café. I let that comfort me, convincing myself I was being overzealous. Which with how good things were going, it was like me to be looking and waiting for the other shoe to drop.

The breeze swept through my hair, and I felt the tell-tale signs of a thrill from swinging higher than I should. For a moment, the sensation made me feel like a kid again. Not the kid who spent most of his life afraid of his dad, but a kid who was free just to be happy.

I slowed my swinging and thought how odd it was to feel like that after so many years being afraid. I felt the emotions overtake me and quickly reached up to wipe away a tear that had escaped. I thought I'd long ago cried out the tears of my difficult childhood.

This time, I felt for the little boy who was never al-lowed to be a little boy. Too many years tiptoeing around an abusive jackass father and a codependent mom. I pushed off again and let myself embrace the joy of the moment.

I leaned back flat on the swing as the air rushed around me, and I laughed. I don't know what magic they were brewing in Crawford City, but it felt like the right kind to heal my damaged heart.

Twenty-Five

Ruther

"**T**HAT WAS STRANGE," COREY teased, biting into the jelly donut.

"Hush, he was just being kind."

"Sure...kind," he said before moaning with pleasure. "This really is good."

I took a bite of mine and had to agree. Not as good as the bakery I frequented in New York, but still delicious. Not that frequented was the right word. I let myself have donuts maybe twice a year. The gesture, though, coming from Clyde, made my heart soar.

I tried not to make too much of it as I took another bite.

We finished the donuts, then took the elevator up to Jake and Lance's place. We'd been there before, but the beautiful, open architecture bewildered me every time.

It wasn't something you'd expect to see in downtown Crawford City.

"Hi, guys," Jake said as he led us inside. "I hope you don't mind. Amos and Doc were both available, and I wanted them to weigh in on your ideas."

I almost cringed. It was too early to get the mayor involved, and the way Corey tensed beside me, I knew he had the same thought. "No, that's great. Why don't you show us more of your plans, Lance?" I said quickly to avoid any misunderstandings about how I felt having them here.

We greeted Emanual and Amos, then Lance dove right in. "As I said last time we spoke, I think building with the older bungalow feel is right for the area, and I've found a few designs and communities that've done it before. Unfortunately, most of the ones I can show you are way too close together for this community. I recommend you create some yards, front or back, to enhance the rural feel your buyers should find appealing."

I nodded in understanding, and Lance continued showing us slides of his ideas. I also subtly watched Amos and Emanual throughout the slideshow to gauge their reactions. Amos was a closed book. Even from my childhood, I remembered that about him, and clearly, that hadn't changed with the years. Emanual, though, smiled through the entire thing.

"This is exactly what Crawford City needs. Do you think you'd like to do this in our town?" Emanual asked me.

I appreciated that he didn't beat around the bush, even if I wasn't fully prepared to answer his question at this point. So, I shrugged. "Maybe. A lot more research needs to happen just to make sure it's feasible, not the least of which is identifying a contractor. Amos, do you think your son can take this on?"

He immediately shook his head. "No, Todd is too booked up as it is. However, we are working with a couple of young men who could reliably do the job. Lance, didn't you already speak with them?" he asked.

Lance nodded. "Yes..." he said, sounding hesitant. "I may be speaking out of turn, but they don't live in Crawford City, and most of their work has been in Nashville. Amos, I recommend that you and Todd take point and subcontract it to them. That way, you can ensure it moves along as expected and stays on schedule."

Amos looked over at Lance, and for a moment, I thought he might scowl, but he smiled instead. "I appreciate your confidence, and Todd has worked hard for his good reputation. The Richards boys are reliable but still a bit green. If you're really interested, Rutherford, I'll ask my son what he thinks and we'll go from there."

I nodded. "If we take this on, I'd need someone reliable. As you know, Corey and I don't live here either, and we haven't discussed who would manage things for us. It's a lot to think about."

The room grew quiet for a moment, and everyone looked at me expectantly as I weighed my options. "If I knew you were spearheading this, Amos, it would make much more sense for us to do it. Lance, Corey has put together a density study of how many units would have to be built to make it feasible. You're correct that heavy density would be a turnoff for this type of community, but the acreage makes this appear lucrative enough."

"And you still believe enough people would buy the homes to make this venture worth it?" Corey asked.

All four men around us nodded. Lance flipped through his slides until he came to one he hadn't shown us. "I spoke to our realtor and asked if she thought she could sell new homes, and she almost jumped on me with excitement. As you can see, she doesn't think she'd have difficulty selling a hundred units in or around Crawford City. She's getting more inquiries than she can handle even now."

"And people aren't just building on their own?" I asked.

Jake shook his head. "No, that's tough, and once you're out of town, there's not much land for sale. We're in a buyer's market."

"Why hasn't anyone bought the motel property then? There's plenty of land there. Do you have a brownfield issue?" Corey asked.

When all but Amos looked confused, I added, "Brownfield, as in waste from the railroad that we'd have to deal with."

"Oh," Emanual said and smiled. "No, that area was mostly cow pasture when Amos and I were growing up. The railroad didn't have anything to do with it. Old man Oliver owned it and built that motel when his wife was still alive. He managed it until he died about ten years ago. You don't need the history lesson, but I doubt there's much to deal with besides razing that old motel."

"We'll want to do an inspection nonetheless," Corey said, and I cringed internally at how that must've sounded. When I glanced around, no one seemed upset, though.

"Okay, well, before we head back to New York, I'd like to have bids and a full understanding of if it's feasible or not. Is there any concern about people knowing what we're doing?" I asked.

Corey gave me a bewildered look, which I ignored. We weren't in New York. If someone wanted to grab the land out from under us, then who would fund that kind of project in the middle of nowhere? However, Jake shook his head. "You'll want to get a contract on it before anyone gets word. I recommend you assume anything that goes wrong in the city could go wrong here, and I'd like to ensure the right people are developing this."

The other men were nodding in agreement, and that, more than anything, made me feel better about this. My father had been an ass, and he'd throw someone under the bus to make a quick buck, but I didn't work that way. He'd somehow had a good reputation despite it, which I'd built up even further when I took over the company.

We were reliable regarding our projects and wouldn't put shoddy work up, regardless of where we built. I would do what was necessary to preserve that reputation, even if I wasn't officially in the business any longer. There were way too many real estate developers, especially in New York, who didn't give a crap about legacy. That would never be me.

TWENTY-SIX

CLYDE

MOVING ON FROM THE park, I wandered downtown and poked my head into the shops I'd only observed from a distance.

I'd met Mr. Cole, my boss's other half, a few times but hadn't spent time talking to him. Still, he recognized me the moment I walked into the drugstore. As we chatted, it became clear why he and his wife made such a good couple. Again, I forced down the grief that I'd likely never have that in my life.

I felt really good by the time I headed back to Ruther's place for our noon meetup. Crawford City really was special. Not that its shops and downtown were that different from any other small Southern town, but its people seemed to be...more. More friendly, more welcoming, more accepting.

I knocked on Ruther and Corey's door and was immediately met by a happy-looking Ruther. "Hi," he said, "come in."

I stepped inside and was perplexed when I didn't see Corey. Ruther seemed to notice and sighed. "So, Corey is buried up to his eyeballs on the project we're considering for Crawford City. I'm afraid I'll have to pry him out of his bedroom."

I smiled. "I take it the meeting went well?"

"Better than we expected, but you don't want to hear about all that, I'm sure. Let me go get Corey, and we'll go to the wine tasting."

I thought quickly. I knew I'd said we needed a chaperone, but wasn't I just being silly? Ruther walked with me almost every night. It wasn't like I was going to jump him in public, although I also knew I wanted him more now than I did before.

"No, let him be. Unless he wants to come, we can let your chaperone sit this one out. Besides, won't someone be there to keep us in check?" I asked and winked, not knowing where my confidence came from all of a sudden.

Ruther laughed. "He won't even remember our plans. When that man gets a new project in his head, he has a hard time letting it go. Let's go. I can't wait for you to try the wine."

I followed him out of the condo and through the hotel lobby. Catherine, a woman I'd only met once, when she and her son, Dr. Allen, came to the café for dinner with Dr. Ash and his kids, met us at the counter.

"So, you're interested in our wine tasting. Lance mentioned you've already been to the winery," she said, and Ruther nodded.

"But Clyde hasn't, and this is my treat."

She smiled, and I didn't see condescension on her face. In fact, she was smiling in a welcoming way, but some internal bullshit made me feel uncomfortable, like maybe I was doing some type of *Pretty Woman* thing.

"Come in and sit down," Catherine said, leading us to a little wine bar area. It all seemed like a big fuss for something as simple as drinking wine. I was immediately embarrassed that I had no idea what actually happened at a wine tasting.

I watched as Ruther swirled his glass and sniffed the contents, cocking my eyebrow before I even knew I'd done it. When he glanced my way, he laughed. "Sorry, I should've asked. Have you done a wine tasting before?" I shook my head, though my blush was probably answer enough. He looked at me kindly, though. "Let me show you then."

The smile never left Ruther's face as he showed me how to swirl and smell, then told me what he smelled in the glass. I looked over at Catherine, who nodded approval, to make sure I wasn't having my leg pulled.

"Okay," I said and followed his lead.

"Now, what do you smell?" he asked.

I bit back the comment on the tip of my tongue that I smelled wine. Instead, I focused on what he'd said earlier. "I don't know, maybe some kind of fruit?" I asked.

"What kind?" he prodded, and I sniffed again, shrugging when nothing came to mind.

"It helps if you close your eyes," Catherine said, and I quickly looked over to see if she was making fun of me. Clearly, she was just being helpful.

I closed my eyes and sniffed, and this time, I thought I smelled cherries and said as much.

"That's right, dark cherries, and I can also smell oak. That comes from the barrels it was aged in."

"I can smell that, yeah," I said, getting into it. "It also smells a little smoky, which is odd, right? It shouldn't be smoky."

Both Catherine and Ruther chuckled, automatically putting my back up. "No, it's a good thing," he said. "The winemaker would want that to be part of the experience."

I nodded, trying not to appear as awkward as I felt. "Now, you taste it," Ruther said, closing his eyes as he took a drink.

I did the same thing, and although the flavor was good, I didn't quite get why there was such a fuss over what was just wine. Sure, even I could tell it was better than anything I'd bought in the discount aisle of the grocery store, but was it worth all this? I doubted it.

"What did you taste?" Catherine asked.

I shrugged. "Not much, really."

"Okay, so this is going to feel strange, but bear with us," Catherine instructed, pulling out a glass from below the bar. "Sometimes you need oxygen in your mouth to catch all the flavors. It's terrible manners, especially down here where people are still worried about such things, but when you drink, let air into your mouth before swallowing." Then she demonstrated how to do it, and Ruther did the same.

"Yeah, that's weird," I said. "I hate to tell you both, but I might be out of my element here."

Catherine laughed. "Dear, everyone is out of their element when it comes to wine at some point or another, but if you aren't comfortable—"

"No, it's not that," I said, knowing this was something special Ruther was trying to do for me. "Okay, show me again. I don't want to end up spitting wine all over my shirt." I knew from experience that getting a stain out of light-colored clothes was a pain in the ass.

They both showed me one more time. I tried it, and, to my surprise, I actually did taste some of the flavors I'd smelled earlier. "Wow, okay, I thought you were just putting me on, but I taste more flavors now."

Catherine winked at me. "We'll turn you into a wine snob before you know it," she said, putting the bottle on the counter.

She opened another bottle and did the same thing again, and I ended up laughing with them as they prompted me about the flavors. I was feeling the effects of drinking too much wine when we were done, and Catherine pushed a bowl of pretzels toward me and instructed me to eat a few.

When someone in the lobby caught her attention, she said she'd be right back, then dashed off.

"This was fun," Ruther said and leaned against me. Maybe it was the wine, or maybe I just really liked him, but I leaned into him and then looked up at his handsome face.

"It was, and I never would've thought tasting wine would be fun."

"Maybe we need to get you out more," he said in a whisper, and when he leaned down, I took his mouth with my own. I pulled back when Catherine came back, and I knew the blush on my cheeks was as much about the kiss as it was the alcohol.

"Shall we dive into another bottle?" she asked, and I immediately put my hands up. "No, absolutely no more for me. I'm already buzzing from what we've tasted."

"Then another time," she said and began putting the bottles away.

I nodded but doubted there'd be another time. "Which wine did you prefer?" Ruther asked, and I pointed toward the pinot. Not because I could tell much of a difference but because that's the one he'd said he preferred.

"Good, we'll take two bottles," he said to Catherine, then turned to me. "Corey is making lasagna, but before you get excited, it's just Stouffer's. I think this would pair well with the wine. Will you join us for dinner?"

"I...sure," I said and glanced over at Catherine, who was smiling ruefully. I didn't take her for a gossip, like most of the town, but she was clearly enjoying how all this looked. I almost said no to Ruther because I was not supposed to be developing relationships, but my brain short-circuited and I accepted his invitation.

Our kiss, brief as it was, had blown my mind and opened the way for more, which I wasn't ready for. Luckily, I think Ruther figured that out because that evening at dinner, we enjoyed listening to music, talking about the project, and eating. Just as friends would.

My mom used to make frozen lasagna as a special treat. Certainly not something we had often because even though it was cheap, we could seldom afford it. The fact that it was something special, though, set the evening apart for me.

As the sun set behind us, I yawned before I could stop myself. "Sorry, I'm used to going to bed early these days. It's been a really nice day. Thank you both," I said and stood to go.

Ruther stood with me and waited while Corey said his goodbyes. We walked out into the hallway, and I was just about to say goodbye when Ruther stepped up to me. I didn't resist. I wanted another kiss as much as he did.

Waves of pleasure rolled through my system as his lips collided with mine. I could've dived in deeper, taken more from him, but even my slightly inebriated brain remembered why I couldn't. I pulled back and placed my hand on his chest. The same chest I'd wanted to explore earlier that day, but instead of indulging in those notions, I shook my head.

"I'm sorry, Ruther, I'm really sorry," I said, meeting his gaze. "I like you and all that, but I'm not...I don't need...sorry." I stopped to catch my breath. Ruther didn't move but kept his strong hands on my sides as I struggled to find the right words. "Things were bad before I moved here, really bad, and they involved a nasty boyfriend. I can't let myself get into another relationship, even if it's just a fling. I can't—"

I bit off the last statement, knowing I'd start bawling like a baby if I went any further.

Ruther leaned down and kissed my forehead. "Clyde, you don't have to explain anything to me. I like you, and if we need to keep things platonic, so be it. But there's no use denying I want you too. The more I get to know you, the more I want you."

I nodded, and the tears fell then. "Give me some time, okay?" I asked, and his warm smile sent shivers all over my body.

"You take all the time you need, Clyde. I'm not going anywhere. I might have to go back to New York at some point, but I won't be gone forever. Crawford City seems to need me, and I think there's something between us that deserves further study as well, wouldn't you agree?" he asked.

I nodded. "Yeah, I guess so."

"Then let's see what happens," he said, but before he could pull away, I drew him into a tight hug and held on, letting myself feel what it would be like to have someone like Ruther hold me.

I didn't really believe there was much to explore or study, as he'd said, but that didn't mean I couldn't enjoy imagining it. Sweet afternoons tasting wine and laughing with friends. Quiet walks home after work, even simple pleasures like an early morning donut. Those were pipe dreams for someone like me.

The reality finally caused me to step back. "See you at the café," I said and walked away before I did something foolish like kiss him again.

"Oh, you weak, weak man," I said to myself as I rushed toward the motel. I'd learned my lesson, though, and despite the happiness I felt from the fantastic day, I knew not to go unaware of my surroundings again.

No one was around except a group of what looked like a bunch of teenagers. There was loud music pumping out of the bar across the street, which made me hopeful that I could get to my room unnoticed.

I locked my door behind me and fell onto the bed. Today had been beyond amazing. I jumped up, brushed my teeth, and got ready for bed.

I touched my fingers to my lips, remembering what it felt like when Ruther kissed me. The scratch of his well-maintained beard, the taste of the wine we'd shared.

Ruther was my fairy tale, but that didn't mean I couldn't enjoy dreaming of a handsome prince for once. Even if they were pipe dreams.

The wine lulled me into a deep sleep, a sedative that worked like no other. I was so content, dreaming of a sexy Ruther, more wine tastings, and sweet walks together.

At first, when the hand came across my mouth, I didn't react. Having been asleep, I'd thought it the caress of a lover. Then I woke up and registered the pressure of someone straddling me.

"Aah, there's the slut. Open your fucking eyes and look at me!"

I jerked and squirmed to get away, but Jimmy's weight had me pinned to the bed. His hand pressed against my mouth, preventing me from yelling for help. "You motherfucker, did you really think you'd get away with stealing my fucking cash? I should beat the life out of you."

I noticed a hand that wasn't Jimmy's slide over his shoulder and saw the biker from the other night. He wasn't smiling creepily like last time. Instead, he looked worried, like he was afraid Jimmy might make good on that promise.

"Get off," I mumbled into his hand, then bit it.

"Ouch, you fucker!" he yelled and hit me across the face.

"No, not fucking again," I said and wrestled an arm free, then took a swing at him. Yeah, Jimmy would probably keep his promise. I didn't know how he got in here, but damned if I'd let him kill me without leaving evidence that he was my murderer.

I managed to scratch him before Jimmy's man helped hold me down, giving Jimmy another chance to get a punch in and causing me to writhe in pain.

"This isn't cool, man. I can't go back to fucking prison," the guy said.

Jimmy paused but didn't take his eyes off me. "You have fifteen minutes to get me my fucking money, all of it. If you don't, I'm going to beat you so fucking hard you won't recover. You understand me?"

I nodded. I'd known my reckoning was coming, I just hoped it wouldn't be so soon. "Okay, okay," I said between agonized breaths, the pain where he'd hit me still ricocheting through me. "I need to get to an ATM."

"An ATM?" Jimmy asked with a suspicious grin on his face. "When did you get uppity enough to use a bank?"

"Do you want the money or not?" I asked, knowing my attitude was likely to land me another punch, which Jimmy looked as if he was about to deliver. But the guy still holding me shook his head and to my surprise, my ex actually listened to him.

"Okay, take him over to that fucking drugstore. They have an ATM outside. Once he's got my fucking money, we'll bring him back."

The guy pulled me out of bed and barely allowed me to pull my pants on before he manhandled me into the pickup's front seat. It was the same black truck I'd seen earlier. Jimmy crawled in next to me, pressing me between them.

I got out of the truck when they pulled up to the ATM and fumbled for my new bank card. I'd yet to do anything with the thing besides call using Mrs. Cole's restaurant phone to activate it.

I had enough in my account to cover what I'd taken from Jimmy. It cleaned me out, but I silently thanked the universe I'd been saving every dime possible since working at the café. Jimmy and the other guy hung back, probably to avoid the ATM camera catching their image, not that it hid my split lip or that I was at the ATM with no shirt on in the wee hours of the morning.

"Hurry up!" Jimmy yelled, and at that moment, I decided to leave myself fifty dollars. It wasn't much, but it gave me something if...when I had to run again.

I shoved the cash and the card into my pants pocket, and handed him the money when I got back to the truck. He counted it and laughed. "This ain't enough."

"Jimmy, it's what I've got."

"You go back over there and get me all of it."

"It is all the money I have, fuck!" I said, hoping someone in the tiny town might hear us and come to my aid—no such luck. Crawford City was dead this time of the morning.

He looked at me, then over at the ATM, and back again. "You might be a piece of shit, but you ain't never lied. Best you ain't lying now, but I weren't kiddin' neither, this ain't enough for what you put me through. I'll be back next week to get the rest, and you best have this much or more waitin' for me, you hear?"

"I won't have that much, maybe half that. But that's it, Jimmy, I ain't got nowhere else to get money."

He laughed. "Trailer trash," he said. "Next week, you best get me every cent you can!"

I nodded and stared at them as they sped off, leaving me bloody and shirtless in the middle of downtown. I held my stomach where Jimmy had punched me. They hadn't let me put shoes on either, so I had to wander back through town barely dressed. At least I didn't have an audience to watch my humiliation.

By the time I got back to the motel room, my feet were bleeding from accidentally stepping on broken glass. I couldn't even cry because there was no one to blame for this fucking predicament other than myself. I locked the door, not that it had done me much good. The son of a bitch that'd helped Jimmy must've somehow gotten ahold of a key.

Ignoring the pain in my feet, I pushed a dresser in front of the door. Damned if I'd let him come back and try again. Even if I knew I wouldn't sleep, I needed at least a moment's notice to get ready to fight.

I was tired of men beating the shit out of me, and if Jimmy came back, I swore to God himself I'd kill the son of a bitch. He'd been paid and needed to leave well enough alone, although I doubted he would. I didn't have much choice but to pay him next week. I had no evidence he'd come into my room in the middle of the night, and he'd been smart enough to stay out of the way of the camera in the ATM, so it'd just be my word against his.

Once the sheriff heard I'd stolen from him to begin with, I'd be going to jail anyway. He had to know, though, I wouldn't become his fucking patsy. If he kept pushing me, I'd take jail over this.

I thought about calling Lewellen. Yeah, she was a piece of shit too, but she'd come if I called. Not that I could call. My motel room had no phone, and I hadn't paid for more minutes. I had been planning to do that the next time I got paid. Now, I wouldn't have the cash.

But I'd make enough this week to pay Jimmy off once and for all. Then, I'd cut town if I had to. No matter how much I loved it here. I was compromised now. Jimmy knew where I was, and he'd likely never let me live in peace.

Twenty-Seven

Ruther

Despite Corey's teasing, I was happier than I'd been in a long time. I got up early the next morning and ran a mile on the treadmill before my ankle started twinging, reminding me it wasn't quite healed.

Not letting that deter me, I went down to the café and hoped I might see Clyde there, but no such luck, so I grabbed breakfast to go for Corey and me. My assistant was already up and madly working on the development project, so I figured I'd ensure he had something to eat.

He barely acknowledged the food, making me chuckle. Nothing showed me this was a viable project as much as Corey's undivided attention.

I let him show me all the details, and, more than once, I wished I'd asked for Clyde's phone number to text him. I'd asked for it once, and he'd just laughed and ignored me.

Maybe now that he'd kissed me, he'd let me have his number. Not that he still hadn't been clear about what his expectation was regarding letting this go further. But at the very least, we were definitely friends now.

I spent the entire day happy. Even seeing my old home in the distance when Corey talked me into going to the town hall to speak to Emanual hadn't caused me any concern. There was just too much happiness inside me for the panic to take hold.

The next day, things cooled off significantly. We went to the café at nine, but Clyde said he didn't have time to sit with us. It didn't look any busier than usual, so I wasn't sure why he was skipping his break. Truth be known, the café looked slower. When I got a close look at him, though, it looked like his lip was swollen.

"Clyde, did you have an accident?" I asked as he swept past us bussing tables.

He hesitated, and his eyes clouded over. "Yeah, I fell, but I'm fine," he said and rushed off.

Even Corey, who was mostly clueless, looked concerned, although he didn't respond.

I showed up that evening for our usual walk, but a concerned Mrs. Cole told me Clyde had already left.

The rest of the week didn't improve. Clyde became more closed off as the week progressed.

The project was the opposite. We'd had nothing but green lights so far. Not only did Emanual and Jake fully support the project, but they discussed it with several members of the town council, who praised the idea and kept saying how much it was needed.

By the end of the week, Corey had put a contract on the land. It was really going to happen. Or it would unless something terrible happened first, but I tried to keep any pessimism to a minimum.

Finally, on Friday night, I'd had enough of Clyde's cold shoulder. He might not be interested in spending time anymore with me, but at the very least, I felt he should tell me so. I waited until he got off work, then confronted him. "What did I do, Clyde? I know you said you weren't interested romantically, and I've respected your boundaries, but at least tell me what I did to make you not even consider us friends any longer."

Clyde paused outside the café door, then shut his eyes. "Ruther, I'm sorry, but I don't have time for this."

"You do, at least time enough to tell me to get lost. If you're done and don't want me around, tell me, but, Clyde, I haven't liked someone like you in years. Maybe not ever. I want to get to know you, be it as a friend or lover. But I'm getting the cold shoulder, and I don't understand why."

"Stop," he said and wiped angry tears off his face. "You don't understand, and you won't ever. I'm a hillbilly with a past as long as you can imagine. I've never had any luck with a man, and you aren't going to be any different. I told you, Ruther. I told you I couldn't do a relationship, and you...you kissed me."

"You kissed me first!" I said and regretted it the moment the words slipped out.

"I did, and I'm sorry about that. I'm sorry, you and I are never going to be anything more than acquaintances. Consider yourself lucky it never went further than it did."

I watched him stomp toward the drugstore and the ATM. It took everything in me to resist following him, telling him he was a fool for not even giving us a chance, but I knew better. I didn't know his history, but the indication that his ex was a bad guy was enough for me to know that if I didn't let him have his space, I wouldn't be any better.

I sighed and turned toward the condo. I caught sight of a crowd of people who'd clearly seen what'd gone down between us. Jake, Lance, Todd, Ash, Amos, and Emanual stood a few feet away, clearly about to go into the café when our argument occurred.

I shook my head and walked past them. There wasn't anything to say. Clyde didn't want me, and I wanted him too much. It wasn't the first time that'd happened in my life. But if I were a betting man, I'd say it would definitely be the last.

I got back to the condo just in time to hear a panicked Corey talking on the phone. "Well, of course, he has insurance. Have you spoken to the contractor? Shit, okay, I'll book a flight out tomorrow. Until then, have the apartment secured."

He looked annoyed when he came out of his bedroom and saw me. "I'm sorry to tell you this, Ruther. There's been flood damage to your apartment back home. Not much damage, but enough to cause problems with the building manager. I have to fly back tomorrow and try to get a handle on it."

"Shit, well, I'll come too."

"You will? But what about...?" Corey paused, but I knew he was going to ask about Clyde.

"Crawford City seems to require a housing developer, but clearly not a lover," I said, walking toward my bedroom. "I'm going to get changed, go down to the gym, and work out for a while. Book me on the flight with you tomorrow. I'll stay at my dad's place until we get the apartment situation worked out."

I didn't linger to see Corey's expression. I couldn't handle that and the loss of Clyde. I knew I'd be back in Crawford City eventually, but my gut told me even if I stayed, Clyde wouldn't give me the time of day. He'd made that abundantly clear.

The next morning, as Corey and I got ready to fly back home, I forced myself to stand on the balcony and stare at the upper parts of the house I'd spent my early childhood in. The place that'd burned me and caused grief most of my life.

I couldn't help but sigh in relief when no panic came on me. Instead, there was sadness, but not because of the home and its bad memories. This fresh sense of loss came from Crawford City almost giving me something I'd wanted more than anything—the love of a genuine and good-hearted man—and then snatching it away.

I cursed the town for making me feel like this, just as I'd begun to hope. I might not be facing panic attacks being this close to the old family estate, but I was facing the fact I would likely never have what I'd always wanted.

Lasting love.

Twenty-Eight

Clyde

I DIDN'T SLEEP FRIDAY night. I kept the baseball bat I bought at the thrift store earlier in the week within reach, and I'd moved the dresser in front of the door. My ex never showed up. Instead, in the wee hours of morning, I got a knock on the door. Jimmy's voice came through it a moment later. "You got my money, darlin'?" he asked, the mock endearment making my skin crawl.

I pushed the money, still in the envelope I found at the ATM, under the door. "That's it, Jimmy. There'll be no more, and if you come around again, I'm going to tell the law!"

He laughed. "You'll be the one rotting in jail then. I'll see you next week!" he said cheerfully. I heard a truck door slam a few moments later and assumed he'd gone.

I slumped on my bed. This sucked so much. He would never leave me alone, not while I was here.

159

The problem was I had nowhere to go. Thanks to Jimmy, I didn't have enough money to put down a deposit on another motel. I didn't even have a phone to call someone, not that anyone I knew would help. Except maybe Lewellen. The bitch.

I left the dresser in place, just in case Jimmy returned, and went to shower. I knew Mrs. Cole would let me eat for free, and last night my stomach had been too upset to eat dinner, so I was starving.

I got dressed and all but ran to the café, determined to avoid Jimmy and his cronies. When I got to the edge of town, I looked over at Ruther's building and froze. Jimmy was leaning up against his truck, talking to Corey.

I felt the blood drain from my face. Shit, he planned this. Jimmy was telling me in no uncertain terms either I pay or he'd take it out on Corey or Ruther. He must've seen Ruther walking me home, or his asshole henchman who'd recognized me told him as much.

I stumbled the rest of the way to the café, although my stomach was tied in knots. I didn't know what to do. I couldn't go back to the motel. Jimmy had seen me when I'd come around the corner.

When I entered the café, I immediately saw Sheriff Pat and her deputy. I think his name was Darren. They appeared to be finishing up their meal. My feet went their way almost without my knowing.

I heard Mrs. Cole behind me, but I couldn't stop. I knew what I was doing would undo my life for good. I was going to get arrested, then I was going to lose my job. I'd be homeless with less than fifty dollars left to my name and not a friend in the world.

That didn't matter, though. Ruther and Corey didn't deserve to get pulled into my bullshit just because I'd done something stupid.

I got to the sheriff's table just as Mrs. Cole's hand landed on my shoulder. "Sheriff Pat, I need to turn myself in."

I heard Mrs. Cole gasp, and the sheriff looked surprised. Tears flowed from my eyes, but there was no going back now. "Clyde, what do you need to turn yourself in for?" she asked, and I could almost see humor in her eyes, like she hadn't believed me. At least she hadn't before the waterworks started.

The deputy scooted over, and I sat down. Mrs. Cole all but pushed Sheriff Pat over as she sat across from me and took my hand. "You see, Sheriff Pat, I stole from my ex-boyfriend. Now...now he's here, and he's getting revenge. I'm afraid he's going to hurt Ruther or Corey, and it's all my fault."

Twenty-Nine

Ruther

I NOTICED COREY TALKING to a strange man and wondered what it was about. We'd loaded up the rental car, and I'd just returned the condo keys to Catherine and came out to see Corey and the man talking.

Corey nodded my way when he saw me, and I got into the driver's seat and waited. When he climbed into the passenger seat, I asked what that was about, and he shrugged. "No idea, just Tennessee overfriendly, I suspect. Nothing to worry about, but we do need to get moving if we're going to catch our flight. You ready to go?" he asked.

I looked around the little town, searching for any feelings of panic, but felt none. "I guess so, mission accomplished and all that."

Corey looked at me and smiled. "I'm glad, but...I'm sorry about Clyde."

I shook it off. "Don't be. I wanted something he wasn't interested in. Not his fault. I'm just a bit of a fool, is all."

"A bit of a fool, is it?" Corey asked, and when I looked over, he smirked. "Let's get you home before you turn into a hillbilly."

I smiled, but Clyde's words from the night before struck me. *Hillbilly.* Was Clyde a hillbilly? I didn't know. Was that even really a thing? Sure, he and I came from different worlds, but he was an amazing human being. One I'd loved to have gotten to know better.

I glanced over at the café, then shook my head. "You're probably right. Let's get going."

Corey nodded, adjusted the satellite radio to the station I liked, and I drove out of town. I knew we'd be back. The project we'd started dictated that. Corey would probably have to come back this way sooner than me, though.

Regardless, it was time to go. I'd come to face the demons of my past, and, for the most part, I had. There was more work to be done there, like facing the librarian and his famous singer husband, and maybe even talk them into letting me tour the house, but for now, I'd fought the devil and won.

At least I could be proud of that.

Thirty

Clyde

WHEN I FINISHED TELLING the sheriff, deputy, and Mrs. Cole all I'd done, I cringed as I waited for them to slap the cuffs on and take me to jail. Instead, Darren, the deputy, pushed me out of the booth, and I found myself in the middle of a group hug. When others who'd heard my confession joined in, I broke down, having to be held up by those hugging me.

It took a long damn time for me to stop crying. When I finally did, and the cluster of people pulled back, I looked at the sheriff and asked if we were going to the station now.

"Oh, goodness, no. You stole, and that was a crime, one you might still have to face, but when the man broke into your home, forced you to pay him, and then threatened others, that shifted the blame onto him. Not to mention the fact that he hurt you."

"But, I have priors. Surely that's gonna hurt."

"Maybe," she said and took my hand, "but we don't make a point of arresting domestic abuse victims, even those who stole money to get away."

"Can you protect Ruther?" I asked. "And Corey?"

She nodded. "I think so, but," she said, looking at Mrs. Cole, "Clyde can't stay in that motel. It's not safe, and I can't afford to have someone stationed there to keep an eye on him."

"Oh, don't you worry about that," Mrs. Cole said, her tear-streaked face set in stone. "We take care of our own."

Sheriff Pat smiled and turned to me. "You lay low until we get that man apprehended."

I nodded, then gratefully slid back into the booth, and Mrs. Cole joined me.

The townspeople who'd heard it all sat back down, too, but they were all still listening, still giving what support they could. "I-I'm so embarrassed, but I couldn't let Jimmy hurt Ruther or Corey. I...not because of me being stupid."

"You stop that right now," Mrs. Cole said sternly. "You weren't being stupid. You were surviving. Ain't a soul here that wouldn't take a baseball bat after that Jimmy character if they could. He don't deserve your thoughts, much less your fear. Don't you worry, Sheriff Pat will find that scoundrel and put him up for good."

I gave a watery laugh, knowing the law didn't tend to put men up for domestic violence. Too many years of watching my mom call the cops on my dad showed me that much.

"I'll be okay if she's going to pick Jimmy up. I should be fine over at the motel."

"Like hell," she said. "You okay to come with me? If so, I'll show you something I shoulda already shown you."

I nodded and thanked all the sweet people who'd stood by me just a few minutes ago, then rushed after Mrs. Cole to keep from losing my shit all over again.

She led me out the back of the café and up a set of steel steps. Then she pulled her key ring out of a pocket and unlocked an ancient brown door at the top.

I followed her into a dusty, slightly musty room. "I lived here until I married my sweet husband. It's a bit dirty, hasn't been used in years. I was going to clean it up and rent it as one of them vacation rentals, but I never got around to it."

She looked around the room and sighed. "It ain't the Ritz, but it was good enough for me, and I reckon it's good enough for you too. You'll be putting some elbow grease in 'cause it needs a good deep clean, but to be honest, it's a heap better'n that old dump you've been staying in."

"I-I can't take this. I don't...hell, I'm surprised I'm not in jail."

"You deserve it better'n any other person I've ever met, and it don't do nobody any good sittin' up here empty. You'd be doin' me a favor, if I'm honest."

"H-how much?"

Mrs. Cole looked at me funny. "Baby, you forgot, you work for me, not the other way around. Money comes from here and goes to you. If you still need it in a month or two, we can talk about rent, but this is yours until you get your feet securely under you. You hear me?" I nodded and wiped at the tears again. "Oh, stop that before you get me to goin' too. Right now, I prefer to be mad at that son of a bitch who came after you. I swear, back when I was a kid, we'd have taken that fella out and given him a good whuppin'. Well, best to let Sheriff Pat do her thing."

She turned to leave, then turned back and pulled me into a bear hug. I clung to her and cried all over again. Then she let go, and without looking at me again, she disappeared out the door and down the noisy staircase.

I sat down on a nearby dining chair and cried for a good long time. Absorbing what it felt like to have support. I'd never experienced such generosity or genuine concern before. Not from my family and certainly not from any former boyfriends.

I didn't know what I'd done to deserve Crawford City, but damn, whatever it was, I thanked the Lord for bringing me here. I finally got myself under control and took a good long look around the room. It was adorable and a heck of a lot bigger than I'd initially thought.

Mrs. Cole hadn't taken much with her when she moved out. There weren't any personal pictures or anything like that. In fact, besides being dusty, it was what I'd expect one of those fancy Airbnbs would look like.

I looked under the sink, found a stash of cleaning supplies, and chuckled. Mrs. Cole was a stickler for cleanliness, something I truly admired in the woman. I slipped on a pair of yellow gloves that were stuffed into a bucket, pulled out the supplies, and immediately got to work.

I had always found being busy preferable to facing my ugly thoughts. I hated what Ruther would think of me when he found out all I'd done, and now that I'd basically confessed all my sins to the sheriff and her deputy in front of the entire town, I knew it was only a matter of time before he knew. Oh well, I'd do it all again just to feel all those people holding and supporting me.

I knew from this day on, I'd never let another man do to me what Jimmy and countless others had done. Did that suddenly make life perfect? Hell, no. But I felt a precious kernel of hope that maybe I was worth having a life without fear—a life surrounded by friends and people who cared about me. Maybe I'd already found it.

Thirty-One

Ruther

I WALKED INTO THE large brownstone my family had owned for years and crashed down on the uncomfortable loveseat my father refused to replace. Looking around, I felt the simplicity of our Quaker roots, even if my parents hadn't really embodied the teachings. My father's true philosophy was more about what you had to do to better yourself.

Having come from a family with deep ties to New York, links that stretched back to when it was a Dutch colony, the city had always felt like home. Even if my distant ancestors had settled in Flushing, Queens, not a brownstone in Manhattan. Although my family also founded Crawford City generations ago, they never fully cut ties with New York. It's ironic how history repeats itself.

I got up and poured myself a glass of whiskey, another Quaker no-no, but one of the rules my father had chosen to ignore, which was good for me. Right now, a shot was what I needed.

I'd been through the brownstone several times since Dad had passed. Mainly to get rid of things I didn't need. I thought about selling it. I probably would, and all I needed to do was reach out to Dad's cousins, one of whom would likely buy it from me. I felt that keeping it in the family was important, rather than listing it on the market, since generations of Crawfords had lived here at one time or another.

I just hadn't been able to let go yet. I laughed at my sentimentality. My dad hardly cared about me. My relationship with my mother was almost worse than it had been with Dad. Then when I was burned, both of them had pulled away. I'd spent too many years wondering what I'd done to make them dislike me.

Was it the fire? The fact that I was damaged, physically and emotionally? My dad had always refused to come to family therapy with me, even when I was young, so I guess I'll never know. All I knew for sure was I'd never be the perfect son they'd expected, even if the fire had never happened.

After putting my tumbler in the dishwasher, I walked up the stairs and entered the room that had always been mine. It felt different now Dad was gone. Empty, but also devoid of emotions. I shook my head. Damn, this place was getting to me.

I peeled off my clothes and climbed into the oversized shower with double rain showerheads. A luxury I didn't understand why my father had installed in the guest bathroom, considering I'd never stayed here and, to the best of my knowledge, he never had guests.

I was thankful for it now, though. The water soothed the hours of travel from Crawford City. After a long shower, I dressed in sweats and climbed into bed, then opened my laptop. I didn't really do social media. I didn't have that many friends to connect with. At least, no friends that frequented those apps.

I found myself logging into Facebook, though, and searching for Clyde. I found him fairly quickly with his unmistakable quirky side smile and timid brown eyes. I missed him. I know I had no right to, not after he'd shut me out.

There wasn't much more than the picture on his profile. Just something from a few years ago saying he'd gone to school. Being a glutton for punishment, I ended up downloading his picture to my computer. Silly, yeah, but I missed our evening walks and daily meetings during his morning break. Clyde had somehow gotten past all my defenses, and he hadn't even wanted to or tried to. I chuckled bitterly because that's probably why he had.

Was I so shallow that I couldn't connect with someone unless they were out of reach? For a moment, I entertained the notion of calling my latest therapist and hashing through it, and maybe I would later. I didn't, however, need a therapist to know it was complicated.

The irony of feeling a deep desire to be intimate with Clyde wasn't lost on me either. Although I was much better now than I used to be, my scarred body still worried me when it came to new lovers. Somehow, I didn't think Clyde would criticize me or shy away just because of the burn scars. I honestly didn't know that for a fact, though. It's possible I'd built up an image in my mind of who Clyde was that didn't match reality.

Okay, yeah, I needed to contact my therapist and schedule a few sessions. I had more work to do.

That didn't mean I would stop caring about Clyde or wishing we were in a relationship. Maybe what it could do, though, was help me process the lost opportunity with him without beating myself up.

I closed my eyes, thought of Crawford City, waited for the telltale signs of panic, and smiled when they didn't surface. I'd accomplished something meaningful during my trip, maybe not the relationship I'd like to be pursuing, but I had managed to quiet the fire-breathing dragon that seemed to lurk in the recesses of my mind.

Clyde was behind that healing. That's something I could cling to. Something I could remember and associate with him. I fell asleep thinking about how happy that thought made me.

Thirty-Two

Clyde

I SPENT THE NEXT couple of days cleaning the apartment. Mrs. Cole had told me to take a couple of days for myself and not come into the café unless I needed food. Not that I needed to considering she usually brought up a plate for each meal. I scrubbed the floors, took out the area rugs and beat them over the back stoop, wiped down all the cabinets, scoured the countertops, and disinfected the toilet. I probably went a little overboard, but the process made the apartment feel like my own.

Once I'd resumed my regular shift at the café, I felt better about my life. Safer, more secure. When Deputy Darren came by to fill me in on their progress with Jimmy, he assured me they would be watching, and if Jimmy showed up at the café to collect his next payment from me, they'd pick him up.

I took advantage of the deputy being close to rush to the motel on my break, collect my belongings, and check out. I'd prepaid for the month, which was money I lost, but I didn't care. I now had something much better, thanks to Mrs. Cole.

The day came and went without any sign of Ruther. At first, I was glad he was giving me space. Until Jimmy was caught, I didn't want him involved. By the end of the week, though, I was fit to be tied. Not just because Jimmy would likely show up any moment but because I hadn't seen Ruther or Corey for days on end.

I'd just decided to go over to their condo and apologize after work when Jimmy came in with a couple of his buddies. One was the jackass who'd been with him before.

They sat at a table between where I was wiping down the buffet and the kitchen, so there was no way I could avoid him. "You got my money?" Jimmy asked, loud enough for several people to hear.

"No, son, he doesn't," Sheriff Pat said as she and Deputy Darren approached Jimmy's table. Another deputy blocked the entrance.

"Sheriff, that man stole from me after he beat me up. I'm—"

"You'll have your chance to share your side of the story," she interrupted. "But right now, I need you boys to come down to the station with us."

"Wait, I ain't got nothing to do with this," Jimmy's jackass buddy said.

"Sheriff, that's the man who held me down while Jimmy punched me," I offered.

"Thanks, Clyde. We have your statement."

The guy gave me a nasty look. I knew he wanted to lay into me but wisely kept his mouth shut. The third guy with them shrugged. "I've just met these two. Said they were coming to get money from his ex. I ain't got nothing to do with it."

Sheriff Pat looked at me, and I shrugged. "Be that as it may," she told him, "you're with them, and right now, I want to chat with all three of you, so if you don't mind."

Jimmy hadn't taken his eyes off me. Anger pulsed around him, and the vein on his forehead stuck out the way it did when he went into a tirade. I didn't flinch. Not this time. I'd fought back, which got me into legal trouble that I knew was not yet over, but it also gave me strength. Strength I hadn't had in past relationships. I'd stood up to Jimmy, and this time, even the law seemed to support me.

The sheriff and her deputies handcuffed the three men without incident and led them to patrol cars. Sheriff Pat returned and told me I might need to come to the station to make another statement. "The county prosecutor might need to charge you, too, but you stand firm, okay? Our local judge doesn't tolerate domestic violence. And even if by force, you've paid the perpetrator back, so that should count in your favor too."

I nodded. She and the deputy had told me that several times. Jimmy had walked in thinking he'd win and probably still thought he'd be out soon enough. I didn't know if he would, but I was pretty sure if he came around again, there's only one way things would finally end between us.

Jimmy might not be the brightest bulb in the box, but he was smart enough to avoid that kind of trouble. At least, I hoped he was.

When the sheriff left, Mrs. Cole came over, put her arm around my waist, and pulled me close. "You go on up and rest. I'll come up soon with some pie I'm just about to pull out of the oven."

I nodded and thought once again about Ruther. I'd like to see him, but after all this, I wasn't really emotionally in a place to make amends for how I'd treated him. I hated that he was uncomfortable coming into the café, though. I'm sure he and Corey were sick to death of pizza, since that was the only option in town besides the café, unless they'd just decided to eat at the condo.

I did as Mrs. Cole recommended, and took a nice long shower. I didn't cry. It seemed like I was all cried out when it came to my bad choices. Yeah, I still had to pay the piper, but at least I could do that and hopefully not end up with a felony charge or something. There was pie waiting for me on the counter when I came back out of the bathroom. Mrs. Cole must've dropped it off during my shower. I ended up eating it by myself and then went to bed.

I felt more than a little guilty about leaving Mrs. Cole shorthanded, but I was exhausted. She seemed to understand that, though, and I appreciated her giving me the leeway. I relished the fact that, by some magic, I now had friends and support, which meant a lot and was one hell of a lot more than I'd ever had before.

The next day, I woke up to Mrs. Cole knocking on the door to the apartment. When I answered, I could tell she was concerned. "I'm sorry that I'm late for work," I said.

"Don't you worry about that." She sighed. "I-I might've overstepped, but Baby, I...we all are worried about you."

I nodded, waiting for the other shoe to drop. "I called an attorney here in town. He owes me a favor, you see, and I asked him if he'd be willing to meet with you. I understand if you don't want to, but he's a nice young man. Smart and knows his way around the law. I wouldn't have done this if I didn't think you might need some help to get you out of this scrape."

I sat on the dining room chair close to the door. "I-I don't have any money, Mrs. Cole. I gave my last paycheck to that asshole Jimmy. I, well, I know it shouldn't be a priority, but I need a phone. I haven't spoken to my family in weeks, not that they necessarily care how I'm gettin' on. But I—"

She held up her hand. "Clyde, you don't have to explain yourself to me or anyone. If Justin, he's the attorney, needs money, we can work it out in your paycheck, but at least meet with him, okay?"

I nodded. "Yeah, I probably do need someone who actually wants to help. Court-appointed is about the same as not even having representation, in my experience."

"He said he could be over here for breakfast around eight. Do you think you can be ready in thirty minutes?" she asked after looking at her watch.

I just laughed. "It doesn't take me all that long to be presentable."

"Well, come on down as soon as you're ready. You should probably get some breakfast in you before you talk to him. I'll warm up one of the cinnamon rolls since you seem to like those so much."

I felt the tension ease slightly at the thought of enjoying Mrs. Cole's amazing cinnamon rolls. She only made one pan a day, except on the weekends. Still, when we ran out, we were out. She said she didn't have time to make rolls all morning with all the other stuff that needed doing around the café.

Her rolls never lasted past noon, and I'd only had one, and only then because it'd gotten smushed when we pulled it out of the oven. She wasn't wrong, though. They were one of my favorite things we served.

I went to the bathroom to brush my teeth while Mrs. Cole waited for me, then followed her downstairs. She placed a giant cinnamon roll in front of me, then sat across from me with one equally big. "I-I could share this one," I said, surprised she was taking two of her precious rolls out of commission.

"No, both of us need something sweet," she said, smearing butter on top, gesturing for me to do the same before digging in.

"Oh, these are good. Did I ever tell you how I learned to make cinnamon rolls?"

I shook my head. We both knew she hadn't told me the story, but I assumed there was a point to her telling me now.

"A woman blew in here, say, thirty years ago now. I was working for my mama and aunt at the time. They owned this before I did. The woman's name was Elizabeth James. Ms. James was beautiful. Tall with dark curly hair that fell to her waist. I was half in love with her myself, although I'd never really thought of myself as bi or anything. Besides, she was way too old for the likes of me, or at least it seemed so back then."

I cocked an eyebrow at Mrs. Cole's apparent coming out, but quickly stuffed a bite full of the amazing fluffy goodness in my mouth before she saw.

"So, Ms. James had lived up in northern Missouri in a small town called Eagleton. She'd worked at a truck stop up there, and I guess these cinnamon rolls were known the world over. I don't know if that's true or not. What I do know is the moment she started servin' her rolls here, people showed up asking for them."

Mrs. Cole chewed another bite as she thought about her story. I didn't interrupt, enjoying the downtime with her. "About six months after Ms. James came into town, she suddenly disappeared. No one knew where she went. One minute she was here cuttin' up with Mom and my aunt, the next, gone."

She put her fork down and sighed. "They found her body along the old abandoned railroad halfway between here and Mayville. Couple of kids out hunting. Traumatized them and the entire town. Found out later she'd been married to an abusive son of a bitch who'd tracked her here, and when he caught up to her, he beat her to death. Killed her and threw her out like an unwanted piece of trash."

Mrs. Cole looked up at me then and sighed. "Baby, I ain't never cried so hard in all my life than I did when we lost Ms. James. I asked Mama some years later if she knew about the husband, and she shook her head. Ms. James kept her personal life to herself. That'd likely caused her death. More than a few people had seen that man come into town. Some had seen her with him. Had we known, well, who's to say, but my gut tells me had we known about her troubles with him, we'd have intervened."

I stared at her, not knowing what to say. Was she chastising me for not speaking up sooner?

She put her hand over mine before I could go down that road. "Clyde, honey, you did right. First, by tellin' me when you got here that something was amiss. I knew to keep my eye on you. The day you showed up with a busted lip, even though you didn't tell me why, I alerted Sheriff Pat, and that's why she and Darren started hangin' out here more often. What I'm trying to say is you are a survivor. You fought that jackass, and because you stood up to him and told the sheriff what he'd done, you are here today. I just wish Ms. James had done the same. I still miss and mourn that woman. I never want to have to miss you like that, you understand me?"

I wiped at the stubborn tear that streaked down my face and nodded. "Now, Justin, he's a good boy," she continued. "Been around these parts all his life, and he might be small-town, but that don't mean he's not tough as an attorney. Let him fight for you. Let *us* fight for you. You'll find the people of this little town will stand up to protect you if you let us, okay?" I nodded again. "Okay, well, you finish that up. I'm going to go get you a cup of coffee. Justin should be here any minute now."

I stared at my barely touched cinnamon roll and thought about Mrs. Cole's words. More than a few times in the past, I thought a man might kill me. Jimmy was certainly one of them. Even now, I think if he could get to me, he'd be a danger.

I looked up to see a handsome man in a tie and a briefcase walk in, and Mrs. Cole pointed toward me. I'd seen him in here a few times, although I'd never gotten his name or heard he was an attorney.

"Mr. Griffin?" he asked as he approached the table. When I nodded, he smiled and put his hand out. "My name is Justin Conner. Mrs. Cole said you might need an attorney."

I spent the next week mourning the fact that Ruther had left town without saying goodbye. I'd seen Jake and Lance come in with the mayor and his husband, and asked about him. "Ruther and Corey went home to New York last week," Jake said, then looked puzzled. He was likely surprised I hadn't known.

It hadn't exactly been a secret that Ruther and I had spent considerable time together.

In the end, it all worked out for the best that Ruther wasn't here to watch as I navigated through legal troubles. Justin, after I officially hired him and paid him a retainer of a hundred bucks, which Mrs. Cole let me borrow against my next paycheck, came to meet me on a Thursday during my break.

"So, I spoke to the prosecutor, and I'll be honest, with your priors, it was a bit of a negotiation to get something worked out," he said. "But, the situation, plus your ex having priors in Georgia and being involved in an ongoing murder investigation, helped me to convince him you were acting in self-defense."

"Murder investigation?" I asked, my stomach turning at the news.

Justin smiled sadly. "Alleged involvement, of course, but a situation not much different from your own. The guy with Jimmy when they came into the café, not the man who held you down, but the other one, was accused of killing his ex-girlfriend. The state hasn't been able to prove it, but the investigation is ongoing. Apparently, they did all know each other before paying you a visit here."

I swallowed hard. "And Jimmy? What were his priors?"

Justin opened his briefcase, pulled out a sheet of paper, and slid it in front of me. "Armed robbery, assault with a deadly weapon, and extortion, just to name the ones in Georgia. Sheriff Pat told me there were others in Alabama, but we're waiting on those to come in."

I gulped. "I walked right into it. Shacked up with a man who would've killed me without a thought."

Justin just sat quietly, letting me process. Eventually, he broke into my thoughts. "Listen, I've spoken to the prosecutor, and in the past, we've done a piss-poor job of protecting victims of domestic violence. Gay or straight. I reminded him of that. He's tentatively agreed that if you commit to therapy, he'd be willing not to press charges."

"Wait, I can't afford therapy."

"Nor will you have to. The Crawford City Clinic has a therapist that comes down from Lebanon twice a week. We also have a retired licensed clinical social worker who volunteers there once a week. In fact, you might know her. She's Jake's mom. The clinic assured me, between the two, they would be able to fit you in, and they don't charge as long as you qualify for their sliding scale."

I laughed. "Qualify? I don't know if I do, but sure. If it'd keep me out of legal troubles, I'd go."

Justin nodded, then hesitated. "As your attorney, I would be remiss not to tell you that the prosecutor is going easy on you this time. That's as much about me playing the guilt card as anything else. He won't do that a second time, Clyde. You'll need to keep your nose clean. I know and trust both women offering counseling at the health clinic. If it can help, if *they* can help, please try to take advantage of that, okay?"

I nodded, knowing what he was really telling me. Don't let myself get caught up in another situation where I have to fight to escape a man. I closed my eyes and swallowed what little pride I had left. I wasn't an idiot.

I knew the patterns he was alluding to. I knew I'd put myself in bad relationships...every time.

However, I hadn't had a fucking clue that Jimmy was the bad man he was. What I did know was I was attracted to men like him. Either that, or I attracted them to me.

I thought of Ruther and wondered if I had also misread the signs with him. I didn't think so. I couldn't see him being violent with me or anyone else for that matter. Unfortunately, the only thing I knew for a fact right now was that I couldn't trust my instincts when it came to men.

I resolved then and there that I would take advantage of this opportunity. No, I wasn't foolish enough to think a therapist could fix me. Hell, my mom and sisters had gone to shelters and taken therapy. It hadn't fixed them.

It had helped my sisters avoid toxic men and bad relationships, though. Maybe that's all I could hope for as well—learning how to live without a man. I glanced through the window to where Ruther had stayed up the street.

I hiccupped as I suppressed the emotions and laid to rest the hope that I'd unconsciously kept in regard to him. He'd already moved back to New York, but I'd indulged in the fantasy that we could be more. And that's all it'd ever been, a fantasy.

I need to stay focused on the positive. I'd begun to build a nice life here, and that was a first. If it meant I would be alone, at least I'd be in a community where I felt wanted.

THIRTY-THREE

RUTHER

A S THE FALL WEATHER began to blow into the city, I felt a new kind of purpose. My sessions with the therapist confirmed that I had, in fact, felt renewed in Crawford City. With his help, I decided I was ready to shed the pain of my past.

I never loved living in New York. I don't think I realized that until now. I mean, I loved my city. I loved the restaurants, nightlife, and Broadway shows. I loved being able to decide to do something on the spur of the moment and have whatever I wanted at my fingertips.

But, as someone now in their forties, I realized I no longer needed any of that. I wanted quiet walks along small-town sidewalks. I wanted people who recognized me and waved or stopped to ask me questions a regular New Yorker would feel were impertinent or nosy.

I wanted what I'd lost as a child in that awful fire that'd taken so much away from me. The panic attacks had lessened, though not gone away. Even now, when I thought about the house, about the fire, I had to do some heavy processing to get past it.

The biggest panic attack since returning to New York came when my therapist recommended that I make plans to tour the house next time I was in Crawford City. "Clearly," I said as I rubbed my eyes with my knuckles, "I'm not ready for that."

Interestingly enough, I didn't have any such reaction when admitting I was going to try to relocate to Crawford City. "I don't know if it'll be my forever home," I told the therapist, "but I know New York isn't. I feel dead here. Everywhere I look, I'm reminded of everything I didn't accomplish."

"Like gaining your father's approval?"

I laughed bitterly. "Exactly. I felt something...something different when I was in Crawford City. A sense of belonging. Does that make sense?" I asked, and he nodded.

"Tell me about the process. How do you plan to move?"

We'd spent the past month talking about the particulars and how I felt about it all. Me selling my newly renovated apartment, contacting my estranged relatives about selling our family's brownstone, and becoming deeply enmeshed in Crawford City.

"What about your assistant?" my therapist asked in our last session.

"That's the hardest part, that and leaving my late cousin Farlow's husband. I feel like I'm going to lose the only people left in my life who I care about."

My therapist and I had talked about my close relationship with Corey several times, so he already knew my feelings were friendship-based rather than anything romantic.

"You need to talk to him, probably before you do anything else," he'd advised me.

He wasn't wrong. I needed to clear things up with Corey. I no longer ran a large company, and while I still dabbled in real estate, my business dealings these days really couldn't be considered more than pet projects. I'd kept my assistant on to help me navigate all the stuff in my life, but even without a therapist telling me so, I knew that was disingenuous.

I invited Corey over after a family member officially signed on Dad's brownstone. I poured him a glass of wine and sat across from him as I explained the transaction details.

He nodded but didn't respond. "Corey, I'm moving to Crawford City. I'm going to liquidate all my New York holdings," I said, deciding it was best to pull the bandage off all at once.

"And what do you need from me?"

I chuckled. "Honesty. Do you see yourself living in Crawford City? In following me there?"

He leaned back in the chair, not touching his wine. "Are you asking me to come with you?" he asked.

I stared at him for a moment. "What are *you* asking?"

Corey stood up and paced. "Ruther, you are more than just my employer. You're my friend, my family. Neither one of us has ever been any good at relationships."

I laughed in spite of myself. "Corey, you and I have very distinct types. You like them tall, thin, and regal. I like my men short, stocky, and full of attitude. We are not compatible."

"I wasn't saying we are, but I have nothing holding me here either."

"You hated Crawford City," I said and swallowed my wine.

"Correction, I *thought* I hated Crawford City. In fact, I liked it very much. I only realized that after we returned to New York."

"Like it enough to live there?"

Corey shrugged. "Enough to move to Nashville. I admit, I prefer a city over a small town, but Nashville is nice and adequate for my needs."

We stared at each other for several moments before Corey sat down again. "I know you wanted to sell your dad's business, and I supported that, even welcomed it. Then you found that property in Crawford City, and your life fell into place."

He looked thoughtful, so I stayed quiet. I knew better than to interrupt when Corey was speaking his mind. "I-I'd like to do more projects like that. Not random suburban builds or conversions for the wealthy. The Crawford City project feels real. Like we're making a difference. I'd really enjoy doing more of those."

I stared at my long-term assistant. It was almost like he was someone else. Someone I'd never known. "But you love New York, the nightlife, the men. You'd be giving all of that up."

Corey laughed. "You're not paying attention, Ruther. I haven't dated anyone seriously for years. I hardly go out clubbing. I find myself increasingly enjoying my own company as the years progress. I admit, if I hadn't gone with you last summer and experienced the place for myself, I would never have considered conservative Tennessee a possible place to call home."

He took the wine and sipped it, and I could tell he was pondering his words. "I want to do something that makes a difference. I know I'm being...well, different from how you've known me, but the Crawford City project has struck a nerve."

I didn't know what to say. I didn't need the money. With the liquidation of the business, even with the debts, I had more than enough money to live comfortably for the rest of my l was wealthy even by New York's standards. Now with the liquidation of my dad's property and my apartment in the city, that added even more.

"So," I said, trying to wrap my brain around what he was saying, "you want to create a real estate development company, similar to the one we just liquidated to do...what? Build small houses for poor people?"

Corey shook his head. "Not poor people, although affordable housing would be something we could consider, but projects like in Crawford City, where there's a need and not many investors who can afford to invest or take the risk."

"And you'd manage it?" I asked, getting right to the point.

"And I'd manage it."

"Shit," I said and poured another glass of wine. "Corey, I didn't plan on ever doing this kind of thing again, not with Dad being gone. I thought I'd retire."

Corey laughed and when I cocked an eyebrow, he asked, "How many pieces of real estate have you found around Crawford City since we left?"

I wanted to roll my eyes, but my smile slipped out before I could stop it. "Your point?"

"My point is you love it. I know for a fact you probably have three other possible build sites located in or around that town. In fact, if you haven't at least made one inquiry, I will shut up and never bring this up again."

I frowned but got up, walked to my desk, and pulled out a folder. When I handed it to Corey, he opened it and laughed again. "It's another property, this one behind the bar," I said. "It's not officially for sale, but it belongs to the railroad, who have all but abandoned it. If the project we've started is successful, we could expand over there."

"So, what say you? Shall we do this?" Corey asked.

"Only if you become my partner."

It was Corey's turn to cock an eyebrow. "We've already established we aren't compatible."

"Hush," I said and did roll my eyes that time as I sat back down. "Not like that. I meant as my *business* partner. Fifty-fifty."

"Wait!" Corey stood up again. "I don't have the revenue to invest fifty-fifty. Besides, you're the expert."

"Corey, don't be ridiculous. You're as much, if not more, of an expert as me. I also don't want to work that hard."

Suddenly feeling resolved, I stared at my employee and friend. "I won't do it without you. Not without you being an equal partner. I like the idea, and I think it'd be fun, lucrative, and, well, emotionally, it'll help me too. But not doing it by myself. If we take this on, you'll be making decisions with me."

He stood stock still for a moment, then a smile grew. "Deal! Fuck, yes! You've got a deal," he said and thrust his hand out toward me.

I shook it, then stood and pulled him into a hug. "I love you, Corey. You're truly my best friend, and being partners is something we should've done a long time ago." The emotions that played on Corey's face when we pulled apart hit me in my own feels. "I believe this is the beginning of a beautiful partnership."

THIRTY-FOUR

CLYDE

T HERAPY. I'D ACTUALLY NEVER had a therapy session, and besides what I'd seen on TV, I don't know what I expected. I guess that was both good and...interesting.

I'd spoken with the therapist who worked for the health center, and Jake's mom, Anita, seemed the best fit for me. She was an older, heavily tatted lesbian who didn't put up with shit. I immediately loved her.

We spent week after week peeling back the layers of my life and childhood. The fact that Anita had spent time working with foster kids might've helped the most. "You're still working through your child abuse," she'd finally said during one of my sessions. "This isn't something you overcome, dear. It's often just something you learn to live around. It's part of you. But with help, you can learn how to keep it from preventing you having a functional life."

I teased her often about needing to invest in tissues since I used so many during my sessions. At first, I was angry my emotions were so big, but she assured me that was just the way of it. "Tears help you work it out, so let 'em flow," she'd told me repeatedly.

By early October, I'd graduated from one-on-one sessions to spending my Saturday mornings in Nashville, where I joined a group for battered spouses. It wasn't what you saw on TV with formal talks about how bad our childhoods were or grumpy participants acting like assholes to one another.

It was liberating. We'd tease and laugh, but just as often, we'd cry and hold one another as we worked through all the shit in our pasts.

Gloria, for instance, showed us her scar from a bullet wound where her husband shot her, barely missing her heart. And Doug's boyfriend had cut off his pinky as he slept the night he'd announced he was leaving.

Not all of us had physical wounds, but we certainly had plenty of emotional ones.

I know I'm sentimental, but as cooler weather finally broke through the intense heat, a dam broke inside me. I was seeing myself as someone who could function as a human being. Date? No, I didn't dare think about that, but I could at least see that my brain wasn't broken.

I'd simply dated men I understood. They felt normal to me. As I served the fall tourist crowds or walked past the bar or motel, I began distinguishing between people who were obviously unsafe.

I hadn't been able to notice the difference or know what to look for before. It's almost like the therapy sessions were teaching me to be observant. When a guy would hit on me, something that happened fairly frequently here, which for a small town the size of Crawford City was surprising, I always said no or discouraged them if they weren't forthcoming, but it helped to consider the men who were interested.

More than a few threw up red flags all over the place, and while sharing with the support group, I talked about how excited I was that I was finally able to see those warning signs.

"Do you think you'll ever date again?" Doug asked me one day. I would've thought he was flirting under other circumstances, but that wasn't it.

I shrugged. "I don't know. Part of me thinks I'll never be able to trust myself with another man, but at the same time, being able to pick up on the red flags might make that a possibility one day."

Doug looked at where his pinky should be on his hand and sighed. "I don't think I ever will. No matter what my heart wants. I-I don't think I will ever trust another man not to hurt me. Next time, it might be my life."

I thought of Mrs. Cole's story about the woman who taught her to make cinnamon rolls. "It does seem like a major risk to trust someone after all we've been through."

The group all nodded but remained silent. There wasn't much to say. None of us were good at picking men, and that's what led us to staring at one another on a Saturday morning.

The group leader broke before the subject could be pursued further, and I passed out cookies I'd made the night before. "A little sweetness makes tough subjects easier to digest," Mrs. Cole had told me when I first started going to the group.

She wasn't wrong, and ever since I started bringing treats with me, others had joined in. It felt good to enjoy fellowship with people I was processing life with. Having a cookie or two just seemed to make that easier.

THIRTY-FIVE

RUTHER

"THAT'S IT, AND YOU'VE got the condo reserved again?"

"I told you, Ruther, we're good. What's going on? You don't usually question me," Corey asked, and I shook my head.

"I'm sorry, Corey. I'm just nervous."

He patted my shoulder. "It's fine. I spoke directly with the owner, Jesse. He said he wouldn't be using the condo anytime soon. We have use of it for as long as we need it."

I sighed. "I hope that's true. I have an idea what I want to build for myself. I just need to speak to Lance about it."

Corey smiled. "Okay, so we're set. Oh, Jake and Lance want us to go to the winery event this weekend. The vintner announced it's time to harvest, and then there'll be a party."

"Weren't we supposed to attend a class before we harvested?" I asked, remembering our first and only trip to the winery.

"Indeed, but the grapes are being harvested now, so we're too late for that, but the party begins this weekend. It's apparently a yearly celebration now. The weekend after the harvest, the town turns up to celebrate."

"Sounds very Southern European," I said, and Corey nodded.

My New York apartment sold for cash within a week of listing it. After the renovations, I wasn't surprised. Aside from its location and views, I hadn't lived in it since the upgrades, so it looked like new construction.

That also meant I was now officially homeless. My dad's possessions had been distributed between family and a museum in Queens, and anything we found relating to Crawford City had been sent to its town library. Speaking of the latter, I still needed to reconnect with the librarian, Chris, after I'd had a panic attack last time I saw him.

I'd kept a few heirlooms I felt close to, and I wasn't ready to part with my own belongings. All that had been sent ahead and stored in a climate-controlled storage facility in Nashville.

There were so many issues to face that the panic almost returned, but luckily, Corey remained strong, allowing me to lean on him through it all.

The flight was easy, a direct non-stop between New York and Nashville. The rental car was waiting for us at the airport, so all we had to do was climb in and go. I hoped it was indicative of the new future I...no, *we*, I thought, looking at Corey, were embarking on.

The drive from the airport to Crawford City took just under an hour. The fact that the airport was on the Crawford City side of Nashville made it faster and, for the most part, allowed me to avoid the city traffic.

See, I said to myself, *another sign I'm doing the right thing.* Damn, now I was looking for signs. I really was struggling with all the changes. I closed my eyes, laid back on the seat, and thought about all the things I'd enjoy revisiting in my new home.

I was excited to dig deeper into our development project, and I was looking forward to eating at the café. Never mind that it'd taken almost the entire time I was in New York to lose the weight I'd gained in the few weeks I'd been in town last summer.

I'd also enjoy the walks around town and visiting the winery. I bit the inside of my cheek. Damn, I'd tried to stop thinking about Clyde. Now I'd be back in the very town where nearly everywhere I looked held some memory of him. The café where he worked. The sidewalk we'd amble down on our evening strolls. The hotel where we'd tasted wine together, and where he kissed me afterward.

Crawford City was full of that man. I was fooling myself if I didn't think he was a big part of why I'd decided to move. No, I wasn't going to creep on him, but his grace had been a big part of my journey toward overcoming my trauma and fear. His sweet disposition helped open the door to my doing this transition.

I was determined to be a friend or, at the very least, a friendly acquaintance. Even if he never knew it, I owed him a lot. Since my life was completely changing, that meant more than he could possibly know.

Thirty-Six

Clyde

T HE CELEBRATION IN THE park across from Dr. Gib and Dr. Allen's home was amazing. I hadn't been to a big community shindig since I was a kid, and even then, it wasn't as fun as this one.

Mrs. Cole had helped the community put out a spread that went for days. We'd even closed the café that day so she could dedicate all our time to making sure the work was done and people were directed here instead of to the café.

Of course, I figured the café would be empty anyway, which was the main reason for closing.

The celebration allowed me to meet many of Crawford City's residents in a different way. Even if I'd seen them in the café, I was usually running around like a chicken with its head cut off, so as I milled around, I had time to talk to people and learn about their lives. Mrs.

Cole seemed to understand how important that was to me, and every time I tried to help her with the potluck, she shooed me off, telling me I needed to socialize.

It was just so strange how, after spending a lifetime alone, I was here, with friends and a community. Even though I didn't know everyone in town, they *all* felt more like family than strangers. How was that even possible?

I sat down to listen to the teenagers who were performing onstage and smiled at their gritty sound. I'd never had a garage band like these kids apparently were. When I was young, an elderly neighbor used to have people over for music once or twice a month, and when my dad wasn't on a rampage, which was rare, I'd sometimes join in. I could sing all the old bluegrass and gospel songs but never rock or modern country like these kids.

"Can I join you?" someone asked, and I looked over to see Derek, Jake's younger brother, standing beside me. His adoptive mom was my counselor, and she'd talked enough about him that I felt I knew him personally.

"Sure," I said, patting the chair. "Have a seat."

He had a plate full of desserts that he dug into the moment he sat down. "They're good, aren't they?" he asked, looking toward the band.

"Yeah, I think they are. Do you know them?" I asked, surprised if he did since he lived in Nashville, not Crawford City.

Derek pointed at the drummer. "He and I went out for a while. Didn't work out, but I think he's got talent."

"You gonna go work for your big brother scouting out talent and such?" I asked, mostly teasing since I knew he and Jake seemed to be carbon copies of one another.

"Nah, I'm going to law school."

"Cool," I said and leaned back to watch the show.

"Did you hear that a descendant of the city's founder is moving to town? Jake was talking about it this morning. They wanted him to come this weekend and do some keys to the city thing, but he's too busy selling up and stuff."

I shook my head, only half paying attention. "No, I didn't know that. The founder's descendant. That's a long time ago, huh?"

"Yeah, but his family kept a house here for, like, decades. That's where Chris and Roth live now. They renovated it."

It struck me then who Derek was talking about. "You mean Ruther?"

Then I remembered. Rutherford Crawford. *Crawford*...as in, Crawford City. How had I not put two and two together?

"Yeah, you know him?" Derek looked genuinely surprised.

"Well, yeah, he was here in the summer. Came to the café a lot. Didn't you meet him?"

Derek shook his head. "No, I was busy with summer school. I was trying to get caught up after taking a semester off."

"Nice guy, you'll like him. I didn't know he was descended from the town's founder, though."

"Yeah, Jake also said he's a nice guy, doing some big project here in town too. His attorney, Justin, said I could hang out with him when they put the legal stuff together. So, it's all cool."

"Ahh, yeah, I know Justin too," I said, but didn't elaborate on how I came to know the town attorney. "Well, I think I'm going to go check the food and make sure they don't need me. Catch ya later."

I wasn't sure why learning that Ruther was headed back to town was hitting me like this, but I figured I might need to wrap my head around it before he arrived. I silently thanked Derek for letting that cat out of the bag, and after snagging a couple of cookies, I hightailed it back to my apartment to take a break.

I planned to return to the party later, when Roth and Chris were scheduled to perform. That was hush-hush since the town didn't want a million reporters or rabid fans to show up, but Lance had told me when it was going to happen, so I could make sure I was back by then.

I lay back on my bed after finishing the cookies and stared at the ceiling, enjoying the sounds of the music that drifted into the normally still apartment. Ruther was coming back to town. He was doing the project he and Corey had been working on.

I wondered how long he'd be here and, for a moment, wondered who I could ask. Then I shook the thought out of my head.

First, it was only a matter of time before the gossip got to me anyway. It was Crawford City, after all. Second, I needed to focus on my feelings about that. Figure out what I felt, then process it with my counselor and group. The tiny spark in my heart told me I wanted Ruther more than just as a friend or acquaintance. I needed to find out if that was possible for me before he showed up and I fucked up all the progress I'd managed to make.

I laughed again as Matt playfully picked a fight with Logan over the grape harvest. The class had been more fun than I'd expected. Logan and Matt had such good personalities and were clearly in love, so they seemed to bounce off each other as Logan droned on and on about how to find only the ripest, sweetest grapes to pick.

"Mrs. Cole, you're sure you can spare me?" I'd asked her before signing up for the harvesting class. "According to Logan, we'll be harvesting Monday to Wednesday."

"Baby, we've got things covered, and I know you've connected with Matt and Logan. Go on and have fun. You've earned it."

I chuckled at her shooing me out of the café. I'd helped her make an extra batch of cinnamon rolls that I could take with me to the class. I'd done that a couple of times when I wanted to bring something to my group sessions, so she'd just smiled when I showed up early this morning and didn't say a word as I pulled down an extra pan and began helping her knead the dough.

"You know, I could take this over from you," I said, making her laugh.

"Honey, if you work one more hour, I'll be paying you overtime. You do enough, just keep on doing what you're doing," she'd said. The same thing she said every time I brought up taking on more responsibilities.

She was right. I worked forty hours and often popped down to help when I wasn't on the clock, but mostly when she wasn't around to fuss at me. Still, she was very flexible with my schedule whenever I needed, like for my support group sessions. Truth was, I loved the café and spending time there, clocked in or out. I loved everything about this little town.

Mrs. Cole wasn't wrong about me needing more social time either. Counseling and the group had taught me that I needed to build my circle of support outside the therapy window. I'd been working on that, not that it was too hard with folks around Crawford City being so friendly and welcoming.

That was one of the reasons why I wanted to take the grape harvesting class. "Okay, I'm going to divide you into pairs. Those who've done this before, you'll be in charge of the newbies," Logan announced.

He walked up to me, then scanned the room for an experienced partner. His gaze landed on a woman I only knew as being engaged to Lia, the winery's store manager. "Millie, you've got Clyde," he said.

"Have no fear, newbie. I'll show you the ropes," Millie said, bumping my shoulder. "If we linger here any longer, Logan will go into another lecture about the sugar content of each grape. We'll never get any harvesting done."

"Hey, I heard that," Logan said.

"I don't take it back. Let people get some work done and stop your yammering," Millie said, her lips curving into a smile.

He just shook his head and walked on, causing Millie to laugh out loud. "We're first cousins, in case you didn't already know, and the guy has always been long-winded. Come on, I'll show you where to start."

I loved working alongside Millie. She talked about her life, including graduating from law school only to find she didn't feel the calling to work in a courtroom. "I'm lucky there are plenty of other legal jobs out there," she said.

She'd taken a job with the former judge in Mayville and was even doing some real estate work in Crawford City. I immediately wondered if she'd met Ruther, but I didn't ask.

Everything seemed to come back to Ruther these days. I'd been talking to my counselor about allowing myself to have another relationship, and she'd been encouraging. "Just watch for the signs," she'd cautioned.

The group had said the same but were much more pessimistic about it. I guess living the life was different from helping others process it.

Harvesting took less energy than I thought. My uncle James used to rent land from his neighbor and do what he used to call truck patching, which involved a hell of a lot of work that, more often than not, I got recruited for. Free labor and all.

This wasn't anything like that. Sure, the chiggers could get you, but as long as you sprayed really well, they seemed to leave you alone.

I loved watching the grapes go through all the fancy machinery at the end of the day, prepping them for the...I couldn't remember everything Logan said. I lost interest when he started getting into the details.

Eventually, I wandered out and plopped down on the bench out front to eat some of the sandwiches Mrs. Cole sent over for the occasion.

"So, what's goin' on?" Amos asked and sat down next to me, digging into his own sandwich. I'd ridden to the winery with him and his husband.

"Oh, nothin' much, just enjoying the scenery."

"Must be different from running around the café all hours of the day and night, huh?"

I just laughed. "Different kind of work, but still work. I love it, though—the café, that is, not the farm work."

Amos laughed too. "Takes a special kind of person to want to spend their lives working the ground. I never felt the calling, but I'm glad our boy Logan has."

I nodded. "Yeah, I don't know much about wine, although it's interesting. I grew up with beer drinkers, with the occasional moonshine thrown in."

Amos looked up at the fields. "My parents and grandparents were from the islands and loved their rum. My mom and grandmother were the fruity drink types. I don't know why, but I didn't get into any of it. If it weren't for Emanual, I don't think I'd drink much at all, other than a nice cold beer after a hot day's work."

"Nothing wrong with a cold beer. How long have you and Doc been together?" I asked, referring to the mayor by his nickname, as nearly everyone else in town did.

"Oh, since we were kids. Off and on. Took us a long time to make it permanent, though."

I let that seep in—two men in a relationship that'd lasted a lifetime. "So, what's the secret of staying together that long?"

Amos laughed. "Ain't no secret except you got to keep trying and apologizing, and don't let your pride and anger keep you from working through things. At the end of the day, what's worked for us, I think, has been friendship and the fact I can't imagine my life without Emanual in it."

"I reckon I never really thought lovin' someone my entire life was possible. My mom stayed with my dad even though he was abusive, until he left her for someone else. My sisters got divorced shortly after getting married. Not even my grandparents lasted, so I don't have a lot of role models."

Amos sighed. "Ain't that many gay role models. More than there used to be, but society's been pushing us apart since the Middle Ages. Listen, if you find someone you love, you dig in, work hard. Don't let nobody knock you around, that's no good, but if someone treats you right, and you treat them right in return, there ain't nothing better. Take it from me. I pushed Emanual and everyone else away for years, then when I finally let him in, let my family in, my life changed for the better. And that's a fact."

I wanted to ask more questions, but mostly because I wanted to hear the full story about the mayor and him. Logan called us back into the barn, though, to show us the next step in the process after the grapes got washed.

Despite being bone-tired, I lay awake that night thinking about what Amos had said. The world did seem to be pushing men who love each other apart. The entire LGBTQ+ community, in fact, but some had survived.

This town was full of men who'd overcome the hatred the world threw at us. Images of Ruther came back to mind, and this time I smiled. If he was coming to town, I was going to enjoy getting to know him again, and this time, there would be no running away.

Thirty-Seven

Ruther

I DIDN'T WANT TO go to the café yet. I just wasn't ready when I had so many other things going on. Corey and I were working with Justin, a local attorney, to formalize our business arrangement. Lance, Jake, the mayor, and Amos needed to meet with us to propose the project to the town council for approval.

I met Randy and Cliff Richards, the brothers working under Amos and Todd as our builders, and liked them right away. They were big, tall, rough construction workers who had a great sense of humor and constantly made us laugh.

They were quick to lean into business as well. They showed me new construction projects they'd worked on in Nashville and the surrounding area, and I was impressed. "We believe in quality, which is what's hurt us getting bids in Nashville. We won't cut corners," Cliff said, looking me in the eye.

"If you're looking for someone who'll build crap to save you a couple of pennies, we ain't those people, but if you're like Todd, Linc, and Amos and believe in a quality product, we're definitely your guys."

I glanced over at Corey, who was smiling. "That's who we are as well."

"Not that we don't expect you to adhere to a budget," Corey added. "We're strict about that. You should be able to predict the supplies you'll need for a development project this size, and buying in bulk should cut costs enough to cover overruns. We're hiring you because we've been assured you know how to control a project's budget."

"That's our specialty, as long as you don't come in wanting fifty changes once construction has started."

Corey chuckled. "We are developers, not individuals. If we have people wanting to make changes to the design, they'll be strictly controlled and will occur prior to any building. This isn't our first rodeo either."

I cocked my eyebrow at my snob of a business partner using such a Southern saying. Then I shook my head. It's not like the accent doesn't rub off on you easily. I just never thought I'd see the day it rubbed off on Corey.

The weekend slipped up on us before I knew it. I'd have preferred to plow forward with the project and get as much done as possible, knowing the ribbon-cutting goal before the first of the year was ambitious even for us.

My plans were for nothing, considering there was a party out at the winery, and everyone we'd be working with made it clear we needed to be there. "This town cares about who's in it. You'd be better off reconnecting before you announce your plans to the town council," Emanual had advised.

I already wanted to go. I liked the winery, Logan and Matt, although I'd only met them in passing, and this small town. I'd moved here to be a part of it as much as anything else.

Corey and I drove out to the winery, following behind Jake and Lance, and parked in the space beside a cute little barn. We walked from there to the mill. I wasn't sure we would ever get there as numerous people stopped Jake and Lance to talk and meet us along the way.

It would take some time to get used to all the small talk around here.

There were hundreds of people gathered around the mill, and a small band played a variety of music, which I was thankful for. Most of the time, it's only country down here.

There were events, too, even bobbing for apples. There were games for the kids running around, laughing and having fun. There were booths selling products like soaps and homemade crafts.

It was like stepping into a Hallmark movie or something. Not that I watched very many of those.

The delicious smell of something roasting caught my attention, and I turned to head toward whatever it was and ran right into Clyde.

We both froze and stared at each other a moment before either of us could get our wits about us enough to speak. "Um, hi," I said first.

He nodded and smiled. "Hi, it's been a while. How are you?" he asked.

I shrugged. "Fine enough. I was just about to go find out what smells so good," I said, pointing toward the booth where someone was selling what appeared to be almonds.

"Same. Wanna walk with me?" he asked.

I smiled and nodded, and we walked to the booth. "I've always loved these," Clyde said. "When I was a kid, there'd be a big fair every fall, and that's the one time a year Dad would give us some extra money for rides and stuff. Each year we'd get to pick something to eat. My sisters always wanted the caramel apples but I always wanted the roasted almonds. They just smell so amazing."

"Two, please," I said when the guy behind the booth acknowledged us, and I gave him some cash.

When I got our order, and I handed one to Clyde, he blushed. "Oh, you didn't have to pay for mine."

"I wanted to, especially after you told me how much you liked them."

I could tell he didn't know how to respond, so I just began walking, hoping he'd come with me, and we could avoid the awkwardness.

A big tent had been set up with picnic tables, so I sat down and grinned happily when Clyde sat across from me. We quietly watched all the hustle around us, eating our almonds.

"I-I made a mistake," Clyde said, catching my attention.

"A mistake?" I repeated, not knowing what he meant.

"Yeah, I, well, when you were here in the summer, I was dealing with some shit. I pushed you away, and you were gone by the time things came together."

I nodded. "I figured you didn't want to see me any longer."

Clyde humphed. "More like I wanted to see you too much. I was afraid of screwing up, again!"

I had no idea what he had screwed up but decided to stay quiet to see if he would explain.

When he didn't, I cleared my throat and launched into the speech I'd planned for when I saw him again. "Listen, Clyde, I-I haven't liked someone as much as I like you in a long time. Because of that, I pushed you when you were clear you weren't interested. I apologize for that. You may have heard already, but I've decided to move to Crawford City. I'd like it if we could be friends, and I promise not to push you, okay?"

Clyde surprised me by putting his hand over mine. "I like you, too, and you didn't push yourself on me. There's a lot you need to know about me, about my past, and it's not stuff I want to tell you here in public. But if you're really interested, want to pursue something, maybe we could find time to talk in private?"

I couldn't hold back my smile, even though I knew I must look like some lovesick teenager who'd just found out his crush felt the same way he did. "Um, what's your plans tomorrow, Sunday?"

Clyde laughed. "I volunteered to come back here and help them clean up after the harvest festival, but if you want to join me..."

"I'd love to!" I said and had to force myself not to jump up and pull Clyde into my arms.

We agreed on a time to meet and had just made it official when Logan took over the mic from the band. "If everyone could gather for a moment, we've got an announcement to make."

We followed the crowd and watched as Matt joined Logan on stage. "As you all know, our winery has slowly grown over the past few years. We've been lucky enough to win some awards and added several new varieties to our inventory. This year, we've conquered one of the most difficult challenges we've faced growing grapes in Middle Tennessee, and that is the taming of the muscadine."

Several people laughed, and I quickly remembered the wine I'd tasted last summer.

"We've tested this year's batch, and y'all...it's amazing. So—" He looked over at a few of the kids lingering close to the stage. "—if you're old enough, Lia and Millie will be helping Matt and me give each of you a sample. I think you're going to be as impressed as we are."

I wondered if they'd indeed conquered the flavor. It was close last year, the flavors melding nicely with the blend of grapes they'd used. Just a bit overwhelming for my taste.

"Want to try it out?" Clyde asked.

"Yeah, come on," I said, and we walked side by side to where a line was forming. While we waited, Clyde chatted about everything that'd happened since I'd been gone. The new items Mrs. Cole had added to the buffet line. So-and-so was having a baby, and a couple who'd just announced a wedding. I didn't know any of these people, but I realized, a few months ago, neither had he. The thought that I'd eventually care about this information filled me with joy. I was beginning a life where I felt like I could belong.

We reached the front of the line, and Matt poured Clyde and me plastic cups of wine and smiled. "Take a sip and let me know what you think," he said, and not wanting to hold up the line, I did as he requested.

My eyes grew wide at the taste. "Really? Damn, how did you get those flavors out of a muscadine?" I asked, and Matt grinned. "You'll have to ask Logan, but it's good, right?"

"Damned good," I agreed.

Logan, who was standing close enough to hear me, beamed. "I'll be back to buy a case later. If you have one."

"We do," Lia said from behind us. Just come out on Wednesday when the store's open, and I'll take care of that for you."

I gave her a nod, then Clyde and I moved out of the way so they could pass out more samples.

"It's really good, isn't it?" Clyde asked as he sniffed the remainder of his sample, then tossed it back.

"It is, just like other Tennessee natives. It's surprisingly good."

THIRTY-EIGHT

CLYDE

I SAT NEXT TO Ruther in the chapel, staring out at the view. We'd finished helping clean up at the winery, and then Ruther told me he wanted to show me this special place. It was spectacular—beautiful views as well as the all-glass architecture—and very private.

"I-I'm not good with men," I said, beginning the difficult conversation about my past. "I don't think anyone in my family is. My dad was abusive, and my mom codependent. Hell, the whole family is fucked up because of them. I-I don't trust myself in relationships, but Ruther, I've been thinking about us a lot since I found out you were coming back to town." I turned to see his expression, and when I only saw kindness, I decided to keep going. "I'd like to pursue something with you, but you gotta understand, I ain't just gonna be able to jump into a relationship. I need to make sure I do it right, take my time, get to know you more." I looked down at my hands and sighed. "Make sure you're safe."

I felt him stiffen. "Clyde, I've never hit anyone in my life. I won't be starting with you."

I nodded. "Here's the fucked up thing about all this, Ruther. If I don't do this with the support I've set up, I can actually make you that way. It's all I've ever known." I stood up and paced. "I-I'm fucked up from my childhood and all the beatings my dad gave me and my mother. I have to do this right, or not at all. That's what I'm tryin' to say."

Ruther stood up and drew me into a hug, which, to be honest, I had to force myself not to resist. I settled into his arms, though, and let myself feel for the first time in a long time how good it felt to be held by a man I liked.

"I'm not in a hurry to push you one way or another, Clyde. I like you, and I really did like the stuff we did during the summer. Our walks, meeting you during your work breaks, eating the donuts you brought over, and our wine tasting. I especially liked the kissing," he said and chuckled. "The thing is, you can take all the time you need. I'm in no hurry, and I'm not seeing anyone else either, so there's no need to feel pressured, okay?"

I nodded. "Okay," I said into his firm chest.

"Now, about that kissing stuff, would you feel okay if I did that now?" he asked, and I eagerly nodded because I wanted to kiss him so bad, I could pop with anticipation.

Ruther put just enough space between us to cup my face and tilt it up toward his, then he gently pressed his lips to mine. The kiss was so tender and felt so meaningful, I might've shed a tear had it not sent me into pure bliss. "I'm not sure I've ever wanted anyone like I want you," I admitted after we pulled apart.

Ruther pulled me back into an embrace and rested his chin on top of my head. "It's the same for me, but since we're coming clean about our pasts, I've kept some ugliness hidden from you too."

He sat back down and gestured for me to join him. "I have childhood trauma that causes panic attacks like the one you saw last summer."

Ruther looked out the big windows overlooking the panoramic view and sighed. "I almost burned to death in a fire. It happened years ago but it still haunts me."

He shuddered, and I quickly reached for his hand. He squeezed mine in acknowledgement of my support, but his gaze remained fixed on a point out the window as he continued.

"My parents weren't home, and the fire started when I was asleep. I was alone in the house...the big house on the hill that the town librarian owns now. I woke to flames, and when the ceiling fell in, it trapped me in bed. Had it not been for the firefighters getting there..." He took a deep breath and let it out slowly. "It's still hard to talk about, and if I talk too much, I'm going to have an attack. But you should know, I've got extensive burn scars from my chest to my feet. Somehow, by some miracle, it didn't burn my face or hands. Probably because the covers shielded me. I'm an ugly monster under my clothes."

I turned to him, aghast at the suggestion. "That's bull-shit, Ruther. You survived, and I don't know what the scars look like, but you are not a monster—you're a survivor." I reached over and slid my hand along his jaw, and turned his face to look at me. "Listen to me, I've been doing therapy since you left, and one thing I learned is that you have to celebrate the part of you that survived the ugly stuff. No more talk about you being a monster."

"You haven't seen me."

"Okay, show me. If...if you're comfortable, show me."

Ruther froze. "I...Clyde, I don't know if I'm ready."

"Then show me when you are. I've only just begun to get to know you, Ruther, but I like what I've seen. Your heart is beautiful, and you're special. I can tell you now, I will never see you as a monster. Trust me. I've seen monsters, and if Sheriff Pat is right, I barely escaped the last one with my life. Having scars don't make you a monster. Hurtin' people for your own twisted gratification? That's what makes a monster."

Ruther ruminated on that a moment, then pulled me into a hug even though we remained seated. He held onto me tightly. I'm not sure if it was for my benefit or because of what he'd disclosed to me. Either way, his arms felt so good around me. I snuggled in and let his presence feed my soul.

THIRTY-NINE

RUTHER

I'M NOT SURE HOW I thought that would go. I had no intention of telling Clyde about my burns or the trauma. Now that I look back, it's a miracle I didn't go into a full-on panic. Except maybe he'd been so candid about his past, about the abuse he'd endured as a child and from his lovers, it seemed appropriate to tell him about my own issues.

I'd been convinced that I no longer thought of myself as a monster. I'd told the therapists I'd overcome that, but when faced with the incredibly handsome man in front of me, the words tumbled out of my mouth before I could stop them.

At first, I thought Clyde was throwing false platitudes at me, then he'd asked to see the scars, which I was so not ready for. I almost stood up to go, but I'm glad I didn't.

Listening to him share his story, it was clear he really had known some monsters in his life. When he told me that treating other people badly is what made monsters, not simply having scars, it struck a nerve but in a good way.

We cuddled in the little chapel until the light faded, then walked back to the mill and my car. We drove back to town hand in hand, but stayed mostly quiet. I guessed it was because we had a lot on our minds. I pulled up in front of the café after Clyde told me he'd taken an apartment above it.

We both leaned in and I kissed him hard, then rested my forehead against his. "You're an amazing man, Clyde, and you've done more for me just by being yourself."

He didn't say anything, and I could feel he was getting emotional, so I stayed close a few moments longer, then whispered, "See you tomorrow at nine? Is that still your break time?"

He chuckled. "Good memory. Yep, and I'd love nothing more than to spend it with you."

I leaned back and grinned at him. "Do I still need a chaperone?"

Clyde snorted. "No need to worry about that. If we get too randy, Mrs. Cole will douse us with mop water."

"Eew," I said, and we both laughed.

He leaned in again, took my mouth with his, and then pulled back and winked. "See you tomorrow morning," he said and climbed out of the car.

I watched him disappear around the back of the building, then I drove the short distance to the condo. Clyde was so much, and I didn't think I could ever get enough. God help me, he was an incredible man.

⤝

"Like a glove," I said to Corey after he asked how I was fitting into Crawford City. He'd spent the last few days in Nashville finding a place to live. Our contractors, Randy and Cliff, were helping him find somewhere he would have easy access to their offices.

"I'm glad things are going good, because, well, I don't want to stress you, but—"

I cocked my eyebrow. "Spit it out, Corey," I said when he seemed hesitant.

"The librarian, the one we sent all your father's stuff to, he's...he found something I think you should see, but you should let him show you."

I paused and stared at my new business partner. "What's this about?" I asked.

"The investment and your heritage, I think."

"Can't you just tell me?" I asked, sad that I was taking the coward's way out.

"I could, but I don't have all the details. He does, and if we're going to be part of the Crawford City community, shouldn't you—?"

I nodded, knowing what he was going to say. "I should, and yes, you're right. I need to meet with the librarian and get it out of the way. But if this is about my dad, something nasty, I shouldn't be meeting with him about that before I have a gentler meeting, don't you think?" I asked before he turned back to his laptop and the email I assumed he was about to answer.

Corey looked back up at me. "I'm sorry, Ruther. I didn't think. I believe they just found some photos about the town. Nothing dramatic or anything like that."

I sighed. "Okay, well, that'll make this easier. But I'm not ready to discuss the house. Meeting with the librarian is fine, just not...no house stuff yet."

"Understood. I'll make that clear."

I returned to the bedroom and paced. The curtains were drawn, and I hadn't been able to look at the view of the house since I'd been back. Knowing someone lived there was a lot to digest. Meeting with them, knowing they were living in that space, was almost more than I could handle.

The knock on my door shocked me out of my head. "Yeah?" I replied.

Corey opened the door and stepped inside. "May I offer a suggestion?" he asked.

I nodded, not really paying attention.

"Why don't you ask Clyde to join us tonight after he gets off work? He seems to make things less stressful for you."

I stared at him. I had thought that myself but hadn't voiced it, and it was strange that Corey had picked up on it.

I sat on the edge of the bed. "I wish this wasn't so hard. You'd think after all this time, I'd have gotten past it."

Corey shook his head. "Listen, boss..." He stopped and smiled before regaining his composure. "Listen,

Ruther. I'm impressed at what you've accomplished in such a short time. If having your guy close by helps, ask him."

I nodded and ignored Corey's slip of almost calling me boss. Things were still relatively new in our new relationship. Good, but new for both of us.

"You're right. Okay, so, this evening at the library?" I asked, and Corey nodded.

"Yes, Chris said he was working late, so you can come in anytime."

"I'll go over to the café and ask Clyde if he'll come too."

"Go over? He doesn't have a phone yet?"

I shrugged. "Yeah, but he hasn't given me the number."

Corey looked down and didn't respond. I'd been trying not to let the fact that Clyde still hadn't given me his number upset me, but apparently, even Corey thought it odd and it was, considering that's something even strangers didn't hesitate to give out.

"I'll let you know what he says," I replied before heading to the café.

Clyde was smiling at one of the guys from town, and, for a moment, I had to push down my jealousy. *No, don't be that guy*, I chastised myself. *He's dealt with that enough in his life.*

When he glanced over and saw me, his smile grew even wider. He excused himself and came over to where I was standing.

"To what do I owe the honor?" Clyde said, the formality of the question sounding funny with his accent.

"I have to meet with the new owners of my old home, the one—" Clyde's smile dropped, and he put his hand on my shoulder. "I wondered if you'd join me."

"Of course, honey. I'd be happy to. When and where?"

I had to catch my breath from having him call me honey, but I managed not to make a scene. "It'll be at the library. I was hoping to go tonight." When I said it, he told me to hold on while he checked with his boss.

He disappeared into the back and returned a moment later, smiling again. "Mrs. Cole said she doesn't need me after four, so come get me any time after that."

I nodded and kissed him before I thought about it. His cheeks blushed adorably, which warmed all the cold parts of me.

Corey was right, again. Having Clyde with me made things better. I didn't understand why, but I didn't need to. It was enough for me that he did.

FORTY

CLYDE

A T FOUR THIRTY, RUTHER and Corey stood patiently waiting for me in the café. I was glad I'd taken a few minutes to rush up to my apartment to shower and change, since I'd been sweaty and smelled like food. Both men smiled as I came out.

Ruther leaned over and kissed me, causing me to blush again. I wasn't used to such public affection, but damned if I didn't like it. I guess it went a long way to show how comfortable I was in Crawford City, not to feel the need to look around to see who'd seen the kiss.

"You smell good," Ruther said quietly.

"Yeah, I got off early for a shower. I wouldn't be much company if I smelled like I'd worked all day."

Corey led the way to the library, and Ruther walked arm in arm with me. It felt so strange that he showed this kind of affection, but like the kiss, I wasn't going to complain. It was just too nice.

The library was a stone's throw from the café, so we hadn't gone far before Corey opened the door for us, and we walked inside. Besides the café, this was my most visited spot in town. I didn't have cable or any streaming services, didn't think I could afford them, but Mrs. Cole had left a TV and DVD player at the apartment, so I often checked out movies from the library for free.

I also loved reading, and Chris quickly learned my favorite authors and was constantly recommending a new book for me to try out.

Chris and Roth were standing together behind the front counter, working. It was still so weird to see a famous music star working in a small-town library. Chris noticed us and smiled, although he looked slightly concerned when he glanced at Ruther.

I remembered Ruther's panic attack last summer when Chris came over to his table, and I immediately tightened my grip on his arm. I'd forgotten that Chris had been the trigger for that incident. I hadn't put two and two together that Chris and Roth had bought Ruther's home. I didn't know much about that, only that Chris's parents lived with him, and his mom had invited me to join them for dinner. Something I hadn't taken her up on yet.

Both men greeted us, then Chris asked Roth to watch the front while he showed us his discovery.

Of course, Roth agreed, and we followed Chris into a room behind the circulation desk. It wasn't very inviting.

The room had no windows, the fluorescent light was way too intense, and every corner was crammed full of books.

"I found an old photograph in the historical material that was sent, well, a while ago," he said to Ruther, clearly avoiding something. "This photo is of the old Quaker meeting house that was here years ago. I only figured out where exactly it'd been located after I received the latest of your family's archive of Crawford City."

He pulled another picture out from behind the first and pointed at a particular area. "See, this is the corner of what used to be called the First National Crawford Bank and Trust. You can see the name on the building. You can also see a road that runs right along the bank, and there's the old meeting house."

We all looked at the photo. I had no idea where this was going, but I was here for moral support, not because I could offer feedback.

"That's interesting, but—" Ruther began, but Chris quickly pressed on.

"Mr. Crawford, Jake told me you're looking to develop the property that runs on the other side of the old railroad tracks. I thought you might like to know, before the railroad came to town, that road in the photograph ran directly into the property you're considering. The road is long gone, of course, and the whole section of town across the street where it used to run has been built up, but I thought you might want to install a monument at the meeting house site. It'd be near the exit from the neighborhood you're building. Something to commemorate Crawford City's pioneer past, especially the part about our Quaker roots."

I stared at the two pictures. The old building looked just like any old church did back in the day. It was a plain rectangular building with planks that ran horizontally, most likely painted white. What appeared to be a bell hung on the roof above the doorway.

"I don't remember ever seeing this picture," Ruther said, and for a moment, it looked like he might get emotional. "I wonder—"

Corey was staring at the picture too. "Do you mind if we take these with us?" he asked.

Chris stiffened. "They technically belong to you, but I've searched through the county records, through our archives, and as far as I can tell, these two pictures are the only ones left of those old buildings."

Ruther laughed. "Chris, I admire your commitment to preserving them. Mind if we snap some pictures using our phones?"

"Of course, go right ahead. I can also scan these at a high resolution and save the digital copies to a flash drive for you."

"That'd be wonderful. Thank you," Corey said.

Chris smiled, carefully picked up both pictures, and darted out the door.

"What do you think?" Ruther asked Corey.

"I think it'd be a great way to enter the community. Make a very public nod to the past and your family's history here."

"Besides the name?" I asked and was surprised I'd said anything. It wasn't like me to comment. Maybe it was because it seemed obvious that since the town was named after his family, that should be enough.

"Yes, besides the name," Ruther said and playfully bumped against me. "My family were Quakers. My third great-grandpa was lynched, probably right where we're standing, because he dared to stand against the Confederacy. I no longer practice Quakerism, but I think it'd be good to honor my roots."

I nodded, feeling embarrassed that I'd intervened.

Corey and Ruther were discussing what they'd do with a building if they put a replica in its place when Chris walked back in with the photographs and handed Corey a flash drive with the digital copies.

"You're thinking about replacing the building?" Chris asked.

"Maybe," Corey responded, "but we need to speak to the mayor and town council. We wouldn't want to maintain it, and what purpose would it serve?"

I did look up then, interested all of a sudden. "Crawford City doesn't have a good, neutral spot for groups to meet. There's the church, but some people aren't comfortable with churches as meeting places, like my support group. It could be a community center, especially if it's just outside the main streets of town.

I thought of when I'd helped Ruther out of the woods. The path we'd followed had looked like it used to be a road or a driveway or something. I knew exactly where they were talking about.

Ruther looked at me and nodded. "It could be a community center. These old buildings weren't fancy; they were built to be anything but. Simple, one-room buildings with hard, uncomfortable benches. We could restore it to be historically relevant, but the benches and stuff could be moved out of the way for meetings."

Chris looked around the room. "What's the potential for building a basement?" he asked.

Both men stared at him, then shrugged. "Not sure, why?" Ruther asked.

"Because this room is getting out of hand fast. If you were to build a basement under the main structure, we could use it to store Crawford City's historical references. That way, it could be part of the library system." He quickly laughed. "Not that we'd have any money to help finance it. We barely have enough funds to function here, but we could staff it with volunteers if it was tied to us."

"That's a good idea, Chris, thanks," Ruther said, shaking his hand. "We have a lot to think about."

I followed them out of the library and noticed that the nerves Ruther seemed to have developed when we'd gone in had vanished. We walked across the street almost like we were drawn to where the meeting house once stood.

The old bank had been converted long ago and now stood empty. We wandered down the dead-end street, and I could see the old motel from where we stood. "So, this is where it used to stand," Corey said, looking at the photo on his phone.

"That's the hardware store back there," Ruther said, pointing along the ridge where you could barely make out the building.

"Nothing's been here for a long time," Corey said, wandering to the overgrown area that butted up against the derelict railroad.

"It'd be a nice museum too," I said. "Most little towns have some sort of historical society thing. I'm surprised Crawford City doesn't."

Both men nodded and then continued looking at the lot. "It's what we said we wanted to do," Corey said. "Making a difference, not just throwing up buildings."

"The structure itself wouldn't cost much, not if we built it like it originally was."

"We could build a separate building for the archives," Corey suggested. "Something that matched the style of the meeting house. I'm sure your family's original home wasn't the mansion."

Ruther cringed. "Yeah," he quickly said, and I could see the tortured look setting in, which caused me to step closer and take his hand.

"I'm sure Chris would research that for you," I said. "He seems to be on top of all that anyway."

Ruther smiled down at me and leaned in. For a moment I thought he might kiss me, but Corey kept on talking about the site, drawing Ruther's attention. "This could be a great way to start the project if the cost isn't prohibitive."

"Could you possibly put a park here too? Would there be enough room?" I asked. "Seems to me that's something missing in Crawford City as well."

Both men smiled. "Sounds like we need to talk to Lance." Ruther looked at me then and squeezed my hand. "Wanna walk over to the pizza place with me? We'll let Corey entice Jake and Lance with pizza, and if history is any indication, it'll take at least an hour to get our dinner."

I chuckled because the one time I'd ordered from there, the pizza was delicious, but it had taken a very long time for them to cook it.

Ruther and I sat in the old pizza place, and I listened as he told me what he knew about his family's Quaker past. I didn't know much about the Quakers. I knew they'd settled in Pennsylvania, but I would've never guessed Quakers had come to Tennessee. I guess that's the point of replicating the meeting house and adding a public monument.

Ruther was buzzing with excitement by the time the pizza arrived at our table. "So, what do you think?" I asked, already knowing they wanted to do it.

He shrugged. "There are lots of components, like the architect, the town council, the mayor, whether the city or library or whatever can maintain it. But, if we can work it out, it'd be a nice legacy to leave the town."

I leaned into him, enjoying how excited he was getting. I'd never spent time with anyone who cared that much about their town or history. My life had just been about surviving another day. It felt good to be on this side of things, thinking about possibilities outside of where my next meal would come from or how to avoid someone who'd lose their temper.

Six months ago, I would've never predicted being in this place. It's crazy how fast someone's life can change.

FORTY-ONE

RUTHER

I HONESTLY THOUGHT I'D be building some midcentury modern structure as my home, imagining something reminiscent of Frank Lloyd Wright, but as we looked over the spot where my family would've once come to worship, I knew that wouldn't be the case. I didn't want a massive home, nothing bigger than the apartment I'd owned in New York.

If I accurately remembered my Crawford City home, the one I was slowly able to think about without panicking, I recalled the central structure as being a very traditional Federal style building. It would have been very plain, no adornments or porches even, although I'd be changing that. I wanted to build it on the other side of where I imagined a plain Quaker meeting house would stand.

The bank building across the railroad tracks was empty, but renovations cost more and were more hassle than new construction, so I didn't even consider it. Instead, we could build matching buildings, one like an old barn. Plenty of old meeting houses in the Northeast had barns close by.

The museum and records could be kept in the old meeting house, where people could come in and learn about the town's history. Both the good and the not so good parts. I'd sent pictures of my ancestor, who'd been hung in the town square, to the library and knew I'd like to honor him somehow too. He'd sacrificed everything for his convictions.

I'd also donated the original document showing my ancestors had purchased the land from the Cherokee who'd occupied it when we'd moved here. Quakers refused to occupy land that oppressed people, another strange custom of the time, especially with Manifest Destiny just getting going.

I could envision that document protected behind glass, where people could see it, read it, and know at least this tiny piece of Tennessee had stood on the right side of justice and equality. History hadn't worked out to benefit that side, making it much more important to show.

I found myself holding onto Clyde as the evening progressed. Corey was so right, Clyde kept me calm and helped me process things that might have led to an attack. However, as wonderful as having him cuddled against me was, it didn't take long for him to start yawning.

Lance and Corey were hashing out the details, including my vision of the barn and my own residence tucked into the woods, away from the public structures but built to exemplify the historical elements of the park.

And a park. That'd been Clyde's idea, and it was a fantastic one. Kids running around the historical buildings just felt right. "I'm going to walk Clyde home," I said, "before he turns into a pumpkin."

"Hey," Clyde protested but laughed. "I'm up early, and you all can lay around with your feet up all day."

"Is that what we do?" I asked, goading him.

"How should I know? I'm at work. Who knows what y'all do all day? Sittin' around eatin' grapes like in those old-timey Roman movies, I suspect." Everyone laughed at Clyde's obvious teasing, and we bid them good night.

I walked him down the sidewalk toward his apartment above the café, his arm securely tucked into mine.

"I really enjoyed tonight," Clyde said as we neared his building.

"As did I. Your presence makes me calmer, Clyde," I said. I cringed inwardly, not meaning to put that into words just yet.

"Glad to help," he said, and, stopping in front of the closed café, he kissed me. "Good night, my handsome prince."

I almost made some retort about that, but, for some reason, being Clyde's handsome prince felt like an honor too good to refuse.

"Good night, my handsome Clyde."

He waved at me and disappeared around the side of the building. Yeah, I was smitten. I looked around the Southern town that was closed and deserted for the night. I wasn't sure if the calm and contentment I felt had to do with Clyde or being in this special place or both, but I was thankful.

Forty-Two

Clyde

"**H**ONEY, YOU HAVE TO hurry up!" I said to Ruther, who'd volunteered to help put up holiday decorations around the town square.

"I just have to finish this last part," he said, and I knew I shouldn't push him. He and Corey were nervous about their upcoming presentation to the town council. We still had thirty minutes before meeting Doc and Amos about the decorating, but I liked to be early to these things.

They were also calling for our first snowfall tonight, and I wanted to walk around the square on my sweet boyfriend's arm. Not that we were boyfriends. No one had made any declarations or anything like that, but that's how I secretly thought about the man.

"Is Corey gonna get here in time?" I asked, staring out the condo's window.

"If he said he will, you can count on him. Besides—" Ruther came up behind me and pulled me against his body. "—you said noon, not eleven thirty."

"I should've said earlier so he'd get here on time."

Ruther chuckled into my ear, and I shivered. "You're a worry wart," he said.

"You're adopting our sayings fast enough. Come on," I said and pulled him out of the condo.

We had Thanksgiving this weekend, and I'd opened my big mouth and gotten a big to-do set up. It wasn't my intention. I had mentioned to Mrs. Cole while the mayor and Amos were in the café that I'd once been in Kansas City over Thanksgiving and didn't know a soul there, so I walked down to Country Club Plaza, a beautiful outdoor mall-like place.

They were having some big show of turning their Christmas lights on. I'd gone to that and had fallen in love with the whole shebang. "Well," Doc had said after I finished my story, "if you're going to organize that, we best get those decorations up."

I honestly hadn't meant my story to result in anything, but this town did seem to love making new traditions. Poor Lance had once scheduled a party in the park for his family, and now it was a huge community thing that drew people from all over the state. This being my first holiday season in Crawford City, well, I was open to adopting any traditions, new or old, that the town had to offer.

Chris made fliers at the library, and I helped him distribute them all over town. Chris and Roth were having

Thanksgiving at their house. Luckily, no one had mentioned it to Ruther. He was still struggling with thoughts of the place, but since he and Corey were going to be in town, Mrs. Cole said she'd open up the café after the meal for hot cocoa and cinnamon rolls.

Of course, that meant I'd be cooking them while everyone else was stuffing their faces with turkey. Not that I wouldn't have turkey myself. Corey, Ruther, and I would meet in my apartment, since I could run down and manage the rolls. I'd already bought the turkey, and Corey said he'd do the sides. If it worked out, this would be the best Thanksgiving I'd ever had.

"He's here," Ruther said as we walked outside. Corey was dressed in a nice-looking, expensive coat and leather gloves.

"Um, dude, what are you gonna do in all that?" I asked. "You know we're climbin' light poles to hang decorations that're older than any of us."

Corey laughed. "I'm sorry, Clyde. I...well, I have a date, and before you get upset, I think it's a date you might approve of."

I cocked my eyebrow and crossed my arms. "Lucy, you bet'r splain," I said in my best Ricky Ricardo accent. My mother used to watch *I Love Lucy* on a rerun loop when I was growing up, and I could quote lines from that TV show at the drop of a hat.

"I was in Mayville finishing up some of our pre-liminaries regarding building permits and such and ran into the talented and absolutely gorgeous Solace Brown."

243

I had no idea who Solace Brown was, but Ruther's expression suggested he was someone famous. "So, what? You're going to go hang out with him instead of helping set up the lights for our shindig?" I asked, mostly teasing Corey since I known he'd probably beg out of the manual labor anyway.

"No, I'm going to meet with him and Roth and see if they will perform some of the music from the new album they're doing together." He looked at me and shrugged. "Jeez, you don't read any of the gossip, do you? Roth and Solace are doing a collaborative Christmas project. It's the first thing Solace has done professionally since he left the business."

"Cool, and you think they'd perform for our silly lighting ceremony?"

"Apparently, Jennifer Cole and Solace are besties. She's gonna be in town and invited him for Thanksgiving. So, yes, he's here, Roth's here, and I think with a little encouragement and a push from Chris, I can get them to do a little music for your big event."

I felt excited about the prospect, mostly because it'd probably go over really well with the townsfolk. "Okay, but you know you still owe me some physical labor. I'm not gonna let you wiggle out of this entirely," I said, causing him to laugh.

I expected to see him walk toward the library, but instead, he walked into the park and toward Ruther's old home.

I felt Ruther stiffen beside me. "Come on, we have work to do," I said, pulling him toward where Doc said to meet him and the other volunteers.

We hadn't really talked about the house since Ruther had come back. I knew it still bothered him, and damn Corey for not making it less obvious where the meeting was taking place.

But decorating offered a temporary distraction, and we were immediately put to work when Doc saw us.

I got volunteered to stand on the cherry picker since I wasn't afraid of heights. Attaching the ancient street decorations to light poles wasn't hard. It was mostly just hanging them on old hooks, which apparently stayed on the light poles all year long, and then plugging them in.

The hard part was replacing all the old bulbs that'd burned out while in storage. That was what Doc had Ruther doing. Poor guy. I had chased down a lot of faulty bulbs in my day since my granny had ancient decorations we used when I was little.

My family never decorated much. Mom was always too busy, and Dad too drunk. Granny probably just felt sorry for us, so she made a big to-do about it every year while she was still alive.

I shook off the sadness around all that—no use thinking about the past. I glanced over and saw Ruther's old home for the first time from my high perch on the cherry picker. It looked like one of those big fancy antebellum houses down South—bright white against the early winter sunlight.

I looked over at where Ruther was laughing with Doc about something and sighed. Both his past and my own seemed to haunt us even to this day. "You done up there?" Todd, who was in charge of driving the cherry picker, called up.

"Yeah, you can move to the next pole," I said and held on as we moved down the line.

Even as grown men, childhood trauma affected our lives. We couldn't control what'd happened to us, but it didn't have to define us either. *New traditions help replace the old, ugly ones*, I thought as I hung the next decoration.

Ruther and I were making new traditions here and now, replacing the old with something new. I looked around downtown from my bird's-eye view and saw other decorating happening at all corners, and the sight warmed my heart. This was what holidays should be like, and it was definitely going to be a new tradition for me.

Forty-Three

Ruther

THE PANIC HIT ME the moment I realized where Corey was going to meet Roth and Solace. I could feel the flames sweeping toward my face and would've given in to it had Clyde not pulled me down the road and distracted me.

That was something so different from how things had been before. Nothing could pull me out of a panic before I met Clyde. Not that anyone had ever tried. My dad was mostly embarrassed by it. As a grown man, I figured his embarrassment stemmed from guilt over Mom and him not being there the night the mansion caught fire.

They'd been coming back from Nashville when they pulled into the driveway and saw all the firefighters battling to put out the blaze. My life had only been spared because the Cross sisters, our neighbors, had spotted the flames and called it in before it reached my room.

The mayor caught my attention before I could get lost in the memories and, luckily, put me to work replacing the old bulbs. The task was tedious enough to distract me from my dark memories.

Emanual and Amos were so funny together. Their love for each other and the town was so apparent. Emanual was fast to adopt something that made the town more connected and more of a community. Amos seemed to go along with whatever his husband did.

Their soft touches and occasional glances showed that even after decades, they only had eyes for each other. I wanted that for myself, and after Emanual said something funny about Amos being particular about how things were decorated in their cabin, I laughed and looked over to where Clyde was hanging the decorations.

Our eyes met briefly, and I smiled and waved. God, that man melted my insides. I wanted so much to sweep him away and into my bed to make love to him for hours. But that wasn't something I could do yet.

There were still so many trust issues he was dealing with. Having heard about his past, I understood. There was a lot of bad stuff brewing there. He went to therapy and the support group religiously. It only goes to show how important the decorating was to him that he didn't go to the group this morning.

Usually, he'd show up at the crack of dawn on Saturday morning and tease me for being grumpy about being dragged out of bed at such an ungodly hour. Still, he'd ply me with donuts before kissing me stupid and running off to Nashville for his group session.

Jake escorted him to Nashville because he said he needed to spend time with his parents, who lived there. I knew it was an excuse to drive him there, which was very kind. Jake's adoptive mother was Clyde's counselor, and you could tell it was a collaboration to give Clyde the support he needed.

When I suggested to Clyde that I drive him, he froze. "Maybe, but I-I need the group to be about me. I'm sorry," Clyde said and began getting anxious about it.

"Shh, I get it, but I want you to know you can lean on me too if you ever need, okay? No pressure, just I want you to know I'm here."

Relief flashed across his handsome features, causing my heart to go all aflutter. So much damage had been done to such a beautiful soul. He didn't know it yet, but I'd turn the world inside out to make him happy. Even in our short time together, I was completely head over heels for him.

"You done with that one?" Amos asked, drawing my attention back to the work at hand.

I nodded. "How many more to go?"

The mayor laughed. "Not that many but after this, we need to check all the lights and hang them on the town hall."

I almost complained, almost said something off the cuff to make Doc and Amos laugh, maybe even act like a sullen teenager, but this made my sweet Clyde so happy, I couldn't even pretend to be frustrated about the work.

I glanced back over and heard Clyde singing "Jingle Bells" at the top of his lungs, off-key, by the way, and Todd telling him to stop before he got them arrested for disturbing the peace. That just caused Clyde to sing louder.

We worked all day on the decorations. When we were done, the street looked good, but damn, those decorations were ugly and outdated. If the project we were doing was half as lucrative as Corey's most recent numbers suggested, one of the first things I was going to do was donate the money to replace all this with something modern.

I had a feeling the lighting ceremony was going to become one of Crawford City's new traditions, and now that this was becoming my town, I wanted to do everything I could to make it a better place. Not just for me but for the people I was quickly beginning to consider my friends. *Maybe even family*, I thought, then shook that out of my head—no need to jump ahead of myself there.

I liked the town, and yes, it was going to be my home, but that didn't mean I needed to have grand thoughts of them being what I'd never really had, at least outside my relationship with my late cousin. Even that never lent itself to the kind of family where people showed up for the holidays or leaned on each other when things got tough.

No, I'd never had that kind of family. If anything, my parents became more distant, my father more tyrannical, after the accident. I shut that thought down. No need to let them and their peculiarities ruin the day.

After we finished decorating, all the volunteers met at Amos and Emanual's house for hot cider and warm cookies that Amos had slipped away to bake. We sat around the comfortable living space while old Christmas music played on actual vinyl records on a massive stereo system that looked like it came out of the nineteen seventies.

I can't say the effect wasn't wonderful, though. Clyde sat next to me on the oversized sofa and snuggled into my side as we watched the other volunteers talk about the day's adventures and then the latest town gossip.

"Who's hungry?" Amos asked when a freckle-faced boy I hadn't seen delivered several boxes of pizza. I hadn't known they were going to feed us, or I wouldn't have had three of Amos's chocolate chip cookies.

Crawford City should've been all this for me through the years. Happy holidays seeping into happy memories. But even if the fire hadn't happened, my parents were more about appearances than anything else.

We were seen and not heard in this town. I think we visited the family estate because people didn't know or relate to us here, which gave my family some anonymity. Well, fuck that. Now I wanted everything this town had to offer.

I leaned over, kissed Clyde's temple, and pulled him against me. His snuggling in further just made this feel even more right. My parents might have seen the world very different from what I did, but their actions had inadvertently led me back to this town that was becoming so important to me. If for nothing else, I had to be grateful for that.

FORTY-FOUR

CLYDE

I LOVED HAVING THANKSGIVING with my guy and his friend. "It's the best Thanksgiving I've had in a long time," I told them. I didn't tell them it was the best I'd ever had. No need for my ugly past to taint such a great day.

When it was time for the lighting ceremony, I was nervous about it all coming together. Turns out, I had nothing to worry about. "The whole town showed up," I said, shocked at the size of the crowd.

"Well, of course they showed up, Baby. You made it sound so fun," Mrs. Cole said, and I smiled through my blush. Most people probably came because Roth had agreed to perform his new Christmas music with the famous Solace Brown, a name I now knew intimately because Ruther and Corey had forced me to listen to his music whenever they were around.

I wouldn't call myself a jazz fan, but his stuff was good. Ruther also seemed to enjoy it, so I wasn't going to complain.

"Gather around," Doc said from the stage that'd been put up in front of the town hall. "It's time to get the festivities started."

Everyone did as he instructed, and as soon as he was satisfied, he looked out into the crowd. "Clyde, can you come up here?"

I froze. "Me?" I asked, and Mrs. Cole and Ruther laughed as they pushed me up on the stage.

"Now y'all, this here celebration is all on account of this man right here, one of our newest residents in Crawford City, and one I know has captured y'all's hearts as much as he has ours."

The crowd cheered, which just made me blush harder.

"Since this was Clyde's idea and because he has worked his little butt off to make this happen, I'm going to let him do the honors. So, let's do a countdown, and Clyde, when we get to one, flip this switch," Doc said and handed me a big box with a switch on top.

I felt a little bewildered by the whole thing and just hoped to heaven I didn't somehow mess this up. I searched the sea of mostly familiar faces for one in particular. When my eyes locked on Ruther, he gave me the cutest little thumbs up, and I felt reassured despite the sudden attention.

"Five," Doc started counting with the crowd. When they hit one, I flipped the switch, and lights filled the night.

"Wow," I said at how pretty it was. Even the ugly fifties décor looked good in lights.

"With that, we're gonna get off the stage and let our masters of ceremonies come on up here and entertain y'all," Doc said and took the box from me, placing it on the ground as a drop-dead gorgeous Black man and Roth came onstage. I'd seen Solace Brown's pictures on the internet when Ruther and Corey made me listen to his music, but damn, I had no idea he was that handsome.

As soon as I was off the stage, I rushed over to Mrs. Cole, and since we had live entertainment, we'd decided to serve the cinnamon rolls and hot cocoa outside. People milled around, and as soon as we began plating the rolls, they all seemed to line up.

Ruther stood next to me, passing me plates, while Mrs. Cole served the hot cocoa, all pre-prepared in a large thermos.

It only took a few minutes to get everyone served. Then, of course, the teenagers came back around for seconds, which I was happy Mrs. Cole didn't object to. I didn't know these kids well and had no idea what their situation was, but I can remember more than one occasion when community events were the only food I got to eat that day.

More likely, these kids were just hungry. I can remember the hunger pains of being a teenage boy too.

Once we were done, Mrs. Cole wrapped up the rest of the rolls and handed them to me. "You boys might need these while the café is closed. If they get stale, you can always make a bread pudding with what's left. Do you know how to do that?" she asked.

I laughed. "I suspect it's the same as how you make your biscuit puddin' but with cinnamon rolls instead."

She laughed. "True, but don't add any more cinnamon, or it won't be fit to eat."

I carried the tray into the café while Ruther helped Mrs. Cole with the thermos.

It was so freaking cold, and the snow from two days ago hadn't done anything but make it feel colder. Once we were done at the café, Mrs. Cole locked up, telling me I could come in later to get the rolls using the key I had to the back door, but to go out and enjoy the rest of the show.

I didn't complain. I wanted to listen to Roth and Solace's new music. It was beautiful. Solace's soulful voice backed by Roth's or vice versa made a sweet Christmasy sound I had no doubt would be playing across the airwaves for many years to come, just like the old songs from my great-granny's time.

I leaned back against Ruther, enjoying his larger, sturdy frame and the warmth that flowed out of him, while we enjoyed the concert. Corey stood a few paces away, his expression filled with longing. I looked up on stage and realized Solace had initiated such a response from the usually stoic man.

I got Ruther's attention and gestured toward Corey, and Ruther chuckled. "Someone's got it bad," he said. Corey looked over at us and frowned.

"You two need to mind your business. Ain't nothin' goin' on over here," he said, using a put-on Southern accent.

"You shouldn't do that. You sound like something got caught in your throat," I said, causing Corey and Ruther to chuckle.

It made me happy to see Corey so enamored with another guy. To be honest, I still worried about what kind of relationship Ruther and Corey had, although they didn't seem to show any interest in one another romantically.

Now that I saw Corey mooning over the jazz singer, I couldn't help but smile. If he was having such a hard time hiding his interest in Solace, he would certainly not be able to hide any such feelings for Ruther.

That made me ponder things even more. I knew I had major trust issues. Since Ruther had come back to town, I seemed to be looking for flaws, some of which I'd found, but nothing pointed to me not being able to rely on him. From my perspective, he was completely trustworthy.

Despite that and the ongoing support of my group and counselor, I hadn't been able to let things progress between us.

Yes, we cuddled, hugged, held hands, and kissed. Kissing Ruther was by far my most favorite pastime. But going further scared the shit out of me.

Until now, I think I was letting my fear about him and Corey keep the boundaries up. Now, would this change things?

I realized immediately it wouldn't. I just wasn't ready for things to turn sexual. Not yet. I needed more time and more of...something. What, I wasn't sure. It's not like I wasn't sexually attracted to him. God help me, I wanted Ruther in every way possible.

And there it was. I wanted him, craved him, hungered for him, and that's what was in my way. Fear that I was getting attached to someone who'd end up not being who he appeared to be. That once we went all the way, he'd turn into Jimmy or one of the other regrettable men I'd dated.

I shook off the ugly thoughts and focused back on the Christmas concert. I wouldn't be solving this tonight, and maybe not anytime soon. But at least I could enjoy being here and sharing this moment with Ruther. Hopefully, he felt the same.

FORTY-FIVE

RUTHER

I LAUGHED AS JENNIFER Cole teased her husband, Jesse, and again admired what a long-term loving relationship actually looked like. Lance and Jake had come down a moment earlier, and Jake was cooking what I assumed was an egg dish from the way it smelled.

Jen, as she'd instructed me to call her, wasn't home very often, on account of her modeling career. I'd met her several times at New York parties, but we'd never really spoken. It was still surprising that such a famous model had grown up here and was now my landlord.

"Where's that handsome man my stepmother can't stop talking about?" Jennifer asked as soon as I stepped in.

"He's at his apartment," I said, almost commenting on her assumption that he'd spent the night with me. Then I figured she and the rest of the town must think we were shacking up, considering I couldn't seem to keep my hands off him in public or private.

"Well, invite him over," she said and turned.

"Okay, I'll be right back."

"Wait, you can't just text him?" she asked.

I swallowed hard, not wanting to admit I didn't have his number, nor did I want to lie. "No, he doesn't—"

"You don't have his number," she said. I shook my head. "Well, never mind, I'll call my stepmother."

I didn't want to look at anyone. How embarrassing was it that we were practically in a relationship, or actually were in one without a label, and something as simple as exchanging phone numbers hadn't happened?

I laughed a few moments later when Mrs. Cole blocked Jen from bothering Clyde. "It's not like I'm going to stalk him," Jen said. "I just wanted to invite him over for breakfast."

She listened to whatever her stepmother had said, then laughed. "Maybe, but it's not fair. You won't make those special for me, and no, I don't want you to teach me how to make them myself."

She listened for another minute, looking amused, then said goodbye and hung up. "Seems you aren't the only one who won't be getting his number, Ruther, but she said she'd text him and let him know we want him over here and with his cinnamon rolls. Which," she said, looking at me accusingly, "you didn't tell me he had."

I laughed. "One must keep one's secrets, and if you must know, I was saving that bit of information for my own selfish reasons."

"And mine," Corey said behind her. He'd crashed at my place after he and Solace spent too much time walking around after the performance—enjoying the lights, Corey had said.

I had a feeling there was a lot more to it than simply admiring decorations, but I was thankful Corey hadn't pried into my relationship with Clyde, so I figured I should return the favor and mind my own business.

Jake had just flipped a beautiful frittata onto a plate when there was a knock on Jen and Jesse's door. Jen got up to answer, and I heard Clyde's voice. "Um, Mrs. Cole asked me to bring these over for you all."

"Oh, and for you. There's also someone here who will want you more than those rolls, I'm sure," she said, leading Clyde into the room. His face lit up with a smile when he saw me.

"I wondered why Mrs. Cole was reneging on her offer for the leftover rolls. I should've known it was because you sweet-talked her," he said, looking at me.

I put my hands up in surrender, then got up and kissed him. "Jen did the sweet-talking. I'm just enjoying the results."

"Like I believe that," he said, then looked over at the crowd of people. "She didn't tell me there was a party, or I might've brought the other rolls I kept back for me and...well, me."

The group laughed. I could tell by Jen's expression that she wanted to ask Clyde questions about protecting his phone number, but she let it drop. When Jake announced it was time to eat, we all went to the table with our after-Thanksgiving treats, which included leftover pumpkin pie, the cinnamon rolls from Clyde, Jake's Frittata, and various other desserts I was convincing myself to ignore.

Jen was hilarious. She lightly teased Corey about fancying Solace, then spent the next few minutes telling him about all her escapades with the man over the years.

Clyde sat silently as the spontaneous party spread across the room. I don't think he knew what to do, and I felt bad for him being thrust into a situation he wasn't prepared for. I didn't know if he did, but I felt the poor guy needed rescuing.

"Well, if you'll excuse us," I said, standing up. "I'm going to pull this one away, and we're going to go on a drive through the countryside if he agrees to accompany me."

Clyde immediately looked relieved I was providing an escape, then quizzical about the car ride. He didn't ask me anything about it, though, on the short walk to my condo.

As soon as we were inside and I closed the door, I asked if he was okay.

"I..." he started in a whisper like they could hear us through the floor. "I don't know how to be around famous people and doctors. Y'all are too fancy for me."

"That's bull. You know Jen asked about you immediately when Corey and I showed up at their door. Said Mrs. Cole couldn't stop talking about you. You fit in with them as much as I do. We're all just people."

Clyde looked perplexed, then sat down on the sofa. "No, I'm a redneck who's never had two pennies to rub together, and ya'll are rich. Plus, you're...well, you're you, and there's Corey, and...a famous model who's married to a doctor, and Jake runs around with movie stars and country singers, and Lance designs incredible buildings all over. I...you know I'll never fit in, right?"

When he hiccupped back tears, I rushed over and knelt on the floor in front of him. "Sweetheart, what's really going on?"

"Why me? Why do you really wanna go out with me? Is this just you slummin' with the locals? I ain't nothin' special, Ruther. I ain't never learned to use fancy silverware or which spoons and forks to use. I buy all my clothes at the thrift store 'cause I can't even afford Walmart. So? Tell me why. What do you see in me?"

Big tears fell from his eyes, and my heart beat faster, knowing if I didn't say the right thing, I could lose him here and now.

"Listen to me, Clyde. You have overwhelmed my senses. Not only are you one of the most attractive men I've ever seen, but you're just as beautiful on the inside. You're so strong, you chase off my monsters. You help me feel complete."

It was my turn to get emotional, and I rocked back on my feet. "I came to Crawford City to face demons that plagued me all my life. Did you know it's going to be thirty years this year? Thirty years ago, Christmas night. Just admitting that six months ago would've sent me into a blind panic. Do you not see it's you that's made the difference?" I asked, standing up and walking toward the window to stare out. "I get you've got some identity issues around Jen Cole. Hell, we all do. But, Clyde, don't you ever think you are less than anyone, especially anyone in this town. Everyone here loves you. They have since you first arrived. In fact, I'm the outsider here, and I know if I ever did anything they thought was out of bounds around you, they'd rally behind you and kick my ass to the curb."

I thought that'd make him smile, but instead, he sat still, tears streaming from his face. "Why me, though?"

I sat down next to him. "I don't know, Clyde. My attraction for you is so strong, I struggle to keep my hands off you. But also, being around you makes me feel so safe. Maybe because you've seen the dark side of life and lived through it? All I know is you mean more to me than I know how to explain."

"What happens if I let you in, if we get serious, and then your fancy New York friends, or your relatives, see me as the white trash I am. What happens then? You'll be embarrassed by me."

He stood and walked toward the door.

"I will never be embarrassed by you, Clyde. Even if I gave a shit about what people in New York thought, I'm not going back there. I sold everything, even my family's brownstone that my great-grandfather bought. I sold it all. I'm all-in here, in Crawford City. I'm all-in when it comes to you."

He stared at me, and I bit back a comment about him not trusting me enough to give me his phone number.

This wasn't the time for that conversation. Even if it hurt more than I could say that he didn't trust me with it, or apparently didn't trust me not to dump him over some theoretical snooty people I didn't even associate with.

"I don't think this is a good idea, Ruther. I think I'm still too messed up, and I'm not strong enough to deal with you when you dump me or look at me like I'm trash. I-I'm gonna go."

"Wait, Clyde, wait. Let's talk about it."

Unfortunately, the door closed behind him. I wanted to run after him, but damn, I knew he'd run harder if I did. He clearly needed space, and even if it killed me, I wouldn't be like the assholes he'd dated before.

I went to my room, collapsed on the bed, and let my tears flow. Fuck my background for coming between Clyde and me. I wish Mrs. Cole had mentioned it was a party. I wish he'd trusted me with his number so I could've warned him, given him the chance to say no.

Instead, we were back to him wanting to run away from me, just like he'd fucking done in the summer. The hell with that. I got up, wiped the tears away, and sat at my computer. Sometimes old-school worked better than new.

I sighed and shook my head as I began typing a letter so it would be easy for him to read. My hand-writing sucked.

Dear Clyde,

I don't know how to tell you how much it hurts me that you still don't feel like you can trust me. I know from what you've told me about your past that relationships are hard. I get that learning to trust again isn't easy.

Maybe you're right. Maybe I need to step aside so you can be yourself without a relationship. Although accepting that scares me and makes me want to yell and flail my arms around like a child having a fit.

Despite that, if you need it, I will give you space.

I'm going to Nashville for a few days to give you that space. I care about you more than anyone I've ever cared about before.

I deleted the sentence I wrote about loving him. Neither of us were ready for me to go there yet, but care about, yes. I could admit that much.

I'm not going anywhere. I'm here for the long-term, and if my wanting more from you is too much, then we can be friends. I'd rather spend the rest of my life with you as a friend than lose you over pushing for more than you're ready to give.

With all my heart,

Ruther

I sent the letter to the portable printer Corey had installed in the condo, then found an envelope in his stash of office supplies.

I wrote Clyde's name on it, and when Corey returned from the party, I asked him to deliver the note after I left town.

"You're leaving?" he asked.

I nodded. "I-I don't know what to tell you, Corey. I know the man needs space, and I can't keep up with the hot and cold, so yeah, I'm going to stay at a hotel for a while and spend some time touring Nashville. Text me when you get back to town, and we'll get together for dinner."

"Or you can just stay at my place," he said, grabbing his key ring from his pocket and handing me the key. "I meant to give you a key anyway. You'll be more comfortable there than in a hotel. I'll see you tomorrow. Unless you need me now, I'm going to stay another night. I've been invited over—"

He paused, and I knew it was because of where he was going.

"You and Solace?" I asked to take the pressure off, and he smiled.

"Yeah, but I'll be back tomorrow. What happened with you and Clyde? You both seemed okay."

I sighed and shook my head. "He doesn't think he belongs with the likes of me. He thinks I'll eventually look down on him because he's not famous or rich or whatever, I don't know. I'm overwhelmed by the drama of it all. It's not like I don't have my own shit to deal with," I admitted.

Corey put his hand on my shoulder. "I'm guessing maybe you need to let him in, let him see the real you, Ruther. No offense, but you can be a bit intimidating with your cool demeanor. And to be honest, I thought you looked down on me for years, until I got to know you."

That took me aback. "What? I never did anything like that."

Corey laughed. "You didn't, no, but...you're aloof, and your father, if nothing else, taught you to put on an air of confidence, which sometimes feels like arrogance. I know it's not. I know you, Ruther, and know your heart is big, often too big for your own good. It's one of the reasons I'd walk barefoot through glass for you, or more accurately, move to the middle of nowhere."

"What do you think I should do? Tell him I'm a fucking mess and that he'd be better off running away and never looking back?"

"No, that's the opposite of what I'm telling you. You should tell him you're human, that you've got as many flaws as anyone, and that you love him. Have you told him that?"

I paused, thinking of the letter and how I'd deleted that admission. "He's not ready for that or all my bullshit. Thanks, Corey, for letting me stay with you, and I'll think about what you said, but please don't forget to deliver that," I said and pointed at the letter.

I was pleased I could stay at his place instead of a hotel. Corey was a real friend, and now we were working together as equal partners, that'd only begun to solidify even more. He knew me better than anyone.

I picked up my bag and stuff I needed for the time I was going to be away and headed out before Corey could give me any more advice.

As I drove past the café, I glanced up at Clyde's apartment, only slightly disappointed I didn't see him in the window. It didn't matter. I was going to need to define this as much as he was because now that I'd written the letter, now that I was giving myself some time too, I realized I needed clarity as much as he needed space.

If it wasn't our time to be lovers, so be it. But rejection stung, and although I don't think he'd figured it out yet, his fear that I might reject him had certainly led to him rejecting me. I wasn't without my own demons, and I'd come to Crawford City to heal myself, not create fresh wounds.

So, I needed to figure out my boundaries and set those into place before things went much further. That scared me because I didn't want to lose a chance to love Clyde. The fact was, I'd come too far to throw everything away just because he saw me as one of the monsters of his past.

He'd once said I wasn't a monster, but his actions certainly said something else.

FORTY-SIX

CLYDE

T HE KNOCK AT THE door didn't surprise me. I figured
Ruther would come, and to be honest, I was feeling
bad about my outburst. I hadn't meant to let my insecu-
rities cause me to lash out at him. It took a long cry to
figure out that's what I'd done.

I opened the door and was disappointed to see Corey.
"Um, hi, come in," I said.

Corey nodded and came in, shutting the door behind
him. "I brought you this," he said, handing me a letter.

He was about to go, but hesitated. "Can I...I might be
overstepping here, but can I offer some advice?"

I didn't know what Ruther had told him, and I was
afraid this letter was telling me to fuck off for good, but
I nodded anyway.

"Can we sit?" Corey asked, and I pointed at the dining
table. "Have you ever heard of Queensbridge?" he asked,

and I shook my head no. "It's a housing project for poor people in Queens. That's where I grew up."

That revelation shocked me. "You grew up in the projects?"

He chuckled. "I did. Listen, Clyde, I don't know what happened. Ruther didn't go into detail, but he told me enough to know you were questioning your social status compared to his. I think I can help you overcome some of that. I applied for a job with Ruther's father twice, determined to get a job working as anything they had open. They were starting a project near where I grew up. I remember envying all the people driving beautiful cars and wearing designer clothes. The only other people I'd seen in those around my hood were drug dealers. But these men had legitimate businesses. Ruther's father was an ass. He might have touted the Quaker heritage, but he was as judgmental as any New York elite. I was determined, though. I knew that if I could get in with them, they might be my way out of the projects."

He paused and looked at me, making sure I was listening. "Ruther's father wasn't there the day I came back to beg for a job. I was willing to clean their fucking toilets if it meant earning a position there. Ruther looked at me in the suit my dad had bought at a thrift store. I was waiting for him to kick me out like his dad had done the day before. Instead, he said, 'Do you know where I can get a good cup of coffee?' I didn't. Honestly, I'd never bought coffee before in my life. Neither of my parents drank it, but I'd seen a Dunkin Donuts down the street from Queensbridge. 'Um, yeah,' I said, praying the coffee I'd seen people taking out of the donut place was decent. He handed me ten bucks and told me to bring him a latte. A word I'd only heard on TV. I ran all the way and cut in front of several people, ignoring their protests and announcing I needed a latte." He chuckled at the memory.

"The barista shrugged and asked what size. I froze. I had no fucking idea. I just told her to give me the biggest she had. It worked. They gave me the coffee, and I almost burned my fingers rushing it back to his office. Ruther saw me come in, took the coffee, tasted it, and smiled. Then he asked when I could start."

A tear slipped out of his eye, and he wiped it gently away. "Clyde, that man shouldn't have given that ghetto boy a chance. No one else would've. He did, and because he did, I went to college and eventually graduated with an MBA. All of which Ruther paid for, using his father's company funds."

He stared at me for a long time, looking thoughtful, before he continued. "You aren't right if you think Ruther would ever snub you or toss you away because of how you grew up. Ruther doesn't judge people, even though sometimes his demeanor indicates that he does, or could."

I sighed and nodded. "I was just about to go over and apologize. I-I should do that now."

Corey shook his head. "No, he's gone to Nashville." He sighed and stood up. "I love Ruther like he's family, so this is me being overprotective by overstepping. You aren't the only person who can get hurt here. I know you've had a hard past. Shit, man, I have too, but Ruther's heart is delicate. He's taken a liking to you, more than any other man I've ever seen him with. I was there this morning when he admitted to Jen that you hadn't even given him your phone number. I saw the hurt he always hides so well. You might not mean to, but you're hurting him by not trusting him. If you're fucking him around because you want someone fun, you should let him go. Ruther has some major shit he's dealing with right now, and I've never been more impressed with him for facing it down. He needs friends, but he sure as hell doesn't need someone pulling his chain and leading him on."

He paused, like he wanted to say more, then took a deep breath before letting it out slowly, staring at me the entire time.

"As his friend and now business partner, I'm asking you, man to man, to do right by him, Clyde. If you want him, hold on because you'll never find a better man to love. But if you don't, for all that's good in this world, let him go before you break him beyond what those of us who love him can repair."

He stood up from the dining table and left without saying goodbye.

I just sat there, stunned by Corey's unvarnished words. He'd dressed me down pretty hard, but he also made me think about things in a way I hadn't until now.

I opened the letter and read. I'll admit it hit me harder because of Corey's words. I could see the pain Ruther was suppressing as he wrote, and I ended up having another long bout of crying.

After I got myself under control, I gave Anita a call. I'd never taken her up on the offer to call her when things were more than I could handle. It never felt right, and I had to force myself to swallow my pride about disrupting her when I knew she was having family time.

When she answered, and I asked if she had a moment, I told her what'd happened.

"Do you not trust him, Clyde?" she asked.

I wiped away the tears that hadn't stopped flowing since Corey left. "I do trust Ruther, and Corey confirmed what I already knew, that he's a good guy. But I-I fuck men up."

"How, how do you fuck men up?" Anita asked. Although we'd discussed this before, the argument felt more real when it concerned an actual man.

"I'm cursed, Anita, if I love him, he'll—"

"He will become the monster your father was?" she asked, and I nodded, even though I knew she couldn't see me.

"I'll make him a bad man."

"Oh, sweetie," she said, using an endearment, which I don't think she'd ever done before. "Listen to me, you're not cursed, you've been hurt, and none of that was your fault. The adults in your life were supposed to protect and keep you safe. Not hurt you, not damage you. They made you think you were the problem, but sweetie, it never was you. You are beautiful inside and out, and even though I know that's hard for you to see, to accept, it's what's true."

"Every man I ever went out with, every single one, hit me, or hurt me, or stole from me—every one of them, Anita. The common theme here is me, I'm the problem."

She paused, and, for a moment, I thought I might've convinced her. "The common denominator here, Clyde, is you were abused by someone who should've loved you, protected you. You didn't make those men damaged or abusive. They already were. They recognized you and were drawn to you because they believed they would get away with being abusive. Let me ask you this. Do you think Ruther would ever physically harm you?"

I shook my head and answered, wiping the snot away from my face. "No, I don't think that's him."

"Did his friend not tell you he was the best man he knew?"

"Yeah," I admitted.

"He won't go bad just because you love him, Clyde. Loving someone good and decent makes them better and even more decent. Loving someone who is hurt and who isn't doing the work to make themselves better? That's a different story. But Clyde, you're doing the work even now as we're having this conversation. You might have to accept the fact that by letting Ruther love you, you might actually be giving him the ability to become an even better man than he is now."

I drew in a breath, shocked at that concept. My mind wanted to reject that line of reasoning even before I could consider it. No way could loving me make him a better man. But then, I remembered when he'd been on the verge of a panic attack, and I'd touched or distracted him, and he'd calmed down.

He'd admitted that and told me my presence made him feel calmer and more in control.

"Is that even possible?" I asked Anita, wanting desperately to believe it to be true.

She chuckled. "It's a given to most people, my dearest Clyde," she said, once again using another endearment. "Love makes most people better, lifts us up, and causes us to see the world differently, through the eyes of another person. Yes, I think that's possible, but the question isn't for me to answer. Do you, Clyde, believe that could be true?"

I nodded, instantly believing and surprised that I could. "Yeah, I-I think so."

"When you know, or feel confident enough to let that be a possibility, then you should let Ruther know. I'm going to come to the clinic on Tuesday. Is that soon enough for us to have another session?"

"Yes, sorry for calling you at home."

"No, stop that. This is the commitment I've made to you, and you're worth it. If you need me in the meantime, don't hesitate to call me, okay?"

"Yes, ma'am," I said.

"Clyde?" she asked. "For what it's worth, I'm proud of you. This is tough for someone who's been through the trauma you have."

The tears hit me again, just hearing those words from someone I admired as much as I did Anita.

"Thank you," I managed to say before I hung up.

I spent the rest of the day in bed, holding onto a pillow and crying harder than I had since I'd been a little boy.

Unlike then, I wasn't crying because I'd been beaten up. Rather, I was crying because I realized I had been standing between myself and my happiness all because I thought something was wrong with me. Something that would turn the beautiful man I knew Ruther to be into my father.

After talking to Anita, I could see that for the bullshit it really was. Ruther would never become my father, and neither would I. But if I didn't step up to the plate or let him off the hook, I was going to, as Corey pointed out, hurt him. Maybe not physically like my dad had done to me, or like the men I'd let into my life in the past, but I was going to cause him pain, nonetheless.

Now was the time for me to decide whether to let him in or not. I just wish I knew what decision I was going to make. I might want him, but that didn't mean I was strong enough to let him in. As I lay buried under my covers, I decided to use the time he'd given me to figure that out.

One way or another, I would give Ruther an answer the next time I saw him.

Forty-Seven

Ruther

T HE WEEK AFTER THANKSGIVING passed in a whirl. After Corey and I returned from our Nashville respite, we dove into our proposal. Lance had drawn sketches of various home designs we'd be using. Most were the same inside as the rest. All had open floor plans, some slightly different from the others, making building the homes more cost-effective.

The exteriors, though, were six different historical designs. I knew, looking at the sketches, the houses would be spectacular. Lance had taken into consideration that people here in Crawford City would likely need bigger yards. But the design of the neighborhoods should also lead to community interaction with the front porches and small front yards, and with the garages attached to the back and an alley running between the lines of homes.

The aesthetic would be beautiful, and since most people would be using their driveways, hopefully the streets could be used for meeting places between neighbors and their kids.

The fact that I felt almost jealous of the kids who were about to grow up here told me Lance had designed this just right. It would reflect the vision we all seemed to have of Crawford City and its future.

I flipped through the sketches and opened the one with the meeting house and barn. They would become public buildings belonging to the city. Doc had managed to get the town council to at least tentatively agree to take over maintenance once we'd completed the build.

Corey had suggested we build them last since we'd be using some of the profits from the development to supplement them, but I'd nixed that from the beginning. Even if it was a loss, the money I'd made from selling my family's properties, including the one here, should be reinvested in their legacy.

Not because my parents deserved it, and not to get attention or make our family name anything more than it already was, but because our family had such deep roots here. A modern Quaker meeting house that would become a museum and an attached barn that would serve as a meeting space for the community was the perfect legacy to honor those who came before me.

I turned the page and stared at the Federal style recreation of the home my ancestors had built all those years ago. The house that'd nearly killed me.

It only slightly resembled what it'd been before additions were added. Including the addition that I'd been in the night of the fire. I had yet to go to see it again. I wasn't quite ready, but at least looking at the beautiful rendering in front of me didn't make me afraid or anxious.

Instead, what I saw in this sketch was the future and hope. Beginnings in a new place, a place that represented community and acceptance. It represented coming home as much as finding a new home.

It was modern inside, not unlike the other houses. A gorgeous open kitchen led to a large, fairly traditional dining room, which I'd requested when Lance had asked me what I wanted.

I had visions of friends gathering around the large, harvest-style table I envisioned in the space. There was a huge fireplace in both the dining room and the living room. Although thoughts of using them almost made me panic, Lance had assured me they could be decorative only. Still, because we were building a traditional-looking Federal home, it only made sense to make them the focal point in each room.

The renderings had confirmed what he'd said. I'd never have an open fire in my home. I'd never trust fire again. But I still liked the overall feel I thought the fireplace mantels gave to the rooms.

There were three bedrooms on the second floor. Two smaller ones, which made me think of having children. That was a shock, since I'd never even considered that before. I guess that was just another layer demonstrating how this town had influenced me. Being a father...well, that would be amazing.

Lance hadn't skimped on the quality of his renderings. I had the money for the high end, and I'd do some of that, of course, but I also wanted to honor my Quaker background and not go too overboard. Simple, elegant features appealed to me.

I tried not to think of Clyde in the space. I was forcing myself to develop some scar tissue over the wound I barely wanted to admit was there but that'd opened up after Clyde had walked out again. I needed to prepare for a partnerless life.

But that didn't have to mean a life spent alone. I wanted to further explore the possibility of having children, and I liked the idea of raising kids in the community Corey and I were building.

Despite that, I could see Clyde in the space. It felt like he'd appreciate the simple domesticity of the place, like the wide porch I'd had Lance add to both the front and back of the home, and the big front yard that bled into the shared space only separated by a white picket fence, reminiscent of the time my ancestors settled here.

I could see a family here, and whether or not I wanted to admit it, Clyde was a part of it for me. No matter how much I tried to force my thoughts away from him, I could see him in my space.

Corey came in, distracting me, and when I looked up from the designs, he was smiling. "It's going to be amazing, and you're sure you want to start with the common spaces?" he asked.

"Yes, and I noticed Jen wasn't drinking mimosas with us, so I'd guess she and Jesse are going to want our condo back soon," I said.

"You think she's...?"

I shrugged. "No idea and I wouldn't say anything out loud until she says something, considering how much the town likes to gossip, but does Jen strike you as someone who wouldn't want Champagne?

Corey laughed. "Um, no."

"The sooner my house is built, the better, wouldn't you agree?"

Corey nodded and sat down across from me. "So, I might as well tell you now so you can be mad and get over it." I cocked an eyebrow at him. "When I delivered the note, I told Clyde off for stringing you along."

"What?" I asked, feeling panicked all of a sudden.

Corey sighed. "Listen, Ruther, I know he's had shit happen in his life, but so have you, and someone needs to stand up for you. Don't worry, I don't think I said anything inappropriate or even offensive. But, you do know you deserve to be happy too?"

I stared at him, the emotions stirring inside me. Two weeks ago, I'd have been upset with him for speaking with Clyde over my head. Now, I felt more appreciative that he cared enough to stand up for me.

"Thanks, Corey, but I don't think Clyde is doing anything to hurt me deliberately."

"But it does still hurt, doesn't it?"

I nodded in agreement. "It does still hurt."

"That's all I said. You deserve to be considered here too, and dumping his emotional baggage on you isn't fair. Although," he said, holding his hand up before I complained, "I didn't say it that way."

I chuckled, having been on the receiving end of Corey when I'd overstepped or ignored my health. He could be harsh, but he'd always been truthful, and his heart was in the right place.

"I've decided to push the issue. He'll probably send me packing, but you aren't wrong," I said. "My feelings should be respected too. Maybe Clyde isn't ready for a relationship, and that's something I might have to just come to terms with, but I'm not going to let things continue moving forward without some sort of commitment from him or at least an acknowledgment he wants this to go forward."

Corey came over and pulled me into a hug. It was strange for Corey to show any emotion, so the gesture caught me off guard, but I leaned in, thankful I had his friendship when I needed it.

"Okay," he said, "let's finish this up so we're ready to meet with Crawford City's town council for final approval."

"Think we'll get it?" I asked, and Corey smiled.

"All the key players have already seen the plans and agreed. The townsfolk will get to weigh in on it tomorrow, and I have no doubt they'll all have opinions, but yes, I think we'll get it."

"If we do, I want to break ground on New Year's Day."

Corey looked at me with shock. "That soon?"

I nodded. "Yeah, I've been reading that it's better for the trees to do the work around them in the winter before they've leafed out. I want to keep a strong canopy for the building sites, and both Cliff and Randy have assured me they can work around the trees we save. I'd like to have the surveyors mark the boundaries, including sidewalks, so we can have our arborists mark which trees we're saving."

"Before we bring in the lumber company?" Corey asked, and I turned to see his concerned expression. Maybe he was upset I was spending the money to preserve the old growth that'd sprung up there over the years.

When I saw his smile, though, I knew we were still on the same page. "Yeah, I want to mark the trees we're keeping before we let the vultures in to take the rest."

We went over our plans repeatedly, and both of us were ready for tomorrow, but the butterflies in my stomach told me how much I wanted this. We'd tested the feasibility with every contingency we could think of, and unless the numbers we had already showing interest in buying were off, we would be fine.

That didn't mean I wasn't nervous. This project had taken on a life of its own, and it was representative of the future I'd planned for myself. A future that involved my new hometown and my best friend and business partner.

Forty-Eight

Clyde

I HADN'T SEEN RUTHER since he left for Nashville. I'd talked to Anita about the letter and about Corey's rebuke. She basically said they weren't wrong. Just because I was hurt didn't mean my hurt wasn't bleeding over onto Ruther.

In the café, I'd overheard Jake and Doc talking about a meeting where Ruther and Corey would be making a presentation about their development project. The meeting was in the evening, so I didn't have to miss work.

I rushed up to my apartment after my shift, showered, dressed in half-decent clothes, and rushed to the town hall. Ruther and Corey were sitting at the front of a packed meeting room. I didn't want to make a scene since I was late, so I slipped in the back but could still see.

Doc, as mayor, called the meeting to order and began discussing topics like the cost of the Christmas concert and lighting this year. I hadn't thought about that, but I guess the event cost money, even though volunteers did most of the work. That just reminded me I needed to pay closer attention to things like that.

"Now," he said once he finished telling everyone that the budget was still intact, "let's get to what we came here for. As you all know, we've been discussing the development of the old motel site across the railroad tracks and have been lucky to have attracted a man who has a long history with our community, Mr. Rutherford Crawford."

There was light applause but some tension as well. Shit, I hoped that didn't mean they wouldn't get their plan approved.

"I'll turn the meeting over to Mr. Crawford and his business partner."

Ruther stood up and scanned the crowd. When his eyes met mine, he paused briefly, smiled, and began talking.

"This project is one we're excited to offer. As you can see, Corey is placing boards with sketches of the project up behind me. Lance McCartney, our architect, is also here tonight to answer any questions you may have about the design."

"Will the houses be affordable?" Mr. Kim Banks called out not far from where I sat.

Ruther nodded. "Construction costs, as you all know, have gone up in recent years. The price will reflect that, but yes, we consider them affordable."

And just like that, questions began pouring out from the gathered townspeople. I could tell Ruther had prepared a speech, but after pausing, he smiled and began answering questions. Sometimes Corey chimed in, and sometimes Lance would stand up and answer questions.

A full thirty minutes passed before Doc stopped the questioning, probably because it was getting silly. "Thank you, gentlemen, for your feedback. At this point, I'd like to open the floor to the public for remarks."

Chris's parents stood up immediately and went to the microphone. "As you know, we moved here after our son Chris took over the library. We had to search for months to find a place to live, and even finding a rental property was near impossible. Had Roth and Chris not redone Mr. Crawford's mansion, we would still probably be looking."

I looked at Ruther just in time to see him cringe when they mentioned the mansion. I was just about to go to him when Chris slipped over and patted his shoulder. That kind gesture seemed to help Ruther shake it off just in time for several more people to stand up and go to the microphone.

One after another, they talked about there not being enough places to buy. "My mother wants to move to Crawford City to be closer to her grandchildren, but there's nothing for sale that she feels comfortable buying," Mrs. Cox said.

"It took five years of searching for my wife and me to find a place," James Lacey added.

Every comment was more of the same. People were frustrated because they couldn't find local housing, some said they had been forced to buy in Mayville because nothing was available here.

"I want to go on record saying I appreciate that these boys respected our history enough to be building houses that look like they belong in these parts. All those ugly boxes others are building these days would be wrong. Just look at these designs. These fellas seem to know us, and for that, I'm thankful."

I didn't recognize the man who'd said it. He was probably in his eighties, but when he sat down, I saw a couple of faces I did recognize. Both were women who sometimes came into the café for breakfast.

"Are there any other comments?" Doc asked when he sat down.

"Yeah, let's get this vote done so they can get started," Donald Chris yelled.

Doc chuckled. "Well, okay, then." He turned to the council and said, "All those in favor of approving the Friends' Development, raise your hands."

All nine members of the council raised their hands. "Seems it's unanimous. Guess you boys better get to work," he said, winking at Ruther.

The applause this time was loud; everyone jumped up simultaneously and rushed over to Ruther and Corey, shaking their hands.

I watched with pride before I darted out the back and toward home. I was so excited for Ruther and Corey. They were going to do some good here. Maybe one day I could buy one of the homes they'd be building. Mrs. Cole said she might give me a raise after the first of the year. I doubted I'd ever make enough money to actually buy a house, but I still liked that dream.

It didn't matter though. I loved my apartment over the café. It was spacious, comfortable, and in a perfect location since I worked so many hours. I'd already decided I would use my raise to pay rent so Mrs. Cole never felt like I was taking advantage of her kindness. Crawford City was now my home, and I'd do everything possible to keep it that way. I needed the kind of stability I'd found here and thanked the good Lord that he'd seen fit to help me find these folks.

As I got ready for bed, I thought of Ruther. That's when it hit me. A letter. Old school, just like he wrote to me.

I was sure I didn't have any paper, but I went to Mrs. Cole's desk in the guest room and opened it to find stationary with the cutest little butterfly on top. I silently thanked her for leaving it there.

Dear Ruther,

555-345-0000

Since I met you, you've been taking care of me. You've been making special accommodations, supporting me, and letting me have space, like you said in your letter.

I've never had anyone care about me. Not like that. People don't make special accommodations for me.

They've used me, pushed me around, and too often hurt me. You didn't do any of those things, and because of that, I think I've had a really hard time trusting you.

No, I <u>know</u> that's why I've had a hard time trusting you. I <u>know</u> that don't make sense, even as I write it. Why would I trust some man who wants to knock me around and not someone who cares about me and is willing to help me?

Anita, my counselor, says it's because we trust what we've always known. I think she's right. I think, because you are special, letting you in scares me.

The fact is, Ruther, I know you were struggling too. But I let my own troubles stop me from seeing yours and supporting you.

I'm ashamed of that, and I vow to be different from now on. I vow to support and nurture you just as you have me.

I love you, Ruther. I love you like I've never loved any other man in my life. Even though that scares me and makes me want to run away, I won't. Even if, after all this, you've decided you just want to be friends, I can be the best friend you've ever had.

If you want more, I will do what I can to be more for you as well.

I know this is probably ridiculous, but tonight as I watched you and Corey answer the town's questions and commit to building desperately needed homes, I felt so proud to know you.

The talk at the café this week and likely many more to come will be all about your project, and I know I will beam with pride every time someone says your name.

Thank you for all you've given me these past few weeks and for the summer we had. You've helped me grow and heal.

I look forward to our growing relationship, whatever that may be.

Oh, the phone number on the top? That's me. It's time I gave that to you.

With all my love,

Clyde

I put the letter into an envelope I found in the same stationary kit and wrote *Ruther* on the front. I placed it on the table and went to bed, determined to get up early enough to drop it into Ruther's mailbox before work.

FORTY-NINE

RUTHER

I WAS SO DISAPPOINTED when Clyde slipped out of the town hall before we could talk. I tried not to make that mean he didn't care. He'd come. That was something, right?

The attendees talked until nine o'clock, when Doc and the council kicked us out, saying they needed to lock up. I think people would've asked questions or talked my ear off more if they'd let us stay.

Jake and Lance invited Corey and me up to the roof of their condo, and we sipped Champagne. "So when do you start?" Jake asked.

"January second. That's when I want to have the ribbon cutting."

"Wow, you don't mess around."

"New chapter," I said and looked over at the mansion that had been a part of so many of my nightmares. It was beautiful from this vantage point. The burned parts must've been rebuilt because it looked like it did in my memories. Yet, it wasn't as sinister.

Corey and Jake chatted beside me as I pondered the house. I had one more demon to fight. One more to overcome if I was going to make this place my home. *That house.*

"Do you think Chris and Roth would let me see the renovations they've made to their home?" I asked, causing everyone to look my way.

Jake nodded, but Corey sat up. "Are you sure, you don't—"

"I do. We're doing something special, Corey, something I hope to be doing for some time. Unless I face what happened, I will always be afraid."

He glanced toward the mansion, gleaming in the lights Chris and Roth had used to accent its pillars, then looked at me.

"If you're serious, I can call and set it up tomorrow."

"I am. I'm ready."

Corey reached over and patted my knee. "I'll be there for you. You know that."

I smiled and nodded. "Gentlemen, this has been a wonderful day. But I think I'm going to turn in. Thanks for all your help, and Lance, your amazing designs are what made it as easy as it's been."

He smiled at me and nodded. I headed back downstairs and got into bed, fighting off the panic that'd swept across me now that I'd committed to tour my ancestral home.

Sweat popped out across my forehead, and, for a moment, I could feel the burning. Then I remembered Clyde sitting in the back of the room. His face smiling at me. I'd forgotten that he smiled throughout the presentation and Q and A.

The panic subsided, and although I was still very anxious about what I'd just committed to, I knew I could do it. I wish Clyde and I had cleaned things up because I would prefer to do that with him, but even if we never did, I was so much stronger now than when I'd first come to Crawford City.

I closed my eyes and instead of fire engulfing me, I felt love. That's exactly how I fell asleep—feeling loved and accepted.

The next morning, I woke to Corey singing in the kitchen and I climbed out of bed, happy to be greeted by a latte. "I made this for myself, but you have it. I'll make another," Corey said.

I laughed. He had started drinking his the same as I did years ago and had spent all those years bringing one to me each morning.

I sat down after thanking him and took my first sip. "Corey, you do know how thankful I am to have you doing this project with me, don't you?" I asked.

He paused and looked over at me. "I...to be honest, no, I didn't know. Not for sure. All these years, I've worked for you. You've always been there for me, and I appreciate it, but I've wondered if maybe you didn't regret making me your partner."

I couldn't help but laugh. "You've missed the signs, but I apologize for not being more forthcoming. Corey, I love you being my business partner. I wouldn't have taken this project on without you and your abilities to keep a project on track. I can't wait to do this with you."

Corey smiled and went back to making his latte. "Oh, this was lying on the floor when I got up," he said, handing me an envelope with my name on it. I opened it and smiled when I saw the handwriting and Clyde's name on the bottom.

I felt the happy tears slip down my face as I read it. When Corey sat across from me, I showed it to him. "I think I might be in love, Corey."

He chuckled. "Tell me something I didn't already know."

"Am I an idiot? He's so much younger and so good-looking."

"And you are just as good-looking and smart, and not that much older."

"I struggle with self-esteem issues, and apparently so does he."

Corey put his hand over mine. "I think most people do, and that's not a reason to not pursue a relationship with someone you care about. Now, if you want my opinion, you should go to the café this morning around nine and spend a few minutes with him. Then you need to set up a time you and he can work through some of this, just the two of you."

I nodded. "You're right, as usual. Thanks, Corey."

He got up and patted my back. "I'm going to head back to Nashville and meet with Cliff and Randy to let them know it's a go. I'd like them to begin buying supplies before the spring building rush begins. Oh, and I've talked with Amos and Todd. They said we can use their storage since they're general contractors. The fact that the hardware store and their storage are attached to the property we're building seems perfect, huh?"

"It does. Okay, thanks, Corey."

I checked and had just enough time to shower and get to the café before Clyde's break. I was on the verge of walking out when Corey looked up at me from his phone. "Um, sorry, but Jake just texted. Roth and Chris want to know if you're free this afternoon to tour the house."

I swallowed hard but nodded. "Yeah, I can do it this afternoon."

"Then I'll stay another day," Corey said, much to my relief. I could use some support if I was going to do this, especially if I had a panic attack.

"Um, Corey, would you mind letting them know I might not be able to do a whole tour? It might be too much."

"Don't worry. I'll go talk to Chris while you're visiting Clyde."

I nodded. "Thanks. I'd hate to make a scene."

He gave me an understanding smile as I slipped out the door.

When I showed up at the café, Mrs. Cole beamed. "Ruther, it's so nice to see you, and I heard the best news about last night. Do you want your usual? I'll go let Clyde know you're here."

She didn't wait for an answer, just disappeared into the back. I chuckled despite the harrowing news that I would be touring my nightmare this afternoon. I was staring at the salt shaker, lost in my thoughts, when I heard Clyde clear his throat next to me.

His face fell when I looked up. He sat down and, in a whisper, said, "You're telling me you don't want me, aren't you? That's okay, I understand." Tears pooled in his eyes, and I quickly took his hand.

"Oh, no, Clyde, I'm here to tell you I love you too. I want you. Hell, I need you, Clyde. It's just...well, it's bad timing, is all. I was stupid enough to tell Jake I wanted to tour my old home. He texted Corey right before I came here to inform me Chris and Roth can do it this afternoon."

Clyde looked stricken, then quickly got up and went to the back. I didn't know what he was doing until a few moments later, he came out carrying one of Mrs. Cole's famous cinnamon rolls topped with enough butter to bake a cake.

"Mrs. Cole has given me the afternoon off in case you want me to come with you." He grabbed a cup and filled it with coffee. "Now, tell me how you're feeling."

I laughed as I looked at the roll. "If I eat this, I'm going to feel sick. Here, at least eat half of it."

Clyde smiled but didn't dig in. "Ruther, are you okay?" he asked, and I had to push back my own tears.

"I'm fucking freaked out," I whispered so as not to up-set the other people with my cussing—something they didn't tolerate here like they did in New York.

"You'd have to be, Ruther. Um, why now?" he asked.

"Because I love this town, and I love you, by the way. I think that got buried before. Your letter. I love you too. I love you so much."

He reached over and squeezed my hand, then quickly came over to my side of the booth and snuggled in next to me.

"I've been such an idiot, Ruther. I want you to know it wasn't ever you. Well, maybe it was you, but more like you being too good for the likes of me."

"Stop that," I said as I put my arm around him, pulling him into my side. "No one is too good for you, Clyde. Certainly not me."

He chuckled and wiped away tears, which I hoped were happy tears.

"Okay, so can I do this with you? Today? Can I be there for you? 'Cause, damn, this is big. You know this is big, right?" he asked.

"Yeah, I'm the one freaking out here."

"I know, dammit, but you won't be doing it alone, not if you want me."

"Thank God," I said and kissed his forehead. "I was really hoping you'd say that."

FIFTY

CLYDE

I WAS BEYOND EXCITED, having made amends with
Ruther and confessing our love in person. Only to
have the event clouded by his going to his old home, a
place I knew terrified him.

Mrs. Cole didn't hesitate to give me the time off to go
with him. I bustled around, making sure everything was
done so as not to put too much undue stress on the staff
I was leaving high and dry.

I had time to rush upstairs and clean up before Ruther
met me at the café, Corey in tow. "Chris said to meet him
at the library, and we'd walk over together," Corey said.

I immediately took Ruther's hand and asked if he was
okay.

"Yeah, I am." The fact that he shivered showed how
not okay he was.

"You know, you don't have to do this."

He smiled and nodded. "Yeah, I do, I really do."

Corey turned, looking as concerned as I felt, as we continued toward the library. Chris met us at the front door. He, too, looked a bit concerned when he saw Ruther's face. He quickly started talking.

"Roth is going to meet us at the house, and Mom and Dad said they'd love to show you their side. I think Roth's sister is in town. She usually stays in the condo you're leasing from Jesse, but she's been staying in the suite we keep for my parents. The place is so different from what it was. We've tried to stay true to the history, but..." Chris's rambling, which was unusual for him, trailed off as we continued our trek. I knew he was probably nervous, but I guess his chatter was to make things less stressful for Ruther. It seemed to work, and I could feel Ruther relax as we walked toward the house.

The driveway wound gracefully up the hill. You couldn't see the house from the road, which hadn't always been the case. The small woodland had obviously grown up between the house and the road.

If I'd lived here, I'd have kept it too, preferring privacy over announcing my wealth.

The moment the house came into view, Ruther stopped in his tracks. None of us moved, then Chris announced he would run ahead and let the family know we were here.

As soon as he was out of earshot, I asked Ruther if he was okay.

"I will be, just...I just need a moment," he admitted.

Corey and I waited on either side of him while he steeled himself. I was just about to tell him we could go back when he launched forward, dragging me with him.

When we approached the front door, Roth greeted him and welcomed us inside. I looked up into Ruther's face, concerned about his reaction, but the moment he walked in, he smiled. "It's...it's so different."

"Yes," Roth said. "We decided to take the central part of the house back to as close to the original as possible."

"It's perfect," Ruther said. "Absolutely perfect. Now I can see where Lance got his inspiration."

When Roth looked confused, Ruther told him about the designs for his new home, the one they would be building as part of the development project. "When I was little, this had more of an antebellum look. The staircase was gaudy. I prefer the original much better. I also like the tiled floors more than the carpet," he said as Roth showed us around.

The house was decorated for the holidays, all very tasteful and beautiful. Nothing ostentatious, like I'd probably have done.

We went into one of the wings after touring the main part, and Chris announced this was the guest house where his family stayed when in town. "This is my sister, Lettie," Chris said as a woman turned to greet us.

She stood and shook our hands. "It's a pleasure to meet you. Chris has geeked out about your family for years. It's nice to put a face to the legend."

Ruther stiffened but smiled. I could tell he initially thought she meant the fire being a legend, but then she said something about the Quaker history, and he immediately relaxed.

"Well, come on through, and I'll show you the bedrooms," Chris said.

They'd turned this entire side into another house, from what I could tell. There was a little kitchenette in the back and a doorway leading out and over to where Roth's recording studio sat.

The walkway opened up to a garden that, in the summer, must be the perfect place to sit and while away the hours.

When we came back in, Roth paused. "Would you like to see the section we rebuilt?"

I knew he was giving Ruther an out, and I appreciated the man more than I could say. Ruther didn't respond right away. "It's hard, you know," he said, looking around the pretty space where Roth and Chris clearly spent most of their time. They hadn't offered to take us upstairs, and I respected that since it was their private space. I'd have felt the same if I were showing my home to others.

"This is all so different from when I grew up, and you've really turned it into a home. More than it ever was when it was in my family. As hard as it might be for me to face it, I'd like to see what you've created out of the fire."

Chris led us through the kitchen and into the new addition. His mom, Mrs. Asbell, met us as we came in. "Oh, I'm so happy to see you, boys. Come on in," she said, sweeping us into her home. It was cute. So different from Roth and Chris's part of the home. The kitchen was off to the side and opened into a beautiful open-concept living space.

Windows flanked the entire area and led out to a quaint little garden. The entire space screamed their personality.

Chris's dad came down the stairs then and shook all our hands. "Well, what do you think?" he asked, waving his hands around.

Ruther looked around before responding. "My parents picked and chose their religious convictions and liked to avoid Christmas. I always felt like I was missing something growing up." He walked over to where an enormous Christmas tree had pride of place in the corner of the living room.

He was smiling when he turned around. "You've brought so much joy to this place. It's practically humming with happiness, with family. Your family," he said. "I-I hate to ask, but I would like to see the bedroom. That's what I've feared seeing the most, but it would be healing to see where...where it happened."

Mr. Asbell nodded and led the way. "I'd like to face this alone," he told me and Corey, and although I feared for him, I nodded and held back.

We all waited patiently, and to my utter relief, Ruther was smiling when he came down.

Fifty-One

Ruther

I DON'T THINK I'D ever done anything as terrifying as going to my childhood home and facing the fire again.

It was hard to force myself up the driveway and through the front door, but I knew the moment I did, things would be different. Somewhere over the ages, probably before the Civil War, my family had converted the old Federal style home into more of an antebellum design.

I hated it, mostly because it didn't seem to fit. Even as a gay kid, I'd been surrounded by design enough to know it wasn't right for this home. Chris and Roth had returned it to how it always should've been. It was nothing like the spooky house I'd lived in, which made it absolutely perfect.

I almost backed out of going into the new addition when Roth gave me an out. I'd come this far, though, so after letting them know I might fall apart, I followed the guys down a back corridor connecting the old home to the new.

It was all different. Of course, the section I'd been in that night was gone, and everything was new. I assumed that wouldn't be enough, but I couldn't have been more wrong. The addition looked as old or older than the original house. Beautiful cottage windows skirted around the walls, with a pretty little winter garden outside, where birds and squirrels flocked to a bird feeder.

The entire place screamed home and Christmas. So much Christmas. Where Roth and Chris's decorations were tasteful, this was full-out gaudy. It filled me with joy.

I knew I needed to face the bedrooms, though. That's where I'd been when my world had been destroyed. Mr. Asbell didn't hesitate to take me up the stairs. Nothing was the same, of course. It had all been replaced, but as we walked through the hallway to the back bedroom where mine would've been, I felt almost like I could smell the smoke.

I shivered but focused on Mr. Asbell's voice as he told me what they'd done up here. When I walked into the bedroom, all my worries subsided. "We wanted a place for grandkids, and the missus keeps it as a nursery just to keep our boy focused."

I saw sprinkler heads adorning the ceiling, but they were inconspicuous, and I sighed. What happened to me wouldn't be happening again, not if this family had thought ahead enough to install sprinklers. I wondered if maybe they'd done that because of the home's past.

There was no conclusive evidence of what caused the fire when I'd been burned, but faulty wiring was suspected. Sprinklers would ensure even that wouldn't put anyone through the torment I'd endured that night, and that knowledge filled me with a sense of calm that I hadn't expected.

"Is there any hope that grandbabies are on the way?" I asked.

Mr. Asbell winked at me. "Well, there's always hope."

I nodded, and when I did, I felt the nightmares that'd plagued me over the years fall away, the burden of fear no longer controlling me and holding me hostage. I realized if I ever got the chance, I'd spend the night here again. Not that I would invite myself to Chris and Roth's home, but I wouldn't be afraid to sleep in this room again. That's when I realized I was finally free.

When we walked down the stairs, I saw Corey first and the relief on his face that I was laughing with Mr. Asbell. Then I saw Clyde, who looked hopeful but unsure if I was really okay.

Our chat earlier had been a confession of love, so I took his hand when we got to the ground floor and thanked Roth, Chris, and their family for letting us tour the home. "It's been healing," I said as the two men led us to their front door.

"Maybe, if it's not too much, you'd like to come to our Christmas party? It's not a huge thing, just friends and family, but we'd like you to be here...if you're comfortable," Chris said.

I smiled and thanked him. "We'd love to come," I said and glanced over at Clyde.

I'd managed to face the biggest demon in my life, and I was able to do it here because of the support around me. Not the least of which was my best friend and business partner, but also my connection to Clyde and the rest of the town.

It was a small miracle.

FIFTY-TWO

CLYDE

T HAT NIGHT, AFTER TOURING his childhood home, Ruther showed me his scarred body. He stripped down to his underwear, telling me he wanted me to see it all. "It's as good as it can ever get. No more surgeries," he'd said, and I could tell he was nervous.

I ran my fingers over the scarred skin, including across his chest. "You're beautiful to me, Ruther. These represent a battle you've had to fight since you were a kid."

I brought his hand up to the middle of my own bare chest and pressed it there. "My wounds are on the inside, but you've seen them just as I've seen yours, and you've loved me in spite of them. Can't you see that's the same? Internal or external, our scars make us who we are, show what we've survived. They're a part of you, but they don't define you."

That night, as we made love for the first time, the stars in my life collided and made the world tilt on its axis. My life felt right for probably the first time ever, and it was only because I'd finally and fully opened myself up to the love of another man.

"I love you," I whispered as Ruther lay with his head resting comfortably on my chest.

"I love you too," he murmured before we both fell into a blissful, happy sleep.

FIFTY-THREE

EPILOGUE – RUTHER

A FULL YEAR HAD passed since the night I'd finally found the courage to tour my ancestral home.

Now, the meeting house, barn, and my new home were just about finished as we once again moved into the holiday season. All had turned out exactly as planned, and on budget, which was a feat all its own. I loved the re-creation, and my extended Quaker family had even agreed to visit the following spring to dedicate the meeting house and honor the Quaker history in this area.

I'd already decided I wanted to move into my new house with the man I'd only grown to love more fiercely than I ever thought possible. Clyde was my light. A piece of me I didn't know was missing until we found each other.

CHRISTMAS HOME

From the outside, we couldn't appear to be more different—my New England roots and his Southern ones—but we genuinely fit together like a glove. I couldn't wait to start my life with him, and if the past year was any indication, it would be an amazing life.

Ten homes were under construction in the community, and all had contracts on them. There was a waiting list a mile long for when we could get the other homes done. Cliff and Randy weren't the fastest builders, even with Todd's and Amos's help, but they were beyond thorough, and I knew the homes would stand the test of time.

Because of my family's history here in this part of the country, I appreciated knowing we were leaving something here that would last the course of time.

I'd spent way more than I should've on new Christmas decorations for the community, and no, I didn't use our revenues from the city. Like the meeting house and barn, I felt they should come from me.

Since the fire had occurred on Christmas, I'd long associated the holiday with my own personal hell. All that changed last year, when I spent my first Christmas here in town with Cliff. Now, promoting the holiday, contrary to my parents' commitment to ignore it, felt healing by bringing happiness instead of ugliness and shame.

But the main reason I purchased the new decorations myself was because it brought my guy so much joy. I'd told Clyde my idea about it all during the summer, on the anniversary of the first day we met. I didn't know if he'd picked up on that, and honestly, it didn't matter. The timing was more for me than him.

One of the things I liked about the Quakers is they believed every day was holy. Every day was worth celebrating. That's how I felt about my days in Crawford City and with Clyde.

Funny enough, it turns out my boyfriend's a full-on Christmas nut. He loved helping me shop for the replacement decorations. I thought he'd go for the garish multicolored lights but instead, he selected all-white decorations that formed Christmas-themed designs.

"I want them to accent the town, show off all its sides," he'd said when I questioned him. "Crawford City is colorful enough that it doesn't need all that to make it special."

I agreed. It was colorful enough without garish decoration, especially the ugly stuff we put up last year.

I then put together my proposal and presented it to the town council. It was a fifty-fifty split about getting rid of the old decorations, but the mayor intervened. "The old decorations are a fire hazard, and I'm guessing they won't be making bulbs for them much longer. Not to mention the fact that they cost a fortune to use. The lights Mr. Crawford is proposing to donate are all LED, meaning it'll cost about a quarter of the electric bill we usually pay."

That seemed to sway the council enough to pass my proposal.

Afterward, Emanual pulled me aside and asked if we could make some sort of winter wonderland with the old lights so the town could say goodbye properly in the new park we'd donated to the community.

"That sounds like a great send-off. Why don't we ask Clyde to head that up?"

"You're going to get into trouble, young man. Don't be volunteering your sweetheart without his permission."

I laughed. "I have a method to my madness. Clyde is obsessed with all things Christmas, especially when it comes to this town. I think this is gonna be *our* season."

Emanual smiled and nodded. I knew he remembered last year when Clyde was nearly overwhelmed by the Christmas concert and lighting events.

We pulled the same ragtag group of volunteers together again, along with Cliff, Randy, and their families, to help put the new decorations up and retrofit them to where the old ones used to go.

Clyde was beside himself with excitement over it all. He kept finding me and did a happy dance and squeal before kissing me silly every time a new decoration went up. I loved seeing him so happy and in his element.

The winter wonderland was a credit to Clyde's creativity. He disassembled the decorations or created ways to prop them up. Then with help from me and the guys—which caused Corey to cringe since we were pulling our crew off to do this instead of finishing houses—we got the wonderland put together.

"You did an amazing job here, sweetheart," I told Clyde as we took in the masterful finished product. "You should be proud of yourself because I sure am."

"We created something beautiful out of what was considered ugly. That's the magic of this place," he said, snuggling into my side.

I knew I'd be funding more decorations next year because now that I'd seen Clyde's winter wonderland, I wanted to ensure it became a new Christmas tradition here in town and for us.

Just like last year, Solace joined Roth for the lighting ceremony. The difference was, after we finished lighting the downtown, refreshments would be offered at the meeting house, and Roth and Solace would perform there.

That was all how I'd arranged it, not letting anyone in on my secret plans. Because Mrs. Cole had adopted us, well, okay, she'd adopted Clyde, and Corey and me by extension, we ended up joining her and several of our friends for Thanksgiving at the mansion that'd always been such a terror.

It still surprised me that I could be there and not feel the panic that had plagued me most of my life. I had so many things to be thankful for in the past year, that being the least of them.

We all gathered on the square in front of the library. I was amazed at how many more people were here than last year. Several hundred, if I were to guess. I hoped Mrs. Cole had enough cinnamon rolls. I shook that off, knowing if anyone suspected how many people would be showing up tonight, it would be her.

When the lights flipped on, excited gasps came from the crowd. Clyde had been right, the white decorations showed off the beautiful architecture of the town. It was like we'd stepped into a Christmas movie.

"As you all know," Emanual said, addressing the crowd, "there's been some sadness about losing the decorations we've all enjoyed these past fifty-plus years, but even the most beloved things wither with age."

Amos, standing at his side, leaned in and said into the mic, "Or get better with age, like me."

The crowd chuckled. "That may be," Emanual said, pulling his husband into his side, "but our Christmas lights weren't enjoying the same fate. To say goodbye in a reasonable fashion, though, our beloved Clyde and his sweetheart, Ruther, have set up a special wonderland over at the new meeting house and museum. So, if you all wander over there, we'll have another lighting ceremony, and Mrs. Cole will pass out her delicious cinnamon rolls and hot cocoa."

I followed the crowd over to the park, smiling with anticipation. Corey looked at me expectantly, and I shrugged. I even wanted my buddy and business partner to be surprised. I knew he'd probably figured out I was up to something, but I was hoping his crush on Solace would distract him long enough for me to do what I had planned.

As soon as the crowd was gathered, Emanual gave me a nod, since I'd talked him into letting me announce the lighting and acknowledge Solace and Roth.

I climbed onto my new home's front porch that we were using for a stage and waited to get people's attention. "As you all know," I began when people had settled, "things have happened quickly since I came back to town last year. In fact, I only recently came to the realization that Crawford City had always been my hometown, even if I never felt that way growing up. But I do now, and that's a testament to all of you, my friends, and the friends I've yet to meet. In the past twelve months, not only did we begin this project and finish the public buildings, which, hopefully, make you all proud as the years flow by, but we were also blessed with the presence of a newcomer. Clyde, can you come up here for a moment?"

Clyde turned from where he was helping Mrs. Cole set out the refreshments. "What're you up to, Ruther?" he asked loudly, getting a snicker out of the crowd.

"Go on up there. Don't keep the man waiting," I heard Mrs. Cole chastise him before shoving him my way.

Clyde walked onto the makeshift stage warily, looking out at the crowd, probably to see who was in on this and if it was some kind of good-natured prank.

"You've changed our world, including all this. It only makes sense that you should be the one to flip the switch."

He smiled wide and took the switch. "On the count of five," I said, mimicking what the mayor had done last year. When we hit one, he flipped the switch and nothing happened.

"Oh, crap," he said, causing me to laugh.

"Oh, wait," I said, pulling a box out of my pocket. "I think maybe this will work better."

He looked perplexed as he took the box from me, and as he opened it, the lights came on. I knelt on one knee, so pleased I'd set up a remote start button because he immediately gasped, first at the ring, then at the beautiful lights around us.

"My sweet and handsome Clyde, you've made my life so much better and happier. I've loved you since we first met and have only learned to love you more as time passes. Will you be my husband?"

No one moved, as if the townsfolk were holding their collective breath while we all waited to hear my sweetheart's answer.

Clyde stared at the ring, then down at me as tears filled his eyes. "Well, give him an answer," someone in the crowd yelled, tugging a laugh out of him.

"Patience, Joey. Give a man time to enjoy the moment," Clyde hollered back through his tears. He pulled me up and smiled maybe wider than I'd ever seen on his handsome face. "With all my heart, Ruther. Yes!"

The crowd roared their approval as I pulled my sweet fiancé into my arms. We stepped back, and I slipped the band onto his finger, then he flashed it to the crowd to another cheer.

"Now," he said, taking the microphone from me, "you all go on and enjoy the party. I've got me some kissin' to do."

They cheered again as he handed the mic to Roth, who readily took it, and then Clyde pulled my face down for a deep kiss before wrapping is arms around me in a tight embrace.

317

"You're so sneaky," he said, pulling me off the porch and out of view of the crowd before hugging me again. "I had no idea."

"That was the plan, glad you didn't say no."

I knew as soon as Roth and Solace were finished performing, hundreds of townsfolk would descend upon us to offer their well-wishes. I welcomed it, actually, because it meant that people cared. Cared about Clyde, about me, about us as a couple, and about us being firmly planted in this town. But right now, in this moment, all my attention was firmly locked on the person I loved most in this world.

Clyde grabbed my hands and brought them to his lips, kissing my knuckles. "I love you so much, Ruther. Thank you for being patient with me and for wanting to be in my life." He glanced back at the home that was covered in lights and decorations and wiped another tear. And you proposed to me at your Christmas house."

I took a deep breath as tears slipped down my face at his loving words. We both looked a mess with our tearstained cheeks, but neither of us swiped at our tears. We were long done with hiding our emotions from one another.

"Clyde, I meant every word of my proposal, and then some, and I'll spend the rest of my days trying to convey my love in every way I know how. You're not only the love of my life, but you renewed my love *of* life, something I hadn't felt for most of my existence. You *and,* being here in this town with you did that. You were wrong about one thing, though."

Clyde looked at me quizzically, obviously replaying his own words back in his mind, then apparently giving up. "And what might that be, fiancé?"

I grinned at my new moniker, and couldn't wait until it changed to husband. "You're wrong about me proposing to you at my Christmas house."

Clyde furrowed his eyebrows and looked from me to the ring on his finger to me again, and shrugged.

I leaned down to kiss his forehead tenderly, then met his eyes. "It's not *my* Christmas house any longer. It's *our* Christmas home."

To read about the wedding and join my mailing list, go to
blakeallwood.com/christmaswedding

A NOTE FROM THE AUTHOR

According to the National Coalition Against Domestic Violence, over twenty-six percent of gay and bisexual men have suffered from domestic violence.

If you or someone you love is a victim of abuse, you can call the Hotline at **800-799-7233** for someone to talk to and/or referrals to local services.

We all deserve love, but we all deserve to be loved free of violence and abuse.

Blake

Aiden's art is his passion, but he's lost inspiration. When he meets the gruff but sexy rancher Devin, his life is changed forever.

Start at the beginning, with Blake's first book: Aiden Inspired

https://blakeallwood.com/booklink/2103084

Join Blake's email list to get advance notice of new books
and receive his occasional newsletter:

www.blakeallwood.com

MM Romance
By Blake Allwood

Transitions Series
Aiden Inspired
Suzie Empowered (MF Romance)
Bobby Transformed

Chance Series
Love By Chance
Another Chance With Love
Taking A Chance For Love

Romantic Series
Romantic Renovations (1)
Romantic Rescue (2)
Romantic Recon (3)

Melody Series
Melody of the Heart
Melody of the Snow

Hearts of Rock and Roll
Changing His Tune (1)
More Than October (2)

Coming Home Series
A Long Way Home
Family Home
Discovering Home
Finding Home
Bound For Home

Fallen Fairytales
After Midnight

Novellas
Tenacious
Moon's Place

Romantic Fantasy
By Adam J. Ridley

Big Bend Series
Love's Legacy (1)
Love's Heirloom (2)
Love's Bequest (3)

The Witch Brothers Series
Emerald Earth (1)
Diamond Air (2)
Ruby Fire (3)
Sapphire Water (4)

Tales from the Tarot Series
Twisted Fates

Haunted Hearts Series
Cordelia Manor

Science Fiction
By Adam J. Ridley

Superhero Series
Emergence

Blake Allwood was born in west Tennessee, then moved to Kansas City MO after earning a degree in Early Childhood Education from Graceland College in Lamoni, Iowa. He met his husband Shaun in 1995 and they officially married in 2015, once gay marriage was legalized; although they still consider Valentines Day 1995 as their true "anniversary date". Twenty-two years later (2017), after fostering 12 children together, he and his husband sold their home, purchased an RV and began traveling the country with their two dogs.

Typically, Blake can be found relaxing in the RV or by the fire with his laptop and their Jack Russell Terrier, Buddy, curled up between his legs demanding attention. Denver, their Siberian Husky mix is often asleep at his feet or playing tug of war with Blake's husband.

Most of Blake's stories are inspired by the places they have visited in their ongoing travels. His first book, *Aiden Inspired*, was released in 2019 and he has now written over 20 books. In 2023 he is releasing the *Coming Home* series which is comprised of ten-plus sweet contemporary romance novels that are based on a fictional town in his home state of Tennessee.

Blake also writes under the pen name of Adam J. Ridley for his urban fantasy fans looking for stories revolving around gay characters. His first series is The Witch Brothers Saga, starting with ***Emerald Earth***.

BIBLIOPRIDE.COM

Books by LGBTQ+ Authors

Made in the USA
Middletown, DE
12 December 2025